RAVE REVIEWS FOR EVELYN ROGERS!

DEVIL IN THE DARK

"Woven with suspense and an evocative flair for the darkly dramatic, this is a perfect midwinter read."

—*Romantic Times*

"No one can tell a story like Evelyn Rogers. . . . Gothics are right up her alley!"

—*Huntress Book Reviews*

SECOND OPINION

"Fans are in for a tender and humorous novel that will bring a smile to the face."

—*Romantic Times*

"This plot sizzles with originality. Poignant tenderness skillfully peppered with passionate sensuality assures readers of fabulous entertainment."

—*Rendezvous*

GOLDEN MAN

"A sexy, sensual story you won't ever forget. When it comes to finding a perfect hero, this book has it all. Fantastic! Five Bells!"

—*Bell, Book, and Candle*

"Evelyn Rogers brings charm and humor to this tale of opposites attracting."

—*Romantic Times*

WICKED

1997 HOLT Medallion Finalist for Paranormal Romance!

"Evelyn Rogers brings this charming story of a man too wicked to be good and a woman too good to be good to life."

—*Romantic Times*

"Evelyn Rogers breathes fresh life into the western romance."

—*Affaire de Coeur*

PRAISE FOR EVELYN ROGERS'S *TEXAS EMPIRES* SERIES!

CROWN OF GLORY

"*Crown of Glory* is an exciting adventure with an unusual approach to romance. Rogers's characters make this story unforgettable!"

—*Affaire de Coeur*

"*Crown of Glory* sizzles with history: rowdy Indian fights, anti-slavery issues, the pioneering days of the beef industry, all peppered with the Spanish flavor of Texas."

—*Calico Trails*

LONE STAR

"Ms. Rogers gives us such vivid descriptions that you feel the pulse of the times. She has gifted her readers with a sensitive, refreshing romance spiced with great characters and a powerful love story skillfully plotted."

—*Rendezvous*

"*Lone Star* is a wonderfully woven tale that is sure to captivate your romantic heart."

—*Bookbug*

LONGHORN

"This is an unforgettable read, beautifully written with vivid descriptions of the land and the feelings of the characters. Ms. Rogers is a very gifted storyteller."

—*Rendezvous*

"Evelyn Rogers has crafted an exciting, emotional romance that is sure to please. The characters are portrayed in such a realistic and touching manner that you will fall in love with them."

—*Bookbug*

A DRAWING FORCE

"Why did you come back?" she asked. "You don't care whether your father lives or dies."

"Would you believe me if I said you brought me here?"

"No. Not any more than you would believe it if I said I had been waiting for you."

He cradled her face. "I supposed you had married." She felt his fingers in her hair, pulling at the heavy pins that held it in place, letting the thick knot tumble free. She heard the pins fall against the wood floor.

"Why do you make yourself look plain?"

She stifled a gasp. "I am what I am."

He stroked the long strands, then in an incredibly erotic caress rubbed the tips of his fingers against her scalp, close to her temple and around to the back of her neck.

"You're beautiful. You've always been beautiful."

"Don't tease. There's nothing beautiful about me. You want a woman tonight, and I am available. Or so you believe."

"I want you." He brushed his lips against hers. "And you want me."

Other *Leisure* and *Love Spell* books by
Evelyn Rogers:
DEVIL IN THE DARK
SOMETHING BORROWED, SOMETHING BLUE
SECOND OPINION
GOLDEN MAN
HOT TEMPER
INDULGENCE
BETRAYAL
THE FOREVER BRIDE
WICKED

The *Texas Empires* series:
LONGHORN
LONE STAR
CROWN OF GLORY

LEISURE BOOKS NEW YORK CITY

A LEISURE BOOK®

August 2001

Published by

Dorchester Publishing Co., Inc.
276 Fifth Avenue
New York, NY 10001

ISBN 0-8439-4880-9

Printed in the United States of America.

This book is dedicated to
the memory of Linda Dinkla,
a thousand points of light unto herself.

With special thanks to three much-loved friends for keeping
the fires burning: Elaine Barbieri, Constance O'Banyon,
and Bobbi Smith.

SECRET FIRES

The Loner

Prologue

Stone McBride's life had come to this: the turn of a card.

The men hunched over the poker table watched with hawklike eyes. Three of the players had folded, cowboys still dusty from the trail, weary from months of herding beeves, their hard-earned money gone after an afternoon in a Fort Worth saloon.

Stone could almost sympathize. He had been a cowboy once, in another life.

Only one gambler separated him from the pile of coins and bills spread out on the table, a professional cardsharp, daring, ruthless, whatever uneasiness he felt clamped down by the iron band of need. Stone knew the kind. For most of the past four years, after finally giving up roping and wrangling, he had been a card-sharp himself.

Right now he was the worst kind of gambler, the desperate kind. One card, that was all he needed, a lousy trey to fill an inside straight. It was a greenhorn's bet, but it was the best chance he had to win.

The gambler flicked out the card, face down. Stone eased it toward him, tucked it in with its mates, closed the hand, then opened it slowly, card by card, his expression unchanged as he read his fate. Folks said his name suited him well. He was proving it now. Instead of a trey, he had matched up for a pair of aces, hardly the straight he was after, but it would have to do. He had learned long ago to play the hand he was dealt.

"You're gonna wear off the numbers staring at 'em that way," the gambler growled. "You gonna bet or not?"

Stone looked at the man coolly, his mirror image in black coat, patterned waistcoat, string tie against an almost-white shirt. It was gambler's garb, far different from the working clothes of the cowboys. He had never got used to the tie.

One glance at the single gold coin in front of him brought him back to the game. Except for the small stash back in his hotel room—his leaving-town-fast money—it was the last of his reserve. With the kind of cash he needed, the coin would do him little good now. He flipped it out to join the others in the pot.

"I paid to see your cards," he said. "Let's see 'em."

The gambler complied, too readily. "Three queens," he said and spread the proof in front of him.

If Stone were a humorous man, he would be laughing. Women had always been his downfall. Nothing really changed.

He dropped his losing hand face down on the table and started to rise, keeping the rage inside, along with the desperation. He hid them both well. He'd had a lifetime of practice.

"Mister, your luck ain't no better'n ours," one of the cowboys said, the youngest by the look of him. Stone quelled him with a glance.

The gambler dragged the money close. "How about a shot of whiskey? I'm buying." Before he had finished getting the words out, the cowboys were headed for the bar, the youngest at the head of the pack.

Stone hesitated. He had a thirst, but like the gold coin, one drink would do him little good. A dozen maybe, but not one. With a shake of his head he turned away, settling his hat low on his forehead, moving steadily across the smoke-filled room, his boots clunking solidly against the sawdust-covered floor.

Outside the saloon he was surprised to find that the pale glow of December sunlight still rested on the town. If he'd given it any thought, he would have guessed the hour close to midnight. His misjudgment came as no surprise. For a long while, time hadn't meant much to him.

But that was before his life had changed.

Pulling out a cheroot, he felt for a match. Paper crinkled in his vest pocket. The letter. It brought him up short. He should have thrown the thing away when it finally caught up with him at the hotel. Why he hadn't, he did not know. Somewhere deep inside he must have known that a day like today would come, the day he would lose everything, the day when it mattered most.

He chewed on the cold cheroot, then flipped it into the dusty street. A wagon rumbled by, stirring up more dust. He could hear the swish of skirts as two women passed close behind him on the wooden walkway. One giggled softly. He glanced over his shoulder to find her staring at him. She looked down quickly, as if he'd caught her doing something bad.

She was a pretty thing, with soft dark curls under a feathered bonnet. Her eyelashes fluttered and a smile tugged at her lips.

Women. Again, women. They seemed to like the way he looked, or pretended to, for a while.

He thought of one woman in particular. He hadn't paid her any mind for a long while. But the letter stirred up memories, each one carrying its own razor edge. He had been gone from her and from the old troubles for four years, but the sharpness of the memories had not dulled.

He moved away from the saloon, stepping into an alley where he could study the unexpected correspondence one more time. It came from Sidewinder, a graceless Texas town a hard two-days' ride from Fort Worth. The old troubles came from there, deadly as the snake that gave the town its name.

He had thought he was done with them, but it seemed they were not quite done with him.

He read quickly.

Dear Mr. McBride:

In accordance with instructions contained in the last will and testament of Thomas J. McBride, dictated to me and dutifully signed and witnessed on this date, the fifth of March, in the year of our Lord, 1886, I am forwarding this letter to all potential heirs to his estate so they may be informed of the conditions for inheritance prescribed in the above legal document.

It is the intention of your father, Thomas J. McBride, to bequeath equal shares of the Circle M. Ranch and all his remaining as-

sets to each of his progeny, and to his wife, Clare Brown McBride. Mr. McBride has stipulated, however, that in order to be eligible for this bequest, his progeny must present themselves at the Circle M Ranch no later than nine months from the date of this letter; to remain there pending the arrival of the other heirs, at which time the details of the inheritance will be specified. Those of his progeny who do not appear within that period will forfeit their shares of the estate. The forfeited shares will then be added to the award of Clare Brown McBride.

Thomas McBride has made it clear that no exceptions will be made to the conditions he has outlined.

The official business of this letter concluded, I feel it is my duty as solicitor to the estate and longstanding friend of the McBride family, to include the information that Thomas McBride is gravely ill, that his condition has been pronounced terminal, and that he is not expected to live out the year.

Hoping to see this matter drawn to a conclusion that is satisfactory to all, I remain,

Yours most sincerely,
William Benton Hanes, Esq.

Behind each of the lawyer's words Stone could read the meanness of his father, the demand that each of his children return to the fold, the threat that otherwise Clare would claim everything, especially the Circle M. Tom McBride calculated well. The woman he had hastily married, only a week after the death of his first wife and mother to his children, was pure evil. Stone had long ago forgotten his religious upbringing, but he knew there was such a thing as evil. It dwelt in the form of his young and beautiful stepmother, Clare Brown McBride.

Who else was waiting there? His brother Tanner, maybe, and sister Lauren. A lifetime ago they had turned on him, or maybe he had turned on them. After so long, it was hard to remember which.

But the troubles did not stop with them. Again he thought of the long-ago woman, of a pair of warm brown eyes, of soft shoulders and tender lips. Too late he remembered the coldness that had come into those eyes and the flat denial that had issued from those lips.

He cursed himself for letting her still twist his gut in a knot. Someone else occupied his thoughts now. He had to take care of her.

And there seemed but one way to do it. He would have to make a few too-hasty arrangements first; then he would hit the trail west.

"Tom," he said, unable even from a distance

to call him *Pa* as he once had done, "before the week is out you'll have your first-born by your bedside. I promise you this, you old bastard. It will bring you damned little comfort."

Chapter One

The main street of Sidewinder shot through town straight as a bullet, separating two rows of clapboard storefronts, one boardinghouse, a run-down hotel, a livery stable, and four saloons.

And a jail, of course. Every frontier town needed one of those, as much because of the gaudy women who strolled the narrow wooden sidewalks as the men going in and out of the saloons.

Nothing had gotten better in four years, nothing had been fancied up, except maybe for a few of the women and, in a more subtle manner, the flowers in front of the boardinghouse.

Stone gave the latter another glance, then looked away, tempted to ride through town as straight as the imaginary bullet, to ride fast and keep on riding until Sidewinder and the Circle M were far behind.

Instead, he reined to a halt in front of a place he was painfully familiar with—the general store.

He had barely cleared the doorway when the proprietor cried out, "Bless my soul, if it ain't Stone McBride."

One of the store's few male customers added, "Looks like you win the bet, Hiram."

Hiram Wiggins nodded. "Looks like," he said, his interest undisguised as he took in Stone's suit of clothes. He had been used to seeing the eldest McBride offspring in denim and leather, not black gabardine.

Then, more like the businessman he was, he added, "Get yourself on in here, Stone, and tell us what we can do for you."

Stone let the door swing closed behind him and stepped deeper into the wide, cluttered room, looking around from beneath the brim of his dark felt hat, doing it fast so that anyone watching would hardly know it. He counted ten customers, each one staring at him, except for the tall, slender woman at the rear of the store by the packages of seed.

Like everyone else, she was standing still; unlike them, she hadn't bothered to turn, as if she had more important things to occupy her time than gawking at a McBride. Stone let his gaze linger on her for a minute, then turned to Hiram.

"I'm looking for Bill Hanes. His law office was dark when I rode by."

Hiram pushed a pair of wire-frame spectacles up his short nose. With the ring of gray hair circling his balding head, he looked a little like a monk. He was an upstanding citizen and family man, as Stone remembered, the kind that laughed a lot and saw the good in people.

In Sidewinder—especially the seedy town that Stone saw today—finding good must be hard.

Hiram grinned. "Most likely, on a slow day like this, Bill's got himself an early shot of red-eye and stretched out in his back room for a snooze. Except for you McBrides, he hasn't been getting much business lately." He shook his head. "Must say, though, on many a day your family's been keeping him occupied."

Stone nodded, noncommittal. Whatever Hiram was talking about, he hoped it was none of his concern.

The man who'd mentioned a bet—a farmer from the look of him in his coveralls and work boots—walked around a table piled high with folded denim trousers and extended a gnarled hand.

"Might's well introduce myself, Mr. McBride.

Lester's the name, Lester Thompson. I come to the county after you and your brother and sister . . ."

One look into Stone's eyes and he broke off, dropping his hand, wiping it against his trousers as if that were what he'd intended to do.

"Anyways, good t' meet you," he said, and backed away.

Stone nodded, the gesture being as friendly as he could get at the moment.

Hiram broke the strained silence that followed.

"We got a few new folks around, but times have been hard. There's one I'll bet you remember." He spoke louder. "Annabelle, you remember Stone McBride."

The woman in black took a long moment to turn around, her bonnet covering her face like blinders on a horse, allowing observers a good look at her only when she faced forward. Stone thumbed his hat back for an unobstructed view and took in her thin cheeks, her pale skin, the pinched look around her mouth, all of her features accenting her wide brown eyes.

Despite the distance separating them, he could see it all.

"Come on up here and say hello," the irrepressible Hiram said. "Got to make Stone here feel welcome. Not every day he comes riding into town."

"No," she said. "It's not every day."

She moved slowly toward him, her skirt and petticoat swishing with each step. It was a womanly sound, and she moved around the tables with a womanly grace that came naturally, despite the straight-backed way she held herself.

"Annabelle Chapin," Hiram said, beaming. "Stone, you remember her father. He used to own this place, before he passed and I took it on. 'Course, that was a long time ago, near ten years now. You and Annabelle were hardly more than young'uns when all that came to pass."

If Annabelle was bothered by the recitation, she gave no sign.

"Mr. McBride," she said with a nod, "you have taken us by surprise." Her voice was cool, steady, the wide eyes unreadable as she looked at him. Tall as she was, she did not have to tilt her head to meet his steady gaze.

Neither of them blinked; neither of them smiled.

"I surprised myself, Miss Chapin. As I recall, you run the boardinghouse. At least, you did."

"Yes," she said. "I did. And I do."

Her eyes flicked to Hiram. "Will you see that my purchases are delivered? That matter we were going to discuss will have to wait until another time."

Stone's position blocked her path to the door. She walked toward him, halting two feet away, her eyes no longer meeting his. She seemed not in the least impressed by his presence, nor very much interested. He held his place seconds longer than was polite, then stepped aside. She quickened her step as she hurried past. He listened to the door closing firmly behind her.

"A good woman," Hiram said.

Stone did not respond.

"Can I get something for you?" the storekeeper asked.

"I'll be needing a few things, but later."

Stone retreated to the street, ignoring the hum of conversation that commenced in the store as soon as he turned his back. Settling his hat low on his forehead, he pulled himself up into the saddle and watched Miss Annabelle Chapin as she walked briskly toward the boardinghouse.

She held herself rigid, shoulders straight, head high. She could not, however, stop the sway of her backside. He was not so lost in his problems that he failed to appreciate the movement.

Reining away from her, he rode toward the opposite end of town. By the time he got to the law office, the light was on, the door ajar.

William Hanes, attorney for Stone's father and author of the letter that had brought Stone to town, met him with an extended hand. This handshake Stone accepted.

"Pardon my appearance," Hanes said as he settled his slight frame behind an orderly desk, smoothing his gray hair as he leaned back. "I was resting my eyes in that little room I've got in the back. It's good to see you again. Have a seat."

"I'd rather stand."

"Saddle sore, I'll bet. That's a long ride from Fort Worth. I take it the letter caught up with you there."

In the answering silence, the lawyer cleared his throat.

"It took me a while to track you down," he continued. "You're the last to get here. I figured you would be. Last to leave, last to return. You made it just in time, too. The sixth of the month is tomorrow, as I'm sure you're aware."

"I take it there were bets I wouldn't come at all."

"You know how folks are around here. They'll spit into the wind and lay money on who gets wet. I'm glad you made it, and that's the truth. Tom'll feel the same way—though, stubborn cuss that he is, he might not get around to telling you."

"His feelings are not why I'm here."

Grunting, Hanes put on his spectacles and studied Stone. "It's none of my business what brought you. As I said, I'm just glad you came."

"I'll make no secret of it. The inheritance brought me."

Hanes nodded. "You always did care for the Circle M more than any of the others."

"Is it still turning a profit?"

Hanes cleared his throat. "Now, why would you ask a fool thing like that? You know your pa is the smartest rancher in these parts."

"He's done some stupid things in his life."

"So have we all, Stone. So have we all."

Stone spared a glance out the window onto the street. He let silence serve as his response.

"Tanner's back," Hanes said.

Tanner. The younger brother, the wild one. Stone had been the one to do right, or at least he had tried, more so even than their sister Lauren. Trouble was, as a man moved through life, right had a way of taking on new meanings. No longer was Stone what he had once been. He sure as hell wasn't so sure of himself.

"He's got himself a wife," Hanes said. "A pretty thing named Callie. Met and married her not long after he returned. Same with Lauren. Remember Garrett Lassiter? He has the ranch next to the Circle M." The lawyer chuckled. "It's the damnedest thing, everybody matching up, like there was something in the water made 'em . . . well, you know, feel the need."

At last he got Stone's full attention.

"Lauren's marrying Lassiter?"

"Already has. They're settled in nice and snug in that fancy house he's got out on the San Reanido. It's a pleasure to see her so happy."

"She's happy with things the way they are? Something must have happened to Clare."

It was the first time in years he had said the name of his stepmother out loud. She was the one person he viewed with pure hate, outscoring his father in that respect. Marrying Tom McBride so soon after he became a widower, causing trouble, fracturing the family like it was a melon ripe to be split, she had a lot to answer for. And would, if there was any justice in the world, which Stone very much doubted.

"Don't take me wrong," Hanes said. "She's happy the way a bride ought to be happy, except when it comes to the Circle M. There's no way I can lie about it. Tom's out there lying on his deathbed, holding on longer than Doc Pierce thought he would, but he's not resting easy. Tanner's settled down a great deal—time and that new wife of his have seen to that—but he can't go into his old home without storming out shortly afterwards, riding hell for leather back to the shack where he's living. Leastways that's what I'm told. Clare does like to see things stirred up."

"Tanner's easily stirred."

"Like I said, he's changed. But you'll have to

see that for yourself. You McBrides are every one a stubborn sort, just like your pa." Hanes hesitated. "There's one other thing you need to hear about so you don't go riding out there and get taken by surprise. You got a brother you don't know anything about. A half-brother, that is."

"Only one?"

Hanes slapped his desk. "Tarnation, Stone, I'd like to see what could shake you. I've never seen the man, or woman, either, that could do it."

Stone shrugged. There was a lot about him that Hanes did not know.

"How about this?" the lawyer said. "Chase McBride's a half-breed. His mother was a full-blooded Indian."

"Where some things are concerned, Tom was never one to show much prejudice."

Hanes's grin lasted as long as it took him to look into Stone's eyes.

"Chase came riding in a few months back, nosing around. As it turned out, he was a Ranger, on the trail of a wanted man, but he kept that little bit of news to himself for a while. He had the letter, of course. Tom made sure I sent it. Chase was acting like he wanted nothing to do with it, though. Get his work done and get out of town, that's what he said."

"He sounds smart to me."

This time the grin lasted. "Things didn't work that way. He's the new sheriff. Damned if he didn't make Sidewinder his home. Lives in that little house off the main street, the one Hiram built when he was thinking of moving out from over the store."

"And did this brother match himself up with a woman?"

"Chase brought his bride with him, a pretty girl, name of Faith. Feisty as Lauren, if you can believe that. It turns out the boy was raised in a mission west of here. Tom knew it, too. A long time ago he gave Chase the McBride moniker, only he forgot to tell anyone. Once folks got over the gossip, they decided it was a right fair thing for him to do."

"Everybody knows how fair Tom tries to be."

For once Hanes did not have a ready response, or a defense of his oldest and most prominent client.

A silence settled in the room, broken by the lawyer.

"Make no mistake about it," he said solemnly, "your pa's dying. He's weaker every time I go out to see him. Doc Pierce would tell you, only he's out of town. What I'm thinking is, now that you're back, Tom won't hang on for long."

Stone could do little more than nod. Hanes would know that any grief he displayed would be feigned. Too much had happened in the misfit McBride family for anything like the gentling emotion a son was supposed to feel.

Weariness settled on his shoulders. Thinking of old times could be hard on a man, especially when those times held so little joy.

"Look, Mr. Hanes," he said, "you're right. It was a long ride from Fort Worth. And I'm not yet settled in for the night. We'll be talking later, after I ride out to the Circle M."

He shook the lawyer's hand and left, using the remnants of his energy to mount and take the reins. His attention traveled down the main street, through town and on beyond, all the way to the far horizon where the sun was spreading its pink and purple rays on the edge of the distant hills.

He was weary, all right, down to his bones, but there was one more piece of business he needed to take care of before he left town. He had thought he could avoid it, but as in so many other areas of his life lately, he had been wrong. He had known it as soon as he stepped inside the general store.

With dusk settling on the ramshackle buildings of Sidewinder, he rode the length of the street slowly, wondering how many townsfolk peered out at him as he passed, wondering how many from the old days were still around. On the sidewalks and in the street, he saw no one he recognized.

When he was well out of town, he circled back, keeping to the shadows, choosing for his return route a little-known trail he had regularly used years ago, when secrecy had been all-important in his life.

He came to a familiar back door, letting himself in without bothering to knock, staring at the woman who stood at the far end of the long, carpeted hall. She showed no surprise to see him, and certainly no alarm. She had been waiting for him, as he'd known she would. She had even left the door unlocked.

"Hello, Annie," he said.

"Hello, Stone," she responded, her voice as cool as it had been in the store, its soft sound drifting down the hall like an autumn breeze. "I used to wonder what might bring you back. I should have known it would be the Circle M."

Chapter Two

Annie wished she could call back the words. They made her sound as if she cared if she ever saw Stone McBride again. She did not. She hadn't in a long while.

He took a step toward her, and then another, passing a closed door to his right and one to his left, moving resolutely, wedging himself back into her life whether she wanted him or not. Light from the wall lamp she had extravagantly kept burning flickered across the harsh lines of his face. She held still, unable to do more than watch him approach.

In a suit and vest, with a string tie at his throat, he was dressed differently from the old days, but he still looked familiar in these surroundings, tall and lean and strong. Yet she knew, without hearing him say a word, that he had changed, and the clothes had nothing to do with it. The reasons that had once brought him to this back hallway did not bring him here now.

The memories came fast, wounding, unwelcome, and for a moment the years faded. In her mind she saw a young man with a young man's swagger, quiet and steady and filled with confidence, his features rugged from hours riding the ranges of his father's land. The man facing her now was still shy of thirty, but he moved with the solid purpose of someone years older, projecting a sense that nothing or no one could stop his progress. He seemed not so much filled with confidence as having the air of someone who simply did not care about the wishes of others.

He had lost the outdoors look, but he had gained a new hardness. It was in his eyes, the way he carried himself, the set of his mouth.

She saw all of this in an instant. No longer toughened by the sun, he had been toughened by other forces she could not determine. And she would burn in hell before she'd ask what those forces might be.

But, heaven help her, he was still handsome, his jaw square, his eyes the devilish silver-blue that had so often set her heart pounding, his hair dark as the night that used to send him to her for their secret rendezvous. Watching him, clenching her hands at her sides, she felt a trembling that was a little bit fear, a little bit excitement, but mostly anger because he dared face her so boldly, after what he had done.

"Stop," she said, when he was halfway down the long hall. "That's close enough."

He took another two steps before he complied, putting himself a few scant feet from her, showing her he would decide what he would do. Perhaps he had not changed so much after all.

"You've changed," he said.

Startled, she almost put a hand to her hair, to smooth it back from her face into a tight knot at the back of her neck. It would have been a nervous gesture. Each strand was firmly anchored in place. She had made sure after removing her bonnet as soon as she returned home from the store.

You've changed.

Of course she had. No longer was she the love-struck woman she had been, the smiling, softhearted creature who had fallen achingly in love with the most handsome man in all of western Texas, one far above her station in life, one who had for a while been hers.

But still, the words hurt. He had not said them admiringly.

"I would ask in what way," she said, matching his bluntness, "but I'm sure you'll tell me."

He nodded almost imperceptibly. It was a nod she remembered: using little energy, typical of everything Stone did. Something inside her tightened.

"I expected you to have married," he said. She knew it was not what he had meant to say.

"Do you want to know why I did not? Could it be because I have been waiting for my runaway fiancé to return?"

"It was a consideration that never occurred to me."

"Nor should it."

In the four years since he'd broken their engagement, she had been presented chances to wed. Her spinsterhood at the age of seven-and-twenty was by choice. But she saw no reason to tell him so. Not one of the proposals had offered the chance of a happy life, or of love.

"And Mrs. Chapin?"

"My mother died."

A world of heartache lay in both the question and the answer. Most men would have offered comforting words. Stone did not do so, for which she was grateful. The words would have been insincere.

"You know why I'm here," he said.

In Sidewinder or in her secluded hallway? She did not ask, instead assuming the former.

"To collect your inheritance. It brought the others back, too—Tanner and Lauren, and even a new McBride. You'll have heard about him."

"Bill Hanes told me."

"Chase is quite a dashing figure with the shining sheriff's badge pinned to his chest. But then, the McBrides have always been dashing. Lauren, too. And they have married handsome people, as everyone expected them to."

She wondered if he understood what she meant. If he had stayed to marry her, she would not have been at home in his family. The only thing dashing about her was the way she managed to keep the boardinghouse clean and to put good food on the table. Even with help, she had to do a good deal of dashing around to accomplish all of that.

Not that she would ever complain—not out loud, and certainly never to him.

The question gnawing at the back of her mind would be restrained no longer.

"I would have expected you to marry. Perhaps you have."

He held very still, as only he could do, scarcely seeming to breathe, proving the accuracy of his name. The moment went on forever, and she felt a sickness in her heart she had no right to feel.

"No," he said at last. "I am not married."

The relief was not what it should have been. He had not told her everything. But then, he never had.

Even as the thought arose, she admitted to being unfair. Once she had asked him to lie. If she had done otherwise, or if he had refused, her life might have turned out very differently.

She took a deep breath. "I told no one of our betrothal. After you left, I mean."

"Not even your mother?"

"She already knew." Annie laughed bitterly. "Our secret was not so secret after all. She had guessed."

His eyes narrowed. Right away he had caught the implication of what she said. The secrecy had been because of her mother's frail health. So many of her family had deserted the frightened, sickly woman—first her husband through death and then her only son, Annie's younger brother Samuel, who had sought to make his way in the world.

Only Annie had stayed, to see to the selling of the store and the purchase of the boardinghouse. She had been too young to take on such responsibilities, but she'd had no choice. From the beginning, the mother had clung to the daughter, making her promise she would never leave. Frail, her mind not always clear, she had left Annie with no option but to reassure her she'd be there forever. Even her mother knew the power exerted by the McBrides. If Stone wanted her, he would have her, and all other considerations be damned.

Or so her mother would have thought. Annie had begged him to court her in private, away from the eyes of the world. No one, especially Stone, had known what that secrecy cost her. She had been so much in love.

But love, she had found, like life itself, was temporal. She did not love him now.

Still, he had the power to fascinate. She looked away.

"I'm sorry such a sad occasion brings you home."

"The deathwatch over my father is not sad. Tom is a bastard."

"You should not say such things. Even now he may have passed on."

"I cannot be such a hypocrite. I came to claim what is rightfully mine."

She let out a long, slow breath. "The Circle M."

He looked at her for a long moment, his thoughts hidden behind cool eyes. But she could feel the tension in him, growing as she watched, building inside him, threatening to burst.

But he was not the kind of man to explode. Except for that one time, of course, when he'd fancied himself in love the last time they were together, a night she refused to remember yet could not entirely forget.

She had shoved the details into the murky

darkness of lost memories. Sadly, the sense of anger and ugliness remained.

"Did you think I meant something other than the ranch?" he asked, more sharply.

Did you think I came for you? His meaning was as clear as it was cruel.

Annie's cheeks stung. "Of course not. You are unkind to think otherwise. Or to taunt me in such a way."

"You were mine once, or so you said."

"Stop saying such things."

But of course he would not. Clearly, something had taken possession of him. He was not the impersonal man who had walked in the back door only minutes before.

"I am weary from the road, Annie."

Her name on his lips was enough to twist her heart. And he was not done.

"I would like a welcome home," he said. "Something far better than anything I will get at the ranch."

Before she could draw another breath, he was standing close to her, so close she could hear the beat of his heart. But no. It was her own that pulsed in her ears and made her head reel. The familiar scent of him filled her nostrils, a scent that was masculine and unique. His hands rested on her shoulders, and her whole body felt the pressure of that touch.

She closed her eyes, lest he take command of all of her senses.

"Please let me go. I have welcomed you all I plan to," she said, regretting the shakiness in her voice. "Be grateful I did not shoot you when you stepped inside my home."

"For which my family does not thank you. My presence serves to lessen their respective shares."

Her eyes flew open. "Always the ranch, isn't it? Always your problems. Always—"

His lips covered hers. In a panic, she shoved against him, pounded his chest with her fists, tried to twist away, but there was no escaping his determination. She fought a force against which she had no defense.

When the shock of his assault subsided, she gave up her struggle, tried to hold herself stiff, her mouth tightly closed. But the warmth and softness of his lips brought back the old sweetness, the yearnings that she had thought forever dead, and she found herself leaning against him, her hands opening to feel the tautness of his body, even through his layers of clothes.

Sensation obliterated thought. Hungrily she opened herself to him, welcoming the probing of his tongue, the taste of him, the scent, the feeling of soaring through air even as she nestled in the comfort of his embrace. She felt special and wanted, warm and protected—all the good things she had not known in a long time. The emotions rushed through her and left her wanting more.

Dimly she became aware of a girlish giggle and, more decidedly, the breaking of the kiss, the firm hands on her shoulders, the pushing away, the coldness that instantly replaced the heat.

Stone let go of her, and she swayed a minute, vulnerable, naked. It took a moment for her mind to clear.

The giggle . . .

She glanced over her shoulder in time to see a dark head pull back from the hallway and disappear through the doorway to the dining room.

Shame burned through her. Stepping backward, she forced herself to look at the man who'd brought her such humiliation. She expected a light of triumph in his eyes. Instead, she saw a dark, smoldering glance, and then a mockery that seemed directed toward them both.

"You've not changed so much after all," he said.

She closed her eyes, but only for a moment, wishing she could crawl beneath the faded, flowered wallpaper that lined the hall. But she could not, and she stared straight at the man she had once loved.

"You are wrong, Stone. True, I have a weakness for you. I always did have, and you know it. I used to welcome that weakness. I do not do so now. Never touch me again."

She could feel him withdrawing, though he did not physically retreat.

"I give no promises, Annie, except that I will make every effort to keep to myself. I ask that you do the same."

She stared at him in astonishment. "You think I would—"

"Please," he said, interrupting. "That was uncalled for. I apologize."

He neither sounded nor looked contrite, but she could do little other than nod and back farther away from him. Above all, she wanted to salvage the fragments of her dignity and watch him leave. This first meeting, as devastating as she could have imagined it, was almost done. There was little reason their paths should cross except occasionally on the street or at the general store.

In public she could handle him. It was in private that her weakness took command. In private, the earth moved under her when she looked into his eyes.

It was the trouble she'd had to deal with lately that made her weak. It had to be.

Desperately she sought safer ground.

"Regardless of how you feel now, I am sorry

about your father," she said. "It is difficult to lose a parent, especially the last one."

"Don't waste sympathy on Tom McBride. He neither deserves nor wants it."

She knew he was thinking of his stepmother, Clare. The woman had been the cause of his leaving, or so he had said. Annie rarely saw her in town, but she knew that her power at the Circle M was close to absolute.

Stone would know it, too, despite the years he had been gone. About some things he had always been astute; about others, he had often judged wrong.

The gulf between them widened. Remembering the family confidences he had shared with her, she still could not understand his lingering bitterness. Despite the troubles her mother caused, Annie had loved her and felt her death keenly. Stone had understood her feelings once, for a while, but in the end he had not. And he did not understand her now.

"Good-bye," she said. "I'm sure you have business to see to. The hour grows late and I must see to dinner."

"Set another place. I need a room for the night."

It took her a moment to realize what he'd said.

"Here?" The question was more of a cry.

"If you have one available."

"I do, but what about the hotel?"

"I've grown weary of such places. And forget about the food. I will need a bath, however. It was a long, dusty ride from Fort Worth. I'll have to stable my horse. See that the bath is ready when I return." He hesitated. "I will, of course, pay for any extra services you provide."

He gestured toward one of the closed doors behind him, the one leading to her private quarters.

"You need to keep the back door locked. Someone could creep in during the night and assault you in your bed."

"I am perfectly safe in my bed," she said. "I keep a gun in the bedside drawer."

"Good for you, if that is what you choose. From now on, I'll come in the front."

With growing dismay she watched as he turned and walked the length of the hallway, letting himself out, closing the door firmly behind him. A hand flew to her lips, as if she would brush away the persistent sense of his touch, or perhaps hold it in. She truly did not know which.

When he had spoken of her bed, his voice had taken on an intimate quality. Or perhaps she had imagined it, perhaps—

"Patróna?"

Pulling herself together, Annie turned to the woman who called from the dining room doorway, a woman who was more friend than servant. A widow, she had come to work at the boardinghouse soon after Stone's departure. She and her daughter lived in the attic. Short and solid, her fine dark features at odds with her strong peasant's body, she was closer to Annie than anyone else in the world.

"Yes, Josefina?"

"I apologize for Carmen's behavior. *Mi niña* does not always behave as she should."

Neither do I.

Annie kept the thought to herself. Josefina's daughter was sixteen, a young girl ripening to the possibilities of life. She would want to observe a man kissing a woman, especially when that woman was the spinster *patróna*.

"We have another guest," she said. "Tell Henry to bring bath water to the upstairs room at the back." *The one directly over mine.*

"He will complain. He does not like to take orders from me."

Annie sighed. Why was it that her only two helpers had decided not to get along?

"Please, tell him I asked. And see that fresh linens are on the bed. We wouldn't want Mr. McBride to have any complaints."

"Señor McBride?"

"Yes. It would seem that Tom McBride's last offspring has returned to await his death. Carmen and I will see to dinner. It is close to six.

The boarders must not be kept waiting."

Once again in control, Annie hurried toward the kitchen to attend to her chores. She had a life to lead that did not include her former fiancé. Complicated though it was at the moment, it brought her satisfaction, if little joy. But joy was an emotion that cost far too much. And, she had learned, one that was far too fleeting. She must see to it that she did not see Stone in private again.

She need not have worried. From the dining room she heard him enter the boardinghouse, this time through the front door, heard Carmen breathlessly give him directions to his room, heard him mount the stairs, and, a half hour later, when she was clearing the dishes from the table, return to the hallway. It was Carmen who informed her later that he had gone directly to the Roundup Saloon next door to Annie's establishment.

She did not hear him return, though the music and laughter from the Roundup, both uncustomarily loud, kept her awake far too long. When she got up the next morning at the first light of dawn, he had already gone. Her sense of relief was genuine. If he had stayed much longer and then made his inevitable departure, she would have had to start forgetting him all over again. As it was, their brief encounter was little more than an unpleasant memory.

In the room that had been his for one night, she threw open the windows to let in fresh air, not wanting even the faintest scent of him to remind her that he was back in Sidewinder. She stood in front of the window for a minute, drawing in several deep breaths, before she turned to the rumpled bed.

Had he slept on it naked? Probably. Unwelcome images formed in her mind, a few details blurred because of her ignorance. But enough remained to make her mouth go dry.

On the bedside table he had left a stack of bills, too many for the one night. She would like to throw them in his face. Instead, she thrust the money into her pocket and viciously attacked the covers, the pillows, the wrinkled sheets. When the room was presentable, even to her critical eye, she hurried out, grateful he would not return.

Stone had gone to rejoin the McBride clan, the father he still rejected, the stepmother whose presence had changed so many lives. Her onetime love had made it clear that he would find little comfort in the family meeting. Despite all the unpleasantness that had passed between the two of them, she could not be glad.

Chapter Three

Stone spurred the horse to a faster gallop, his eyes on the rolling landscape ahead. A mile passed and then another and another, but his thoughts were focused elsewhere, on a tall, slender woman with an old-maid's knot of hair at the back of her neck and a defiant gleam in her marvelous brown eyes.

The gleam had got him, and the memories. She had looked distant enough in the store. Alone with her in the isolated hallway, he saw the truth in her eyes. His return had affected her as much as it had affected him.

What fools they were. He should have kept his hands off her. What in hell had possessed him to touch her, to taunt her, to kiss her? The gleam, of course. It had been the gleam.

She had liked what he did, too much, and then she hadn't. He felt the same. About some things they had always thought alike.

But he was the bigger fool. Right now he needed to concentrate on where he was going and what he would say when he got there. A few days ago, deciding to return had seemed an end in itself. He had been wrong. The decision was just a beginning. What was he to do now that he was here? What was he to say when he looked into his father's eyes?

How much longer have you got, Tom? I'm told you can't keep hanging on, but you and I know how tough you can be.

Even he could not be so crude.

When he'd spoken of his father to Annie, he had not been completely truthful. Deep inside him, almost undetectable, lay a sense of regret over the old man's condition, not so much because he was dying—death came to everyone—but because of the wasted years when they could have been together, working at the ranch, making plans.

It was a fool's regret, he knew even as he acknowledged it. During the best of times, when Emily McBride had been alive to keep peace in her family, he and his father had never worked well together. Worse, the troubles between them had led to other troubles—dissension between him and Tanner and Lauren, dissension that grew worse as they left childhood behind.

But Stone had always hoped that if he tried hard enough, everything would turn out right.

Until his mother's death. Until Clare Brown reared her lovely, avaricious head. During his mother's last year, Clare had been his father's mistress, kept in a house not far from town. Her existence became known as soon as Tom was free, when he paraded her before his grieving children and quickly made her his wife.

How much longer have you got did not seem so crude after all.

But pawing Annie Chapin was another matter. Like so many others from his former life, she had disappointed him, but in ways no one else could approach. But he shouldn't have grabbed her as if she were a saloon whore.

And he shouldn't be thinking now of taking the pins from that ugly knot and letting the thick hair tumble free, hair the color of golden autumn pastureland under a noontime Texas sun. Hair that smelled of that sunshine, hair that could curl around his fingers and—

Cursing himself, thrusting her from his mind, he topped a rise and reined to a halt. On this brisk December day, except for the scattered live oaks and evergreens and the occasional rude outcropping of rock, the land stretching out in front of him had already turned the golden color of Annabelle Chapin's hair.

In fields he could not see from the hilltop, the cattle would be searching for sweet grass, and for water, too. He wondered if the creek was still flowing. Bill Hanes had assured him all was well, but Stone had grown too cynical to accept good news readily from anyone.

He thought of Fort Worth. It was time to quit dawdling and move on.

Slowly he reined his horse down the uneven terrain, across a stretch of flat land, and through the gate with the *Circle M* letters burned into the worn curved plank overhead. A sense of dread, and inevitability, went through him. He was officially home.

And then there it was, the ranch house nestled in a patch of green a quarter mile away. He stared unblinking. Anyone watching him would have no idea of the tightness in his gut as he stared at the place where he had lived most of his life, a place he had thought never to see again. He clicked the horse into a walk, taking in the two-story frame walls, the dark shutters, the flower beds stretched out beneath the shrubbery across the front.

It was the flowers that got him, with their autumn colors of dark orange and gold. His mother had put in those beds. Someone had seen that they were maintained. It wouldn't be his father. Tom had never cared for anything that did not bring him gratification or money.

It must be Clare—for some devious purpose, he was sure. She was not the kind of woman who would like to dig with her hands in the dirt.

On beyond the house lay the well-tended barn and next to it, the corral. Empty. At mid-morning the horses would be out to graze. The bunkhouse would be empty, too. He wondered if he knew any of the men who still worked there. Jeb Riggs, maybe, the foreman for as long as he could remember. If he had any warm feelings toward the place, they would be for Jeb.

For only a moment he shifted his gaze to the east, in the direction of the road he should have taken from town. Instead, he had chosen to ride cross-country, a shorter but harder route. He could not take seeing that road today.

But his mind forced him to picture it, especially the sharp dropoff of land just out of sight of the house, the arroyo where the accident had occurred. After five years he could still feel the reins of the wagon horse in his hands, hear the creak of the wagon, smell the dirt stirred by the horse's hooves and the turn of the wheels.

It was the start of a journey he had made a thousand times, taking his mother to town for her weekly shopping, the two of them alone for the peaceful, long ride into Sidewinder and the same ride back, talking about not much in particular, though he knew her thoughts were sometimes as heavy as his own.

On that fateful day they never reached their destination. The right front wheel had snapped, the wagon had canted, the horse had lost its footing, and over they had gone, down the rough, steep slope to the bottom of the arroyo. He closed his eyes, remembering the fall, the weak cry of his mother, the damnable sensation of being out of control.

Except for a few bruises and a twisted wrist, he had emerged from the dry riverbed unscathed. Emily McBride had not been so fortunate. Doc Pierce said her neck had snapped. She'd died right away. Stone had not taken much consolation in the knowledge.

Tanner had been responsible for fixing the wheel, before the start of the journey. But he had not done so. And that had been the end of life as all of them had known it. Nothing had gone right since.

Unable to look more than an instant in the direction of the arroyo, he concentrated on the house. Who awaited him inside? He would rather ride through the fires of hell than find out.

But he was desperate. He had no choice.

He quickened the horse's pace and covered the distance fast. Best to get this first meeting behind him.

Without knocking, he let himself in the front door, with its shiny pane of beveled glass and the brass doorknob his mother had polished every day. It shone brightly now, reflecting the early winter sun.

In silence, he looked around the parlor. The sight of a hundred details knifed through him. Like the outside of the house, it was exactly as it had been when Emily McBride was alive—the same comfortable furniture, the same music box on the table in the corner, the same vase that each spring day held a fresh bouquet of her beloved bluebonnets.

Today the vase was empty. Spring was a long time gone.

He took off his hat in deference to her memory and ran a hand through his hair. He was dressed in black trousers and coat, but he had chosen to pack away the tie and waistcoat he usually wore to gamble. His white shirt was open at the throat.

For a moment he wished he had taken the time to buy the clothes his mother had been used to seeing him in—the work trousers and shirt, the leather vest, a bandanna at his neck to wipe away the sweat and dust from riding the range.

The vest had been a gift from his mother when he turned twenty-one. Fringed, fancy, it was as close to elegant as anything he had ever owned. He still had it, tucked deep in the valise that carried his few belongings. Much as he liked to travel light, he could not get rid of that vest.

Coming here was a mistake. He was turning to leave when he caught a movement by the door to the dining room. A stranger nodded to him, a short, thin man with small, watchful eyes as dark as his hair. He wore an apron around his middle, and his shirt sleeves were rolled halfway up his arms. Stone took him to be the cook. He did not look surprised to see an intruder in the parlor, nor did he look alarmed.

"Anyone else here?" Stone asked. "Besides you and Tom."

The man touched his mouth with his fingers and shook his head.

"You can't talk?"

The man nodded.

He was a mute. Clare had chosen as her cook a man who could not talk back. Somehow he knew the choice had been hers.

"Is she here?" He did not identify the *she.*

The cook nodded and pointed toward the ceiling. Nursing dear old dad, Stone thought, seeing to his every need.

Like hell.

He tossed his hat on a chair near the stairs and took them slowly, one by one, coming to a halt in the second-floor hallway, turning toward the room his parents had shared. As soon as he opened the door, he caught the yellow smell of approaching death. It stung his nostrils as he stepped inside.

What stopped his progress was the sight of his father, lying on his bed beneath a light cover in the middle of the room. Ignoring the woman who stood beside the bed, he studied Tom McBride, wasted by illness, eyes closed, his gray hair long and lank on the pillow, his skin a paler gray, his cheeks sunken, his body frail beneath the sheet.

Only the slight rise and fall of the cover gave evidence he was still alive. Stone waited for some emotion to strike him—anger, pity, disgust. But he felt nothing. He was a hollow man.

Tom had always been powerful, larger than life; whatever power he still retained was not in his physical being. Stone walked close, keeping the bed between him and his stepmother. His father's eyes opened, and the two stared at one another. Stone saw the power right away. Tom McBride had not yet lost his will.

The old man's thin lips twitched. "I knew you'd come. The Circle M brought you back."

His voice was low, hoarse but steady. He did not bother with sentiment, with expressions of relief and joy that his firstborn had returned. To do so would have been a farce. Father and son knew each other far too well.

Stone looked away, toward the closed and

curtained window. The room was hot, stifling, despite the chill of the day.

"How is the ranch?" he asked, choosing the one safe topic he could think of. "Is Jeb Riggs still the foreman?"

"He is. And the place is good as ever, no thanks to you."

"I'm glad to hear it."

He spoke the truth, and his father knew it. The one thing in common between them had always been love for the Circle M. In his treatment of the land and the stock, Tom had come as close to honor as he ever could.

"We had almost given up on you," Clare said.

Her voice was low, throaty, challenging. The sound of it was obscene to his ears. Was he supposed to believe she had wanted his return? Could she possibly think she had him fooled?

A long, slow minute passed before Stone looked at her. She wore a dark green gown, cut too low for daytime, showing all too readily the delicate yet womanly figure that had captured Tom McBride's interest. Her fair hair, bare of any covering, was worn in a fancy style, pulled high with wisps of curls brushing against her face.

No wrinkles marred her pale skin. She must never frown or smile, he thought, then remembered that she was not much older than he.

Her gray eyes darkened as she watched him studying her.

It was Tom who spoke. "Don't get any ideas about her, boy. I ain't dead yet."

The idea was so preposterous, Stone almost laughed. But he could see his father was serious. Dead serious.

"Don't judge me by you, Tom."

"Tom, is it? Not Pa?"

Stone did not respond.

"I didn't kill your ma. Don't go blaming everything that happened on me."

"Where our troubles are concerned, there's enough blame to spread around to all of us," Stone said. He looked at Clare. "Though some carry a bigger share."

She met him with a haughty stare, sharp enough to cut rawhide. "You can't hurt me with words. Your father has been ill a long while. Where were you to hold his hand and wipe his brow during the long days and nights since his affliction struck? Not here. Never here."

"Is that what you've been doing, holding his hand? I would have thought your talents lay elsewhere."

She turned to face him across the sickbed, her bosom heaving with indignation. It was as if the man in the bed did not exist.

"I have many talents, Stone. Don't push me too far or you will learn what they are."

"Is that a threat?"

"A promise."

"You confuse me. Am I supposed to watch myself or you?"

Tom raised himself a fraction, looked from one to the other, then fell back against the mattress. "I'm telling you again, boy," he growled, "leave her alone."

As always, his father misunderstood his first-born son. Stone looked from husband to wife and back again. "I'll keep in mind the warnings from you both."

"See that you do. Tanner's already got his old ideas about her, and him with a hot woman waiting in his bed."

Ah, so nothing at all had changed. Stone felt a disgust he did not try to disguise.

"The hot woman, I assume, is my brother's wife."

Tom nodded. Stone would have missed the fleeting look on Clare's face if he had not glanced up at her. He'd seen that look before, in the narrowed eyes and snarled lips of a wild-cat as it pounced upon its prey.

Was she repulsed by Tanner's advances? Or could she be interested? With Clare, the truth was hard to figure out. Whatever her attitude, it would be the one most likely to cause trouble.

As far as Tanner was concerned, he never bothered with how his actions affected anyone.

"Where is Tanner now?" Stone asked.

"Here, Brother. Right here."

Clare drew in a sharp breath, and Stone looked toward the bedroom door. His younger brother stood watching him, and Stone wondered how much he had overheard.

"Tiny told me you were here," he added.

"The cook?" Stone asked. "I took him for a mute."

"We manage to communicate."

"He's a meddlesome fool," Clare said.

Stone formed an immediate liking for the man.

Leaning against the door frame, Tanner made no effort to come closer. He hadn't changed much, still tall and dark, his features strong. Was there a new maturity about him, a confidence he had not possessed before? Or was Stone simply looking at him with more mature eyes?

"Come on in," Tom said. "Stone doesn't bite. He might stare you to death, but he doesn't bite." He took a ragged breath. "Just don't stay long. I haven't changed my mind about that."

"I didn't think you had," Tanner said, remaining where he stood. He thumbed his hat to the back of his head. "We'd about given you up, Stone," he said. "Today's the last day you could get here and still claim your share of the place."

"Sorry to disappoint you." Stone glanced at

Clare, and then to his brother. "After you got the letter, did you come running right away? I understand you've been around long enough to take yourself a wife. Did you bring her with you today, or do you usually come to the house alone?"

Tanner's eyes narrowed. "Some things don't change. And some things do. Your task, Big Brother, is to figure out which is which."

He looked past Stone and Clare to the pale, prone figure in the bed. "Jeb sent word the mare's ready to foal. He seemed to think you'd be interested."

Tom grunted, his only response.

After another quick glance at Stone, Tanner left. The sound of his footsteps on the stairs echoed in the sickroom.

"And a hearty welcome to you, too, Little Brother," Stone whispered under his breath.

"You spent years defending that boy," Tom said. "Don't think I didn't know it. Are you gonna keep it up?"

"I quit a long time ago."

He stared at the open door. The regret he had felt out on the trail returned, but only for an instant and then it was gone.

"The rules around here are a little vague," he said. "The letter indicated I was supposed to stay at the ranch. But Tanner and his bride are at one of the line shacks, or so Bill Hanes said, and Lauren's with her new husband. And of course, there's the sheriff, who's living in town."

He made no other comment on this recent addition to the family, and neither did Tom.

"Exceptions had to be made," his father said.

"Make another one. I'm not staying out here."

"Good. I'd hate to have you checking on me all hours of the day and night, seeing if I'm still breathing. It sort of depresses an old man."

"I can see where it would."

The two men stared at one another. A look of darkness, or maybe pain, flashed across his father's face.

"Things are a mite more complicated than you boys know," Tom said.

"Such as?"

But Tom had closed his eyes, lost to the pain and the darkness in which he lived.

Stone looked at Clare. He would like nothing better than to throw the letter in her face and get the hell gone. But he couldn't consider only himself.

So Tom thought things were complicated, did he? He had no idea how much.

"I'll be around often enough," Stone said to no one in particular. "It's time I got back in the saddle and did some honest work."

He left fast. No one tried to stop him. Aware that Tiny, the cook, watched him as he crossed the parlor, he grabbed up his hat and went outside, drawing his first deep breath since he'd arrived.

The faint scent of chrysanthemums stopped him. They had been his mother's favorite fall flower. For just a moment he felt her death all over again. Why were the flowers still here? Like their former mistress, they should have been buried long ago.

He looked around slowly. Tanner was nowhere in sight. Stone thought about riding out to find Jeb, maybe help with the foal, then decided that tomorrow would be soon enough to take up his old life. For all he knew, even the foreman might not welcome his help.

A movement caught the corner of his eye. He turned. By the edge of the house was the dark, squat figure of Manuelo, Clare's toady and pet. The man made no effort to retreat, but instead stood in place and stared. Stone was not surprised that Manuelo was still around. Clare was a woman who liked men to fawn, and no one did it better than Manuelo.

If the man was challenging him to a staring contest, Stone was in no mood to accept. Besides, right now he had something else to take care of. And more than he needed air, he needed to put distance between himself and the Circle M.

He made the hour-long ride back into Sidewinder trying to keep his mind clear, trying to forget what had just passed and what awaited him in town, pretty much failing at each.

He made straight for the boardinghouse. Hitching his horse to the post in front, he untied his valise from behind the saddle and went inside. He had told Annie he would be using the front door, and so he did.

A Mexican girl met him in the entryway, a young, dark-skinned beauty with the saucy eyes of a woman. Her full lips curved into a smile and she stood straighter, thrusting out the high, full breasts beneath the soft white cotton of her blouse.

He wanted to tell her she was wasting her time on him, but he knew she wouldn't listen. She was far too eager to experience things that could bring her only pain.

"Tell Miss Chapin I need to see her."

The light in her dark eyes dimmed, and she tossed her long black hair over her shoulder. "I can help you, señor."

"Carmen, *venga aquí*."

An older version of the daughter stepped out of the dining room, a middle-aged woman more heavyset but with features just as fine.

"Come here," the woman said. "We have work to do." Her worried gaze settled on Stone. "You wish to see the *patróna?*"

There was wariness in her voice, as if she had

put herself between him and her mistress as a guard.

At that moment a dark skirt became visible on the stairway behind the girl Carmen, and then a narrow waist, slender shoulders, a tilted chin, and deep eyes that registered a hint of surprise.

Annabelle stopped her descent a half dozen steps from the bottom. Her black dress looked exactly like yesterday's, or perhaps it was the same one, he couldn't be sure. And her hair was similarly thrust back into a knot, this time with a square of black lace pinned atop her head. She looked at him coolly, the way she had done in the store. And once again, they both fell silent as their eyes locked.

Stone was the first to speak. "I need a room."

Annie smoothed back her hair. "For another night?"

"At least. Maybe a week, a month. It depends on how long Tom manages to hang on."

Faint frown lines around her mouth deepened. He had not expected her to be happy over his announcement. Though he had been sent for, no one was glad he had come, with the exception of Hiram Wiggins, who had won the bet over whether he would return.

And Bill Hanes, of course, pleased that all his letters had found their mark.

"This time I'll take my meals here," he said.

He gave Annie credit for keeping control.

"You can have the same room. But do not expect clean sheets every day, or a bath to be brought to your room."

"I expect very little, Annie," he said.

Her hand turned white on the banister, and she looked away from him quickly. "Josefina, please set another place for Mr. McBride."

With that, she whirled and returned to the second floor, leaving him to watch the sway of her hips and the familiar, proud way she carried her head. The wisp of black lace bounced atop the knot of golden hair.

Without a glance at the all-too-observant mother and daughter, Stone followed her up the stairs.

Chapter Four

Annie did not speak until she and Stone were upstairs behind the closed door to his rented room, in the privacy she had vowed to avoid. She had a dozen things to say, none of them dignified or controlled, but she limited herself to one word, just as she limited her vision to the open collar of his shirt.

"Why?"

If he caught the tremor beneath the softly delivered question, he gave no sign. Nor did he insult her by pretending not to understand.

"I need a place to stay," he said, tossing his hat on the bed. She followed the motion, then returned to his collar.

"Other than the ranch."

"Yes."

So it had not gone well with his father. Nor, more likely, with Clare. Annie could not feign surprise. She wanted to touch Stone in consolation, and to shake him, too, for his stubbornness where his family was concerned. She kept her hands hanging loosely, awkwardly, at her sides.

"And you've grown tired of hotels."

"You remember."

"Our conversation was only last night. I don't suppose you considered bunking with the sheriff."

"He has a new bride. And so does Tanner."

"Which leaves only my place."

No reply this time, not even a nod.

A sense of hopelessness wrapped around her. All of this seemed so inevitable, the way a brick tossed out a window dropped quickly and inevitably to the helpless ground below.

"You're assuming I'll rent you this room."

"I'm not assuming anything. But you're a woman of business. I want nothing more than to pay for the accommodations you provide."

Something in his voice made her heart quicken. She could hear each breath he took and the shift of his boots against the thin carpet. His throat became a dangerous place to look. Clasping her hands at her waist, she stared at them.

She truly ought to order him to leave. Nothing else made sense.

"What accommodations do you expect?"

He took a moment to answer. "A bed, of course. An early breakfast, if I can get it, and occasionally a late supper. It's a hard hour's ride to the ranch. I'll be spending my days on the range."

And your nights in this room.

Annie took a deep breath and gazed out the window at the wooden walls and closed windows of the Roundup Saloon. He had to know she didn't want him here. They had a past. No peaceful present was possible, and certainly no future. What he did not know was that she already had enough to contend with. He was a complication. All she wanted was a simple life.

For four years, despite her troubles, she'd had simple. But now Stone was back. In her heart she knew that nothing would ever be simple again.

She tossed a key on the bed. It fell like the brick she'd been imagining.

"You know the rates. Supper's at six. If you don't show up, Josefina can set aside a plate for you, but I can't guarantee the food will be warm."

"Fair enough."

Annie stirred. Why did he keep looking at her the way he did? Staring out the window, she could feel his eyes on her. He had no idea what those eyes had always done to her, and, God help her, did to her still.

"Breakfast should be no problem," she said. "I'm up before dawn anyway."

She forced herself to look at him, at the black hair mussed from his ride, the sharp cheeks, the tight mouth, and, of course, the eyes. Why did he have to look so good? Why did troubles tighten him, make him stronger and more darkly provocative, make him leaner and more intense so that a woman felt a hundred warm urges quicken her blood, make her want more than anything in the world to soften all his hard edges in any way she could?

She held back a sigh. She could shoot him and put them both out of misery. So what if she paid with her life? Right now, dangling from the end of a rope did not seem such a terrible fate.

Or maybe she could wound him in the arm or shoulder, crease him just enough to discourage him from hanging around. With her luck, she would probably miss her target and hit something vital.

She settled on trying to shake him from his composure.

"You haven't led a happy life, have you?"

His eyes narrowed slightly. "It has had its compensations."

"Such as?" The question came out fast and

unbidden. Her cheeks reddened at her own audacity.

"You don't want to know, Annie. You don't want to know."

So much for shaking him.

She managed an answer. "I will, of course, take your word for that. I should not have asked."

He glanced around the room. He must see the shabbiness, the worn gentility of the furnishings that no amount of cleaning and polishing could mask. Worse, he would know the whole boardinghouse for what it was: a barely adequate public house with pretensions of being a home.

"And you?" he asked. "Have you been happy?"

Annie stood tall and straight and told the truth, at least part of it.

"I know it's hard for you to believe," she said, "but I am content with my life. I serve a purpose here in Sidewinder. And I have those who care for me, and for whom I hold a deep affection."

She saw no need to tell him she spoke of Josefina and her helper Henry and even Carmen, trouble though the girl could be.

"So your life, too, has its compensations."

"It has a purpose. I'm not sure that's the same thing."

Suddenly the room became too close and he

became too overwhelming. Tired to the point of exhaustion, she tried to walk past him to the door, but he took her arm, his grip light but enough to hold her in place. She stood beside him shoulder to shoulder, facing in the opposite direction, their heads turned to one another so that their eyes met.

They stood that way a long moment, until the floor moved under her. She swayed. He had to feel the movement. Cursing herself, she pulled away. He let her go, and she hurried from the room, closing the door firmly behind her, fleeing down the stairs, striding past a wide-eyed Josefina and her watchful daughter through the dining room and into the kitchen.

Too well she knew the source of her exhaustion. Standing so close to him, breathing in his scent, she had remembered not only the anger and recriminations of their last meeting, but also the way she had shamed herself before him on that long-ago evening, then far more than now, more even than the way she had welcomed his kiss last night.

For years she had kept that memory at bay, but today it rushed in like a snarling, snapping dog, not only wounding her but also terrifying her with the knowledge that it would not go away again.

She threw herself into the task of chopping onions in case she was tempted to cry.

* * *

Stone stared at the closed door. He had been wrong to come here. Annie didn't want him near. He reminded her too much of the past, of lost dreams, of that last hour together when they had each said and done things they would always regret and, later, when they had said their bitter good-byes.

She was right. He shouldn't be here, but not for any reason she could guess. The urge to throw her on the bed had hit him hard, to kiss her and stroke her and make her want him again the way she used to do. He blamed it on the soft tendrils that escaped the dreadful knot to curl against the side of her slender neck. On the proud way she held her head. On the hints of remembrance that darkened her fine brown eyes.

Love had died a long time ago. It was an emotion lost to him. But lust lingered. He wanted her as much as he had ever done.

He thought about all he wanted to do to her, and his body grew hard. A knock at the door brought him reluctantly to reality.

"Come in," he said gruffly, knowing his visitor was not Annie come to share his lust, but wanting to see her anyway.

A man entered, a pitcher of water in his hand. He was tall and lanky, his long brown hair streaked with gray. A scraggly white beard trickled down the front of his shirt like spilled milk, giving him the look of old age. His clothes were wrinkled, his pants held up with a rope for a belt. When he spoke, he revealed a missing front tooth, and a voice too young to go with the beard.

"Miss Annabelle thought you might be wanting to wash up."

"Did she?"

"She didn't put it in so many words. Sometimes I have t' read her mind."

A stiff leg gave him a decided limp as he walked across the room and poured the water into a bowl on the dresser by the bed. He set the pitcher aside and turned.

"You'd be Stone McBride." He did not say it as a question. "I went t' work at the Circle M right after you left. Henry Jackson's the moniker. Just call me Henry, though I answer to most anything."

"You work for Miss Chapin."

Henry nodded brusquely. "And proud of it." There was defiance in his pale eyes. "Some say I took a big tumble in self-respect, coming here after riding the range for so many years. Only the last few were for Tom McBride. I been all over. Tried my hand at cook a time or two, and didn't get no complaints. And then one little fall"—he slapped his stiff leg—"and I get tossed out like dried manure. I was a good worker, too. Didn't get no complaints, even after it happened."

Stone made a guess.

"Clare McBride."

Henry clicked his teeth. "You're fer damned sure right there. Can't have no cripples drawing full wages, she said. The foreman tried to argue, but when that woman gets her back up, there ain't no more talking. And the old man, laying up there waiting for the Lord to take him . . ."

He broke off and scratched his beard.

"That'd be your pa," he said, his voice softened. "Sometimes my tongue gets the better of me."

"You spoke no more than the truth," Stone said. "He is waiting to die, though I doubt it's the Lord who'll be staking a claim on his soul."

Henry's pale eyes assessed him. "They said you was a cold one," he said, then muttered an obscenity. "There I go again, saying more than I should."

He limped to the door. "Long as I've gone too far already, might as well get this in. Miss Annabelle is a fine woman. When I was let go, no one would talk to me about work, wouldn't even look me in the eye, all except for Mr. Wiggins at the store, but he said he just didn't need no help right now. Only Miss Annabelle took me in. She give me a place to sleep, a shack out back—not much of a place, but the roof don't leak and the wind comes in no more'n a half dozen cracks, and then only when it's blowing real hard."

He cleared his throat. "What I'm saying is I sure would take it personal like if anything happened to upset her."

Stone tamped down his irritation. "I have no intention of upsetting Miss Chapin. As you said, she's a fine woman. It's a relief to know she has such an able protector."

"Don't know how able I am, but I can shoot a gun. Not as good as she can. That's something else to keep in mind."

He closed the door firmly behind him, and Stone listened to his uneven walk down the hall. *Sir Henry* he dubbed the man, Annie's knight. Maybe there were others. Sooner or later he would probably find out.

After a moment he let himself out of the room. Only the girl Carmen watched as he descended the stairs and went out to the street. After a visit to the general store, he left his horse at the livery stable, then returned to his room, cleaned up using the water Sir Henry had brought, and, wearing a clean shirt from his valise, went down to supper.

Annie was nowhere in sight. Josefina and her daughter did the serving. Three other boarders sat at the table. They introduced themselves: a Bible salesman, a rancher from south of San

Antonio, and a plump, grim-faced widow of middle age.

The rancher would be pulling out in the morning, he said, on his way to visit his married daughter who'd settled down on a ranch fifty miles to the west, awaiting the birth of her first child. The Bible salesman, giving hints he wasn't faring too well in Sidewinder, would be catching the stage in a couple of days.

Only the widow indicated she was staying on.

All stared at him, waiting for word about who he was and what his plans were. He gave them only his name. A knowing glint flickered in the widow's eyes. She had obviously heard of the McBrides.

"You be around here long?" the salesman asked him. "If so, you might be wanting something to pass the evening hours. Nothing like the Good Book to give a man comfort."

Widow Simpkins smirked. "I don't believe Mr. McBride is interested in reading."

Carmen chose that moment to set a plate in front of him. Her body brushed against his. Widow Simpkins, watching, nodded to him knowingly, as if her words had just been proven.

"How about an atlas, then?" the salesman said. "I've got a few of them as well. Does a man good to know where he is in the world. With an atlas, he can study the options about where he wants to go."

Before he could decline, the rancher spoke up. "I'll take one of those. That little girl of mine don't know where she is, stuck out on the mesa with that young know-it-all for a husband. I tried to tell her not to marry him. She could do better, I said, but she was not of a mind to listen. If any of you are parents, you'll know what I mean."

While the two men struck a bargain, Stone ate hastily and excused himself. He needed no atlas to tell him his options. Right now he had only one, the Roundup Saloon. His one visit there had been profitable. He needed a hundred more such nights, and then a hundred more.

If Sir Henry only knew, Annie need not fear the man from her past. He wasn't worth the trouble.

Chapter Five

On his second journey to the Circle M, Stone rode past the house and headed for the open range. Wearing the denim pants and work shirt he'd bought yesterday at Hiram Wiggins's store, topped by the fancy leather vest his mother had given him so long ago, he felt at home riding across the rolling hills. With winter coming on, the foreman, Jeb Riggs, would probably be grazing the cattle on the protected fields in a valley to the south.

Stone figured right. Jeb sat tall and angular in the saddle, his skin leathery and lined, his eyes squinting to narrow slits as he watched his onetime boss ride up.

As Stone drew near, he saw a smile tugging at the foreman's thin lips. It was the first sign of a genuine welcome he had received. The smile didn't last long, but then Jeb had never been one to demonstrate much emotion, instead showing his regard in other ways.

He'd been around as long as Stone could remember, teaching the McBride boys, and Lauren, too, how to ride. He'd shown Stone, especially, what it took to handle beeves, demonstrating a patience Tom never had.

Stone should have thanked him. It seemed a little late to do it now.

"I been expectin' you," the foreman said, drawling out the words as was his way, showing no more emotion than if the two of them had been together the evening before, swapping lies over a deck of cards in the bunkhouse.

"You knew I was back?"

"Word spreads. I get the feeling you surprised most folks. I knew Emily's firstborn would be comin' home. She'd want you to show respect."

Stone grunted. What would the foreman think if he knew the real reason for the firstborn's return? The last thing Stone planned was to show Tom McBride respect.

He stared at the small herd grazing in the valley, but he was thinking about the big house nestled in a patch of green not far away.

"How is he today?"

"The same," Jeb said. "Or so I'm told."

"You don't talk to him directly?"

"When he sends for me. Which ain't too often. No need for us to talk now that Tanner's here."

"Tanner's in charge?"

"Not exactly."

"Then who—"

Stone stopped himself. He thought of Clare, of her sharp gray eyes and delicate features, of the body her clothes revealed all too well. Mostly he thought of her need to be in control.

"When I was at the house yesterday, I gathered Tanner didn't spend much time there."

"Not so much. On his good days Mr. Tom looks to him for reports, like maybe he's still running things the way he always did, leastwise 'til he took sick. Your brother mostly stays out on the ranch. When there's callin' to be done, Miz Callie usually does it."

Smart woman, Tanner's wife, keeping her husband away from the charms of the soon-to-be-widow. If what she too obviously displayed could be called charms. Stone thought of her as a spider, the kind that devoured its mate.

For a moment he forgot about Tanner and women and thought about the man whose dying would change a lot of lives. Whatever came over him, it wasn't grief, or even regret over Tom's fate. But it held on. He had to shake the feeling off.

He nodded to the stretch of valley in front of him. "Not many beeves."

"They're scattered. Zeke's got another herd down by the creek."

"Many of the old hands still around?"

"Just me and Zeke. Manuelo's still around, of course, but he don't do much outside the house."

"I met a man in town who says he used to work at the ranch."

"That'd be Henry."

"He said he was let go after being injured."

Jeb kept his eyes on the distant hills. "Henry likes to talk."

"He said that, too. Are you denying his story?"

The foreman took a long time to answer, and it seemed to Stone that a kind of sadness settled on him, or maybe it was resignation over matters he could not change.

"Things around here ain't the way they oughta be, but you know that well enough. Ain't my place to go jabberin' on about those that give me my paycheck every month. All I can say is Henry was a good hand. The boys and I were glad he found work at the boardinghouse."

Mention of Annie's place brought sharp memories of her. Already he'd been picturing his onetime love too much, beginning right away when he'd got up this morning and decided to skip a visit to the kitchen.

She had never been to the Circle M, but in his mind he associated her with the place. She was supposed to be its mistress one day, caring for the house and the flower beds and most of all the children the two of them would bring into the world. He had thought she would provide stability for the McBrides, her only fault being a tendency to defend Tanner and Lauren too quickly when he complained about their antics.

Ironically, it was that very trait that told him she'd be a fine mother. And then she had told him she couldn't be his wife.

A sense of bitterness struck him, its sharp point twisting in his mind like a knife. Searching for something else to consider, he remembered the old breeding bull. He didn't try to figure out why.

"What about Samson? He still doing his duty?"

Jeb cleared his throat and spat. "We had to get rid of him."

"The cows started complaining?"

It was a jest, something Stone didn't attempt very often. The moment seemed to call for it. He needn't have bothered. Jeb's only reaction was to shrug.

"He got . . . ornery," he said after a moment's hesitation.

"Hell, Jeb, he was always ornery."

Again Jeb shrugged. He was holding something back. Stone was about to put another question to him when he saw a pair of riders coming fast across the valley toward the rise where he and Jeb were talking. They were astride their mounts, but they weren't the usual hands Stone might have expected.

"You hiring women now?" Stone asked.

"I don't do the hirin'. Not in a long time."

Curtly said. Stone let it go. The way he remembered it, when help was needed, Jeb picked the men he wanted, with the understanding that his choice could be overridden if any of the McBrides objected too much. It never had been. He had always picked well.

But that was a long time ago.

One of the women, the one in the rear, Stone had never seen before. The other caught his attention. Maybe it was the red hair flowing from beneath her hat, or the skilled way she sat in the saddle, or maybe it was because he had once known her well. Or thought he did.

Lauren McBride Lassiter reined to a halt in front of him, her deep-chested stallion stopping fast and close to him as if she had drawn a mark in the dirt. Stone's own mount stirred restlessly, but he held him in place and stared at the sister who had once given him so much grief.

Lauren was breathing hard, and damp hair clung to her cheeks. Her face was thinner, her cheekbones more pronounced than when he had last seen her. In her fringed leather jacket and split skirt, she seemed slimmer all over, yet somehow more womanly.

The fire in her blue eyes was definitely something he remembered far too well. She had flashed that fire every time he tried to keep her in line.

Some things never changed.

Sister and brother stared at one another a minute. She thumbed her hat back, and a breeze caught the fiery curls. She *had* changed. She was more beautiful than he remembered. But she also appeared in no mood for a compliment.

"You came back," she said. "I predicted you wouldn't. But here you are, right at the last. You always were one to do things your own way."

Her voice was rich, carefully modulated despite her anger.

"Should I leave?" he asked.

Her face softened, and so did the look in her eyes.

"Of course not." She smiled. It was enough to light the day. "I'm glad you're here. And I've done a very poor job of showing it. Aunt Eugenia and Uncle Morgan would be ashamed of me."

Eugenia Colfax was their mother's sister. After Tanner left, Lauren had been shipped back East to Eugenia for civilizing. At least that was what Clare had said. Everyone, including Tom, knew it was to get her feisty stepdaughter out of the way. Tanner was gone, and the existence of the half-breed bastard Chase McBride was not even a faint rumor. That had left only Stone standing in Clare's way of total control at the ranch.

"You didn't linger long after I left," Lauren said.

"It's been a while. I can't recall."

"Of course you can. Why?"

No use pretending with Lauren. She had always been the blunt one in the family, the one who spoke her mind.

"You know why," he said.

"Clare."

His beautiful sister put a lot of venom in the word, a trick she could not have learned from Aunt Eugenia.

"She was why we all left," he said.

"What I meant was, why not sooner? You didn't get along with her any better than the rest of us."

I stayed to protect you.

She wouldn't believe him. He saw no reason to describe the argument that had erupted between Tom and Stone in their late mother's gentle parlor, a room that had never known ugliness until after her death, father and son preferring to keep their disagreements outside.

But on that afternoon, Stone had been unable

to hold back, to pretend that matters among the McBrides would work themselves out.

And then had come the break with Annie, only a short while later. The details of both scenes he would carry to his grave.

He looked beyond his sister to the slender, brown-haired woman waiting in silence astride a powerful-looking chestnut. She, too, was pretty, but in a softer kind of way. Whatever she was thinking about the McBrides did not show in her eyes. With a start, Stone realized that she was now a McBride herself.

"You're Tanner's wife," he said, lifting his hat and nodding.

"Oh, my," Lauren said, "Aunt Eugenia really would be ashamed of me. Stone, this is Callie, my sister . . . and yours."

Callie McBride returned his nod. "There was some discussion about whether we would ever get to meet," she said, looking at him straight on, her expression of welcome tinged with a hint of wariness. He wondered what she had been told about him, and was afraid he already knew.

"We McBrides tend to do the unexpected," he said.

"I know," she said.

"It's not a bragging point."

She gave him a small smile. "I rather like it in Tanner. And he seems to like it in me."

"He would be a fool not to."

Stone meant it. He liked Callie McBride right away. If Tanner was still fooling around with Clare, or even thinking about it, he was a worse bastard than their newfound brother Chase could ever be.

He looked beyond Callie to another rider approaching across the valley.

"Speak of the devil," he said softly, and they all watched as Tanner rode to the top of the rise.

The look that passed between husband and wife seemed affectionate enough to Stone, but affectionate looks were something he did not know much about and he could do no more than guess.

"I see you've met my brother," Tanner said, then glanced at Stone. "And you've met my wife."

"I've had the pleasure."

"I'm glad you see it that way."

"You've done well." *Better than you deserve.* The unspoken words hung in the air.

"She's the best thing that ever happened to the Circle M," Tanner said, defiant as ever.

Stone did not see that as much of a compliment, but like most of his thoughts, he kept this one to himself.

"You two are living at the line camp, or at least that's what I heard."

"She's made it home," Tanner said.

"It's a long way from the ranch house."

"That's the way we want it. And Pa, too. For once we're thinking alike." The words came out sharp, Tanner still defying his brother to question anything he said. "I heard you're staying in town."

"That's the way I want it."

Stone couldn't say the same for Annie. It was another unspoken thought.

"But don't worry," he added. "I plan to be out here every day."

"You always did look at the ranch as yours."

"I had no choice. Somebody had to do the work."

"For heaven's sake," Lauren said with a sigh of exasperation, "if I close my eyes I'm a girl again listening to you two flail away at one another. Why don't you get a pair of dueling pistols and get the fight over with?"

Stone did not ask which of them she would prefer to survive.

"You were in the East too long," he said. "I believe six-shooters are the weapons of choice in Texas."

"Are you a better shot than you used to be?" Tanner asked.

"Let's hope no one has to find out."

He spoke coolly, hiding the anger. He hated these moments with his brother. They weren't what he wanted, or would ever have chosen.

But the two of them had never seemed capable of speaking a civil word to one another, not when they were growing up and Tanner had been the wild one in the family, and, it seemed, not now.

Lauren, naturally, took Tanner's side.

"After I got the letter and returned, when Garrett and I were still having trouble understanding one another, I don't know what I would have done without Tanner," she said. "If it's all the same to you, I would prefer to keep him around."

"I feel the same," Callie said.

"Then there goes the duel," Stone said.

"Has anyone been to the ranch house today?" Callie asked.

The peacemaker, Stone decided. The McBride clan needed one, but he wondered if she was up to the job.

"Yesterday," Stone and Tanner said in unison.

"Jeb—" Stone looked around, but the foreman had gone. Smart man.

"Callie and I were on our way there when we saw you," Lauren said. "How did he look? Bad, didn't you think?"

"Bad," Stone said.

He watched as his sister's eyes watered. If anyone wept for Tom, it would be she.

"I don't see how he breathes in that room,

with it all shut up like it is," he said.

Lauren and Callie shared a glance.

"She's supposed to let the air and sunshine in," Lauren snapped. "I specifically told her to keep the curtains and windows open."

"Well, guess what, little sister," Stone said. "She didn't listen."

"Then I'll have to go tell her again."

It was a scene Stone would have liked to witness . . . almost. But he wasn't quite ready to venture again to his former home.

"Come to dinner," Lauren said. "You need to meet my husband."

"I knew him. From before."

"You knew him as the son of Papa's enemy, or so Papa used to call him. That's not the way things are now."

"Tom approves of your marriage?"

"He arranged it. It took me a while to see the wisdom of his decision. Garrett helped me along with that."

"You're happy with the marriage?"

A glow settled on her. "Completely."

If she had given a different answer, he could not have done anything about it. In the old days he would have tried; in fact, far too often he had attempted to keep his too-young sister away from the mature and dashing man on the neighboring ranch. Not now. He was through interfering in anyone else's life. He'd made enough of a mess of his own.

"How about Sunday?" Lauren said. She looked at Callie and Tanner. "The two of you come, too."

"We've got plans," Tanner said before his wife could reply. "Some other time. I'd better be getting back to work." He glanced at Stone. "Somebody's got to."

The two women and Stone watched as Tanner reined away and rode down to the herd.

"What about you?" Lauren asked. "Do you have plans for Sunday?"

Stone thought of Annie.

"No."

Lauren settled her hat back on her head. "Good. We'll see you at two."

When he was once again alone, an unusual sense of loss came over him. He shook it off. Alone was how he preferred to be. He thought of Fort Worth. Well, almost alone.

He spent the rest of the day riding the range, following the fence line, making mental notes of the places that needed mending, the supplies he would need, thinking all the time that something wasn't right at the ranch, though he could not decide what that something was.

It occurred to him that Jeb never had answered his question as to who was running things, making the business decisions that Tom could no longer take care of. It wasn't any of Stone's business, not with the way he and Tom had parted, but he couldn't keep from worrying about a place that had once meant the world to him.

For reasons far different from the old emotional ties, he needed more than ever for all to be well, at least financially, at the Circle M.

In his riding, he did not go near the house, nor close to the arroyo, the scene of the accident. Some things would take some time. Tanner had been right to avoid a family gathering at the Lassiter ranch.

Among the McBrides, family gatherings had a way of turning ugly. Stone allowed himself to remember the last time he had tried to approach his father, the day after Lauren was sent away, against her will and against his. He had spoken up not only for his sister, but also for Tanner, though no one would ever believe him.

He hadn't been subtle. Subtlety was something Tom would never have understood.

Clare is the ruination of this family. Either she goes or I do.

Stone had flung the words at his father in the middle of the parlor, a room bittersweet with memories of the woman who had furnished and loved it so.

But his father, healthy then and full of vinegar, had roared right back.

Get out of this house. You are no longer my son.

It had been one order Stone could readily accept, especially with Clare standing halfway up the stairs and smirking down at him, controlling the scene as if the men were puppets and she held the strings.

And now, four years later, he was back, returned to the bosom of a far-from-loving family. Sent for by a dying father who had denied he was his son.

He thought about the brother he had never met, Sidewinder's new sheriff. Chase McBride had taken his new wife and adopted son out of town for a few days, Hiram Wiggins had said, leaving his deputy in charge. Maybe Lauren could give a party for them all, taking care to disarm everyone first.

If she tried it, he would have to come up with plans that would keep him away, like Tanner.

He rode back into town late, thinking he would skip the poker table tonight. Leaving his horse at the livery stable, he entered the boardinghouse through the front door.

Right away he heard a woman's laughter—Annie's gentle almost-giggle—coming from the parlor. Right behind it was the deeper chuckle of a man. There was no avoiding passing by the parlor door. For him, there was no way he could keep from pausing and looking inside.

She was seated on the sofa by the fireplace, her hair still combed severely back from her face, her black gown high-necked and long-sleeved. But there was a softness in the way she held herself and in her expression that he had not seen since his return.

Mostly he saw her smile. It lit up the room. His gut tightened. He could not move.

She looked up at Stone and the smile died, transformed into something else entirely. If he didn't know better, he would have thought it was embarrassment, as if she had been caught doing something wrong.

Following her gaze, the stranger beside her looked over his shoulder. Stone put his age around thirty-five. He was an even-featured man with brown eyes and hair, the hair parted off-center and combed smoothly back. There was nothing distinguishing about him, nothing displeasing except that he was making Annie laugh.

Stone fought an urge to rip out the man's throat.

He looked at Annie, and she looked at him.

"Supper's done," she said at last. "Josefina left a plate for you in the kitchen. Do you mind getting it yourself?"

So there were to be no introductions. Nor should there be. This was, after all, a boardinghouse and not a private home. Stone would have liked to suggest she toss the food out to whatever dogs might be passing, but that would make him sound upset. It wasn't his business who sat with her in the parlor. It wasn't his business who made her smile.

Besides, he was hungry. And he had changed his mind about that poker game.

In the kitchen, he stood at the stove to eat, thinking he would wash the food down with whiskey at the saloon, trying not to think about anything else. He was half done when he felt the presence of someone behind him. He turned sharply. Josefina's daughter, Carmen, was leaning with her back against the door frame, as if she had carefully positioned herself to display her already-obvious figure.

Her black hair was thick, lustrous, long, and her white blouse had been tugged off her shoulders to reveal an expanse of smooth, dusky skin. Ample breasts pushed against the soft cloth. She was too wordly for her years, a fact she continued to prove by licking her full red lips.

"Are you pleased?" she asked.

He wanted to advise her on being less obvious, on the trouble she could attract by displaying herself in such a way. Even if she listened, she would not have believed him, or have cared. He wasn't so old that he could not remember being young.

"The food is fine," Stone said. "Thank your mother for me."

The lips puckered into a frown. "I did not mean the food, Señor McBride." And then she smiled. "But you knew that, did you not? You tease poor Carmen, thinking she does not understand."

"I think you understand a great deal. And I do not think of you as poor Carmen."

"In this you are wise. But I knew you would be. I saw you watching the *patróna* and her new friend. Señor Woodruff is our new guest. Right away he and the *patróna* were *simpático*."

"Good for them."

"Is it?" A glint flashed in the girl's dark eyes. "In this I think you do not tell the truth. I also believe that Señor McBride should find someone who would be *simpático* with him."

There was little doubt who that someone was supposed to be. Was she right, at least in determining what he needed? He did not have to think about the question long.

Definitely not.

No longer hungry, Stone set his half-filled plate aside. He waited a moment for Carmen to make way for him; instead, she rested her back against the door frame, hands on hips, daring him to pass.

He slipped past her, avoiding contact, but her laughter reached him as he crossed the dining room and entered the front hall. Without going near the parlor, he headed for the door, his destination the saloon.

All in all, he told himself as he went out on the noisy street, it had been a hell of a day.

Chapter Six

"What an unpleasant fellow," Robert Woodruff said.

Annie stared in the direction of the closing front door. From where she sat, she couldn't see it, but she could imagine Stone storming out into the night.

Unpleasant? Mr. Woodruff did not know the half of it.

"The man has a room here, I assume," he said.

Annie nodded, not wanting a paying guest to think that glowering strangers walked in off the street every day.

"And works in town?"

"He's a rancher." It was the simplest way she could come up with to explain Stone's situation.

"But chooses to live here. How strange."

It was also Stone's right, as long as she rented him a room.

She looked coolly at Woodruff. "As long as they cause no trouble," she said, "I don't question the choices of my guests."

If he caught her irritation, he gave no sign.

"I noticed a saloon next door, and several more along the street. No doubt one of these establishments is his destination. Women, whiskey, and cards. What a waste of time."

Her newest resident shook his head sadly, as if in his life he had seen too many men with such wastrel ways and disliked every one.

At another time she might have agreed with him, but not tonight. For some unidentifiable reason, his reactions were irritating her more and more. Immediately, and irrationally, she wanted to come to Stone's defense.

Stone's expression as he stared into the parlor had affected her more than she had realized. Why she should feel guilty over the situation, she had no idea. She was sitting on the sofa on one of the rare occasions she allowed herself to visit with a guest. Robert Woodruff was a friendly one, too, not at all like the man who had scowled at them and then gone without so much as a nod.

She ought to chase after him with a lecture on civility. In the process, she would make an even bigger fool of herself than she already was.

She smiled at Woodruff, hoping he did not know how much the smile was forced.

"You were telling me about your home in Louisiana," she said.

A look of unhappiness stole over Woodruff's even features.

"My former home. After my wife passed on, much as I loved the plantation, I could not find peace there any longer, nor in New Orleans, where we had passed so many happy hours. If we had had children, it might have been different, but as things were . . ."

His voice trailed off. Annie tried to be sympathetic.

"And so you began traveling," she said. "I believe that's what you said when you first arrived. You're not a traveling salesman, just a traveler."

"For a long time now I've been looking for something I have yet to find."

His brown eyes settled on her, as if he just might find that something in a boardinghouse parlor in Sidewinder, Texas.

Annie stirred uneasily.

"Tell me about your travels."

He did so readily. She tried to concentrate, tried very, very hard, but as his even, softly drawling voice droned on, her thoughts kept drifting back to Stone, especially the way he had looked at her from the parlor door, not bothering to take off his hat the way any gentleman would, just standing there as arrogant as ever.

What did he have to be arrogant about? Certainly not his appearance. Having abandoned his suit and tie, he was back in the work clothes she remembered too well. Dust from his long ride clung to his trousers, his shirt was unbuttoned at the throat, the lines of his face seemed deeper than ever, and, worst of all, his eyes were blue ice as he looked her over.

She could read his thoughts. Those eyes had branded her a harlot—innocent Annie, as pure as the day she had been born. At least she would have been pure, if not for Stone.

Could a woman be almost pure? Probably not.

With that cold stare on her, she had felt a strong urge to take Mr. Woodruff's hand and clutch it to her bosom. She would show Stone McBride what kind of harlot she could be.

But she was not a woman to lose control. Except once. Once was more than enough.

Besides, except as a paying guest, she wasn't the least interested in the personable Mr. Woodruff, nor he in her. Whatever hints he gave otherwise she knew came from the long stagecoach ride that had brought him here. The man was exhausted, not beguiled.

As much as she appreciated his friendliness,

she was at the moment more interested in his money. The rancher had left that morning. The Bible salesman would be leaving the next day, earlier than he'd planned.

"I fear I'm boring you, Miss Chapin."

She looked at Woodruff guiltily, starting to deny the accusation. But he had already figured her out.

She smoothed back her hair. "It's just that I've got a lot on my mind."

"I understand. You did say you were the owner and sole proprietor of this establishment, did you not? It must require a great deal of work."

"I have help."

"But still, a woman alone in a town like this cannot have an easy time."

"I'm used to Sidewinder. It has been my home since I was a little girl."

"And your parents?"

"Both gone."

He nodded sympathetically. "As are mine." He hesitated a moment. "I was an only child. And you?"

She started to tell him about the younger brother who had gone west so many years ago, seeking his fortune. But the existence of Samuel Chapin and his home in the New Mexico Territory was none of the man's business.

And, for all his pleasantness and gentlemanly

ways, he made her feel restless in a way entirely different from Stone. The truth was, she was not entirely comfortable talking with men of any kind.

"I've kept you too long from rest, Mr. Woodruff." She stood, giving him little choice but to do the same. "Please let me know if your accommodations are satisfactory. Breakfast is at eight."

With a nod, he bade her good night and went up the stairs to the room she had shown him when he first arrived. It was across the hall from Stone's. She wondered how the two men would greet each other if they chanced to pass. She could not imagine two greater opposites—the friendly and polite, if overly inquisitive, widower and the grim, private man she had once loved.

Now Stone was more a stranger to her than the widower.

Idle hands lead to dangerous thoughts, she decided as she hurried down the hallway toward the sound of an argument at the back door. Josefina and Henry were going at each other again. This time, it turned out, her dear friend and assistant was berating the handyman for harvesting a crop of tomatoes too soon.

"A freeze is coming," Henry said. "Had to get 'em in."

Since he'd shown up at her back door a few

weeks ago seeking work, Henry had taken over the tending of the vegetable garden behind the boardinghouse. Sometimes he overtended, as was probably the case here, but Annie was so grateful for his help she did not complain.

Not so her assistant.

"It is too early in December for a freeze," Josefina said.

"We'll set most of them aside to ripen," Annie said, "and fry the rest for breakfast. None will go to waste."

Josefina shook her head in disgust, while Henry stroked his scrawny white beard, a gesture he frequently used to show he was pleased.

Annie walked back down the hall toward the door to the kitchen, thinking Josefina would follow. Instead, she lingered outside, not quite done with arguing. Why her two helpers chose to bicker, Annie did not know. They simply did not like one another. Sometimes Annie thought she did not understand people at all.

There was Iola Simpkins, for instance. She had taken a room at the boardinghouse a year ago, moving from her farm soon after Mr. Simpkins died. Childless, she had sworn her stay was only temporary. Any day now she would be leaving to live with her niece in San Antonio. It was a threat she made every time she was approached about an overdue bill.

Annie ought to insist that she do as she

threatened. Instead, because the woman eventually paid, she put up with her, wishing as she did so that the woman would not eat quite so much.

In the kitchen she kept herself busy laying out ingredients for the biscuits she would make early the next day, seeing that enough eggs had been brought in from the chicken coop beyond the garden, setting out the dishes for her few residents, putting aside a plate for Stone, so that he could eat early before leaving for the Circle M.

Had Josefina or Carmen remembered to take a fresh towel to his room? Where the worry came from, she did not know, but it refused to leave her mind. There was only one way to find out, short of interrupting the back-door argument or seeking out Josefina's elusive daughter.

Simpler to look and know for sure.

Taking clean linens from a back shelf of the pantry, she walked quietly up the stairs, not wanting to disturb any of her guests, letting herself in Stone's room with her master key. She closed the door behind her and stood in the dark, willing her heart to slow.

She had every right to be here, and he ought to realize it. He knew his room was freshened regularly. Who did he think did the freshening? Elves?

She chided herself. A freshly aired room was

hardly of importance to him, no matter how much it mattered to her. Though their paths crossed far too often, they did not live in the same world.

And what of his world? Despite the troubles between them, she could not keep from wondering. How were his hours spent at the ranch? Were they as bad as they had been before he left?

In the early days, when they were first getting acquainted, he used to talk about the Circle M, about his dreams for improvements, his main complaints centering on how Tanner shirked his responsibilities and Lauren ran wild. Loving him, wanting to make him feel better, she nevertheless had defended his younger brother and sister.

Her reasons were personal. As she watched the pair when they came to town, Tanner reminded her of her own brother, Samuel, a little wild and centered on his own concerns, but never mean, never cruel. Lauren, beautiful and laughing, a little too flirtatious maybe, and reckless as she rode, was the sister Annie would have adored.

But no argument she could offer had softened his opinion. He was the strong one in the family, he had implied without saying it outright. She had to understand that while his mother struggled to hold the family together, he was left the task of seeing that his brother and sister did as little harm as possible, to others as well as themselves.

Annie never tried to defend Tom McBride. Stone talked about his father's stubbornness, his lack of regard for anyone other than himself. But she had observed other men like that, when they came into the store. To her, they had never seemed particularly bad.

Secretly she thought Tom had passed some of these traits on to his firstborn child.

Stone also mentioned his father in connection with women, though not often, nor in detail. She always thought that in his reticence he was protecting Emily. But others talked, though she tried to ignore them. When Emily died and Tom remarried right away, the whole town knew the talk was true. At last she understood completely the relationship between father and son.

But what of Clare? Maybe the second wife had made the mistake of falling in love with a man who lacked a conscience. Women did such things. Annie knew.

She seldom saw the woman, and then only briefly as she guided her horse and carriage through town, always at a fast clip. But she saw enough to know that Clare was a beautiful woman, and too young for her husband.

Clare rarely did the shopping for the Circle

M, as Emily McBride had done. Instead, she sent someone called Manuelo, a sullen man who did not encourage so much as a friendly greeting.

A heaviness settled in Annie's heart. That was how she first saw Stone, when he brought his mother into town to shop at the Chapins' store. He had been no older than sixteen, already a man, the handsomest one she had ever seen. Watching him from behind the counter, pretending to be busy, she had fallen in love, completely and, she had thought, for all time. Eventually he had noticed her. After a while, after her father died and her mother bought the boardinghouse, his courtship had begun.

Holding the linens close, she crossed the room to the window, pulled aside the curtain, and stared down at the Roundup Saloon. Music and laughter drifted up to her on the cold night air. Through the years she had learned to ignore the sounds. But not tonight.

Women, whiskey, and cards. That was what Robert Woodruff had said drew men to such places. He wasn't telling her anything she did not already know. She saw the rouged women on the street; she saw the drunken men stumble through the swinging doors; she'd even witnessed a couple of gunfights over a game of cards.

Since Chase McBride had taken over as sheriff and hired a deputy, the gunfights had almost ceased. But the women, whiskey, and cards were still there.

Would Stone return with a saloon woman's face paint smeared on his shirt? Would he have liquor on his breath? Would his pockets be crammed with gambling money or empty after a run of bad luck?

The biggest question was why she was standing here close to his bed wondering about such matters.

She was setting the clean towel and washcloth beside the basin of water when the door opened. She jumped and turned, swallowing the pounding in her throat.

Stone stood in the doorway motionless, then eased slowly inside and closed the door behind him. Moonlight filtered through the window. Though it wasn't light enough for her to see his features in detail, she could picture them far too well. Mostly she could picture surprise in his eyes and then, worse, amusement, or possibly scorn.

The room was quiet, too quiet, the saloon noise faded. She fancied she could hear the beat of her heart.

"I brought you linens," she said, too loudly. "I didn't think you would return so soon."

"The cards were against me tonight," he said. "I've had bad luck all day."

Just as she'd thought, things had not gone well at the ranch.

"I'm sorry," she said and meant it, though she knew her sincerity did not show.

He took a step toward her. "Maybe the luck's about to change."

His voice was low, insinuating. It wrapped around her like a warm fog. For a moment she felt the way she used to when she watched him in the store, entranced, intrigued, vulnerable.

But she had been a child. She was a woman now.

"I told you why I came up here. It's hardly a matter of luck. Unless you put a great deal of value in a clean towel."

"If I value anything."

"Do you?"

It was a silly response on her part, worse than sympathy. He must not think she cared. She did not know him, not like before, and that was the way it should be.

He seemed to give the question thought. "I value peace. A quiet time. Sit with me, Annie, and talk pleasantly, the way you did downstairs with your friend. Tell me stories. Laugh gently when I tell you mine."

She caught her breath. Here was a man almost like the one she had loved, the man she must not love again.

"Mr. Woodruff is not my friend." As if that

were the worst thing Stone had said.

"What is he?"

This time his voice was hard. The quick changes in him made her head reel. She answered him in the same tone.

"A paying guest. Like you." She started to walk past him. "It's late. I need to get to bed."

"There's one in here."

"If you're trying to shock me, you're going about it in the wrong way. Don't play games with me. I have no intention of sleeping with you, nor you with me."

"It might bring us peace."

"Peace I already have, or did until you showed up."

"Then how about a good time?"

The high collar of her dress choked her, and the wool cloth felt heavy on her skin.

"Don't do this, Stone."

"Are you afraid I won't please you?"

I know that you would.

She needed air, fresh and cool, a breeze that did not bear his scent so that she could once again breathe. He was close, too close, at once both a dream and a nightmare, the promise of joy in her narrow, cheerless world, a threat to her hard-won sense of safety.

"Whatever was between us is long dead," she managed.

"I know. I'm not asking for love. If I were, I

couldn't return it, even if I wanted to."

"Why don't you just hit me? It would be kinder than the ugly things you're saying."

His voice grew husky. "I don't want to hurt you, Annie. I want to kiss you, now, more than I've ever wanted anything."

She closed her eyes to stop the welling tears. "To make up for your bad day."

"To kiss you. To feel your lips under mine. To taste—"

She covered her ears. "Stop," she said with a sob. "Please stop."

She felt his hands on her shoulders, sensed his head bending close to hers. Pressing her hands against the smooth warmth of his leather vest, she looked up at him.

"You're not going to do what I want, are you?" she said.

"Yes, I am, only you don't yet realize it." Moonlight carved shadowy hollows on his face. The heat from him singed her hair. "I can smell the need on you, Annie, like the sweetest of perfumes. Unless you order me to stop, I'm going to do everything you want."

Chapter Seven

Annie could not look away from Stone's lips. His words were so strong, she could read them on the air.

Run. Tell him to stop and then run as fast as you can out the door.

But her legs held her in place; her throat squeezed back the command she wanted to throw at him. If he touched her, she would splinter into a thousand pieces, each part of her wanting him. He knew it. Already he had made that stunningly clear.

"I don't love you and you know it," she said. "You've certainly let me know you don't love me."

"Ah, Annie, you use that as a defense. I know your feelings. But it's not love we will share."

He stroked her cheek. Her skin burned. She rubbed where he had touched, then dropped her hand, embarrassed because he had caught her.

"Why did you come back?" she asked. "You don't care whether your father lives or dies."

"Would you believe me if I said you brought me here?"

"No. Not any more than you would believe me if I said I had been waiting for you."

He cradled her face. "I supposed you had married." She felt his fingers in her hair, pulling at the heavy pins that held it in place, letting the thick knot tumble free. She heard the pins fall against the wood floor.

"Why do you make yourself look plain?"

She stifled a gasp. "I am what I am."

He stroked the long strands, then in an incredibly erotic caress rubbed the tips of his fingers against her scalp, close to her temple and around to the back of her neck.

"You're beautiful. You've always been beautiful."

"Don't tease. There's nothing beautiful about me. You want a woman tonight, and I am available. Or so you believe."

"I want you." He brushed his lips against hers. "And you want me."

"You'll leave again."

"Do you want me to stay?"

"No." She spoke the truth.

"Then I'll leave. But not tonight."

He kissed her again, and this time he ran his tongue over her lips, parting them, slipping inside and out again, a mock invasion that heated her blood.

Annie's hands, beyond her control, held him by the shoulders. He felt solid, strong, dependable, though she doubted he was any of those things. But he felt it. Tonight could it be enough?

He broke the kiss.

"You think too much," he said huskily. "Let yourself feel. Let yourself go."

"I can't."

He rubbed the back of her neck and her shoulders, then eased his hands lower, to her waist, cradling her against him, enfolding her in the cocoon of his arms.

Solid, strong, dependable. Yes, yes, he was all of those things. And if he weren't, she did not care.

Wrapping her arms around his neck, she returned his kiss. Fires burned within her, consuming flames that had been a secret even from her. She felt hot, constricted by her clothes, but she could bring herself to do no more than hold tight to him and keep her mouth against his.

Stone took control, one clever hand freeing the buttons at her throat, then moving down the front of her gown to her waist, pulling aside the coarse wool, bending his head to taste the skin he had bared, the rise of her breasts, and through the silk chemise, the nipples hard and pointed and eager.

Her head dropped back, and a low moan escaped her lips. The darkness whirled around her. She had to hold on tight to keep from spinning into space.

"It's been so long," he whispered against her skin.

Too long. No man had ever touched her like Stone. No other man ever would.

But he could do whatever he wanted. She felt wanton, unable to imagine his doing anything that would hurt her—not now, not again.

His hot breath sent waves of pleasure skittering across the surface of her skin. She looked down at him and saw his tongue moving across the peak of one breast. He teased her with expert ease, a practiced lover who knew how to arouse.

It was at that moment she discovered she was not completely lost to reason. The word *harlot* drifted into her mind. His eyes had accused her of being one, on this very night when he'd seen her in the parlor with someone else.

Now she was proving him right. Just as she had done four years ago, only then had been worse, much worse. Heat turned to chill. She thanked Providence that she had at last been able to remember what had happened that night, and how she had felt afterwards.

Never could she endure such humiliation again. It mattered not how good he made her feel. It mattered even less that she did the same for him.

He must have felt her stiffen, for he eased away, still holding her but his eyes now searching her face for whatever her expression might reveal.

"Stop."

She could not pull free, but she could say the word he'd claimed would end the torture.

"You don't like it?" he whispered.

"You know I do. You found that out the first night you returned. You kissed me then, you're kissing me now. I like it."

"But not enough."

"Not nearly enough."

Not enough to compensate for the hate she would feel for both of them tomorrow, and the disgust she would always feel for herself.

He let her go, and she swayed. Regaining her balance, she hurried around him and opened the door, desperate to put distance between them. She wished she could flee the earth itself. At that moment the moon did not seem too far away.

But such an escape was not given to man, or to woman.

"Your gown," he said.

The reminder stopped her in place.

"Oh," she said, and hurriedly covered herself.

"I don't plan to apologize," he said.

"I'm sure you don't."

"You wanted everything I did to you. I wanted everything and more."

"I have given you all that I can."

"I don't believe you."

"Believe this, then. I have given you all I'm capable of giving. If you ever had any respect for me, please do as I ask. Do not bother me like this again."

She felt him draw away, not physically, but in a manner that put an impenetrable wall between them.

"You really don't need me, do you?" he said.

"I really don't. Not in any way. I have learned to take care of myself."

"You do it very well."

"I have to."

She wanted to go on, but her voice broke. With a sob, she hurried down the hall, only vaguely aware of his closing the door, of the picture she must present to anyone who might look out at her, the unbuttoned gown clutched together in her hands, hair wild, the stricken look of denied passion that must mark her countenance as she flew down the stairs.

She made it to her room unobserved. Locking

her door, she leaned against it and waited for her heart to quit pounding.

How close tonight had come to that last scene with Stone, the last time she had seen him until he walked into Hiram Wiggins's store a few blistering days ago.

That final night came back to her in all its knifing detail. They'd been behind the boardinghouse in the shed that had been the scene of so many clandestine meetings, the same shed that now served as Henry's home.

Stone had been beside himself, pacing, gesturing, not at all the controlled man she knew and loved.

"I told him I could no longer live under the same roof as that woman," he had said.

Annie had understood, or thought she did.

"She's your father's wife. What else can you do?"

She had badly underestimated the depth of his anger and despair.

"I gave him a choice. Either she goes or I do." His face had twisted into an ugly contempt she had never before witnessed. "He chose her."

Two proud McBrides had thrown ultimatums at one another, neither willing to compromise. Annie had sided with the son, totally, but that was not the issue. She'd felt that she must be the peacemaker; she must soothe the hurt from his heart.

But he had given her no choice. "I'm leaving," he'd said. "Come with me."

The words had stunned her.

"I can't. You know I can't. My mother—"

"She's stronger than you think. I'll see that she has help."

On that night, in his desperate, self-centered view of things, he'd thought he could clear away all her doubts.

"I can't," she had repeated.

"We can take her with us. To your brother, if you want."

He'd thrown out suggestions one after the other, clearly not thinking them through.

"You ask too much."

"I ask that you love me. I need you on my side."

"I am."

He had kissed her passionately. "Prove it."

He meant by coming with him. But she couldn't. And she'd thought of another way to offer the proof he demanded, proof he should never have needed.

Tugging her blouse free of her skirt, she'd unbuttoned it and tossed it aside. And then she had pulled off her undergarments to bare her breasts. It was an act of such love and submission, she'd thought he had to know.

She could still feel his eyes on her. She had

been offering him everything. But it had not been enough.

"Cover yourself, Annie."

She hadn't understood him at first, certain in her heart that he loved her as she loved him, that he would know she was doing what she could. Never had they gone so far together, though their kisses had been full of passionate promise. Above all else, it was a promise she had wanted to deliver. In her mind, she was binding herself to him in the only way that was open to her, in the one act that would keep him by her side.

But what she offered had not been enough.

He had stared at her nakedness. She had seen in him not the love and understanding she wanted, nor even the lust. What she had seen was sadness. It had broken her heart.

"Cover yourself," he had repeated. "I need more."

With those final words, he had gone. She had not seen him again for four long years. For much of that time she had wanted to die.

The final irony had come when her mother heard that he had left the Circle M.

"You've sacrificed too much," she had said, letting her daughter know she knew about the secret betrothal. A short while later, she was gone.

And Annie had been left alone. Until Stone returned and reignited the fires inside.

But not her love. Such feelings could never be.

He had once rejected her, and now she rejected him. If this truly was a game to him, the score was even between them. That was the way it must remain.

At least, she thought, there was no one other than Josefina who would be able to read her emotions or guess what she was going through. Presenting the strong, cool front she had long fought to maintain, she would gather her waning strength and get on with the rest of her life.

If that life was not as perfect as she had made out, if she really was not doing a good job of taking care of herself, that was her secret to keep, her problem to solve.

In truth, her financial troubles were not much of a secret. Josefina knew, and so did Hiram Wiggins, but only because he had been extending her credit at his store. Expenses were up, especially since she had taken on Henry, and business was down. It was the only reason she hadn't refused to rent Stone a room.

A small voice told her she was lying to herself. She refused to listen.

Somehow she would get past these difficulties. Stone would leave. And once again, all would be well.

Upstairs, Robert Woodruff stood by the open window of his rented room and blew cigar smoke into the cold night air.

A smile of satisfaction rested on his face as he thought of what he had seen and heard in the hall. Miss Annabelle Chapin, prim and proper, leaving a man's room in the middle of the night, half-dressed, her hair wantonly free as she ran down the hall.

I have given you all that I can, she had said, and then a moment later, *I have given you all that I'm capable of.*

Woodruff figured exactly what that *all* included. Stiff-backed Annabelle was clearly capable of a great deal.

He flicked ash outside the window.

Her darker side was not all that he considered. She had as much as admitted that she was financially secure. This was a matter that had concerned him. But not anymore.

Ah, the benefits that came with being a sleepless man. He had heard the door to the rancher's room open and close twice. Ever alert to opportunity, he had peered outside and witnessed her departure.

It had been very interesting. His task now was to figure out how to use the revelations about his landlady to his own good.

Woodruff was always concerned with his own good.

Right now, inspired by the sight of a disheveled woman hurrying from a man's room, he needed, if not a good woman, a woman who was good at being bad.

The Roundup Saloon would offer such a woman, although it seemed too close, leaving him open to discovery. The proximity was no problem. He liked the idea of risk. It made him hard.

Besides, for all her nighttime dalliance, Annabelle would be unlikely to converse with whores. What a hypocrite she was. She deserved what was going to happen to her. Most women did.

Slipping into his coat, leaving off his waistcoat and tie, he ran a hand through his usually carefully combed hair and quietly went out of his room, tiptoed down the stairs, and left the boardinghouse.

The Roundup was just as he'd pictured it—one wide, smoky room of gambling tables, a long bar to one side, to the other an out-of-tune piano played by a musician slumped over the keys and lost to the crowd around him. And, of course, the women. There were a half dozen to choose from, each one gaudily dressed, faces painted, most with their arms draped around the shoulders of a gambling man.

One stood apart, a woman with wild dark hair, hungry, close-set eyes, breasts not quite fitting into her low-cut blouse.

Perfect. He had never cared for subtlety. Subtlety was one thing this woman would not understand.

She saw him as soon as he entered. He nodded, she nodded back. One shot of whiskey, a brief negotiation, and they were leaving through the back door, headed for the crib where she plied her trade.

She said she liked it rough. That was the way he gave it to her. But as he came, it was not her hair or her eyes, not even her breasts or insincere cries of protest that burned in his mind. It was an image of Annabelle Chapin lying beneath him, her face contorted with passion, her body pumping wildly against his.

It was an image that he knew would become reality one day before long. Until that time, however, he must be patient and play the part he had perfected over the past few years.

Chapter Eight

Clare McBride stood in the bedroom doorway and stared at her husband, lying helpless in bed.

What a disgusting man he was. He always had been, even when he was lustily healthy and strong-willed. Now he could rarely control his bodily functions.

She was supposed to clean up after him.

Some things she would not stoop to, not even if he ordered all his family to leave the county and bestowed his fortune on her and her alone. She left it to Tiny to perform the nastiest chores. He couldn't even complain, the fool, not out loud, though his eyes were far too openly critical of her for a lowly cook. She must not forget to see that he was punished for that look—after Tom was gone, of course.

"Clare."

Tom's voice was shaky, but she heard him all too clearly. From his deathbed he shouldn't have been able to see her, but he always knew where she was, or if he did not know, he asked. Though Tiny was dumb, he could usually supply the information. She had to be careful, very careful, to protect herself in these waning weeks.

Already her husband was showing signs of distrusting her, watching every move she made in the sickroom, questioning her about how she passed the time, bringing up past occasions when troubles had arisen on the ranch.

How was she to know he would berate her for firing that cripple, Henry? Jeb sided with the useless cowhand, but he would naturally take up for one of his kind. But Tom? In all their years together, she had never known him to show sympathy for anyone but himself.

Clare gave herself a shake, told herself not to grow faint of heart, not to be mealymouthed like so many others in this cursed family. It could be that she was imagining his suspicions, what with all his repulsive brood hanging around.

She did not put Tanner in that category. Walking to her husband's bedside, she smiled down at him, but it was the younger son who was on her mind—his tall, hard body, the way he held his mouth, the strength in his hands. The details blurred her revulsion for the cadaverous man staring up at her.

She had to be careful not to look too hungry. Even Tom was not so foolish as to believe she could hunger for him.

"Yes, darling," she said softly. "What can I do for you?"

She could make the offer, as long as he did not ask her to touch him. She had not the imagination to continue seeing Tanner's strong, muscled body when she touched the wasted man in the bed. But she could smooth the sheets and the blanket, making a great show of worrying that he was comfortable.

"Where is everybody?" he asked.

She shrugged. "How would I know? You told your children you did not want them hanging around, waiting for you to die."

If only you had told me the same.

"I don't want to see them," he snarled, showing a touch of his old cranky self. "I want to know what they're up to."

"I see them ride in, I see them ride out. That's about all. They're still around, if that's what is worrying you. They're not about to give up the inheritance you promised. Why you made that promise, I don't know. I've been the one who stayed by your side through the years."

It was an old argument, one she had brought

up repeatedly since first hearing about the letter his lawyer had sent out.

As usual, he ignored her.

"And Chase?"

"I keep forgetting about the bastard. He's probably off shooting people. Isn't that what he's paid to do?"

He looked away from her, the eyes once so vividly blue now paling to gray. Like his skin. Like his hair.

"Open the window. I want air."

What a complainer he was. Next he would be asking for water, or a sip of Tiny's chicken soup. He wanted air? He would get it. Tiny would approve, and so would Lauren. So what if a harsh wind was blowing a norther across the Circle M? Maybe he would catch pneumonia. With his already weak lungs, he would not survive long.

She did as he asked. A chill swept through the room. She shivered. Tom's eyes were closed. She ought to get him an extra blanket, she wouldn't have to pull it all the way over his chest. Debating whether to just leave him, she saw Manuelo gesturing to her from the hallway. Murmuring about having to get to work, she left the room and closed the door behind her.

"He's here, Señora Clare," he said in his raspy voice.

She understood right away. "Where?" she asked breathlessly.

He motioned to the far bedroom door. Her heart began to beat fast. Tanner. She licked her lips. She could scarcely breathe.

"Get downstairs and keep Tiny busy."

"How? He does not listen to me."

"I don't know," she said impatiently. "Lie about some emergency outside. Tie him up if you have to. Give me an hour up here alone."

Frowning, Manuelo agreed to do what he could. He always did what she ordered. It was why she had kept him around for so many years.

When he was gone, she turned her attention to the far bedroom and to the man inside. From the moment she'd first laid eyes on Tanner, when she was a bride, she had wanted him. She knew, too, she would have him. He pretended not to want her, but that was only because he did not understand what she could offer.

He needed to know.

Unfastening the top buttons of her gown, making sure a more than adequate expanse of her breasts showed, she hurried down the hall.

"Tanner," she said as she entered the room, then came to a sudden halt. An open valise rested on the bed. The man standing at the chest of drawers against the far wall slowly turned. Hard eyes stared at her out of a hard face. Only the lips moved. They flattened in contempt.

"Stone," she hissed. "What are you doing here?"

"Getting the rest of my belongings, something I should have done four years ago. Lauren told me they were still here."

Clare smirked. "When you went to dinner at her beautiful ranch house. I heard. How cozy for you all."

He turned back to the chest. "I'll get out of your way in a minute. Then you can return to caring for your beloved husband."

How sarcastic he was, how arrogant. He knew she was no more a nurse than he. What made him feel so superior? Not once since his unexpected return had he offered to bathe his father's soiled body or change his dirty sheets.

She ought to beat Manuelo for not being clearer about who was in the room. Stone, the McBride she saw as her biggest threat.

Or was he? It could be that he wasn't totally useless to her. She looked over the fit of his clothes—the leather vest that stretched across his broad back, the trousers that hugged his rear and his long legs. Black hair curled against the collar of his shirt, and she could see a red bandanna tied around his throat.

She studied his rear. Not bad, not bad at all. Not Tanner's, of course, but not scrawny like that of the man in the bed.

Her body warmed, especially the part low in

her abdomen. She wanted another man so much, she could make do with this one for a while. No, she could more than make do. Her hatred of him, matched by his disgust of her, acted like an aphrodisiac. Warm turned to hot, and she felt a sexual pulsing between her legs that was as demanding as it was unexpected.

She had been without a man far too long.

A thought struck. She almost laughed out loud, it was so perfect. Things were far too placid at the ranch, everybody outwardly getting along though she knew they did not like one another. She needed to shake up a few people. Tell Tom his firstborn had made advances, give the old fool a few shocks that might stop his heart.

Most of all, she would let Tanner know he wasn't the only man around. She had been too obvious with him. Let him know she could want someone else.

Or better yet, make him see her as a woman who needed the protection of a strong man. It would be a lie, but she had lied before, to everyone but herself.

She closed the door, turned the key, and dropped it into her pocket. "Take your time."

Stone watched her cross the room toward him.

Her eyes assayed his front as carefully as they had studied his back. Nothing displeased. She could make out the bulge between his legs, not distended just yet, but filled with potential. Her breasts swelled until they almost spilled over the edge of her dress.

She licked her lips, giving her tongue a long time to get the job done.

"What do you do for sex?" she asked. "You're a McBride. I know you want it. Do you get it?"

Scorn was plain in his eyes, just as she'd known it would be . . . for a short while. She did not mind. It wasn't his admiration she was after, although when they were done it was one of the things she would get.

She smiled, her body so wet she could lift her skirts and take him right away.

But she did not want to hurry. It had been so long.

"Poor Stone," she said, unbuttoning the rest of her gown, slipping it from her shoulders, letting him know she wore no undergarment across her bosom, exposing her ripe breasts to his narrowed eyes.

She caressed herself, her thumbs playing back and forth across the hard nipples.

"Did you ever wonder what your father saw in me? Why he wanted me so much, not just when he could steal away but all the time?"

"I know what he saw in you. Except when he married my mother, he never showed much class."

"Wouldn't you like to know how low I can get? Ask your brother. He'll tell you what I did to him. You can tell him what I did to you. That way you can compare."

She got no rise out of him in any way that was visible. She needed to speed things up.

Her gown dropped to the floor, leaving her naked to the waist, the bottom half of her body covered by full-legged drawers, stockings, and shoes. Two more buttons, another discarded item of clothing, and she wore only the stockings and shoes.

She played her fingers through her private hair.

"We can be quick about this," she said. "No one need ever know."

He did not turn away, a fact she took as victory. She knew the picture she presented—smooth ivory skin covering dark-tipped breasts, narrow waist, full hips, and long legs that could wrap around a man and squeeze him half to death.

She finished the killing when the man came inside her. At that moment she destroyed his will.

Stone would be no different. He needed but to gaze on all she offered and he would be hers.

"No."

She took a moment to realize what he'd said.

"No? What are you talking about?"

"No, this won't work. Put your clothes on. You look ridiculous."

"Ridiculous?" she shrieked. Rage overtook her. How dare he! She threw herself at him, fingernails bared to scratch out his eyes. He grabbed her wrists and shoved her aside, as if she had been no more a threat than a wayward child.

He turned from her, grabbed the remaining garments from the drawer, and threw them into the valise, snapping it closed.

"I'm getting out of here. Don't approach me again. I'm not interested."

Hate was bitter on her tongue. She fought for control.

"You'll pay for this," she hissed, her bosom heaving with a fury that she had never known.

"I pay for everything, didn't you know that? Now give me the key."

He reached for her gown; she grabbed it before he could and edged close to the window that opened onto the front of the house. A cold wind chilled her backside, but she scarcely noticed. In one quick gesture she got the key from the pocket and threw it out onto the grass. It was at that moment she saw Tanner approach the house on horseback.

Acting instinctively, she screamed, "No, Stone, don't!" And again, "No! No!"

She put real panic in the scream. Turning her

fingernails onto herself, she scratched her neck and bosom, gouging deep enough to abrade the skin.

"Good God," Stone said behind her.

She shifted to smile at him in triumph.

"You underestimate me. Everyone always does."

Footsteps pounded up the stairs and down the hall, and the doorknob rattled. She screamed for help again, throwing herself against Stone at the moment the door to the bedroom crashed open and Tanner stumbled into the room.

Stone thrust her aside, and the two men stared at one another.

"Thank God you've come," Clare sobbed.

She hurried to Tanner's side and huddled against him, seeking protection from his would-be rapist brother at the same time that she took pleasure in the roughness of his clothes against her bared skin.

He looked down at her, concentrating on the scratches, ignoring everything else she wanted him to see.

She rubbed herself against him like a cat and wrapped her arms around him.

"He was an animal," she said raggedly. "I caught him going through the drawers, and when I asked him what he was doing, he went wild." She breathed against his neck. "Oh, Tanner, I needed you so much."

His hands wrapped around her arms and pulled her away from him.

"Get dressed," he said to her, but he was staring at his brother. "Did you go too far with him, Clare? Did you start something and then change your mind?"

She covered her face to hide her fury. "I told you what happened. You don't believe me."

"He believes you," Stone said. "At least the important parts."

She had never heard such loathing in anyone's voice. It was the one moment in the scene that brought her pleasure, except when she had rubbed against Tanner.

"You're making up my mind for me?" Tanner asked.

"It's not the first time."

"No, it's not."

Clare stared from brother to brother, unable to believe what she heard. Here she was, naked, willing—if one of them had the sense to figure it out. Hell, she would take on the pair of them. And what were they doing? Bickering as they always did.

She grabbed her clothes from the floor, giving them both a chance to see her backside. Surely they weren't so stupid as not to look.

"To hell with it," Stone said. "Don't worry

about being second in line, little brother. She's about as fresh as she can get. I did not complete the rape."

Jerking up his valise, he was through the broken door and gone in three long strides, leaving Clare to smile at the man she really wanted and to plump her breasts, urging him to stroke their pebble tips.

Stone hurried down the hallway. He wouldn't look in on his father as he had planned. He wanted to put as much distance as he could between himself and this hated house, and do it fast.

Footsteps on the stairs brought him up short. The lawyer Bill Hanes and Doc Pierce blocked his path.

"Where is everybody?" Hanes asked. "There was no one downstairs, so we let ourselves in."

"Just a little family gathering," Stone said. "McBride style."

"Which means trouble," Hanes said.

"How's Tom?" Pierce asked.

"You'll have to see for yourself," Stone said.

Pierce scratched his beard. "Seems every time I come out here, something's going on. It's a miracle that man is still alive."

"It's the trouble that keeps him going."

Pierce opened the sickroom door.

"Good God, you could store ice in here. You awake, Tom?"

Stone waited until he heard his father's grumbled answer, then hurried past the lawyer down the stairs. He had one more stop before leaving. He would make it quick.

His purpose took him to the barn. During the awkward meal at the Lassiter ranch, Lauren had mentioned not only his clothes but also a saddle he had bought with one of the few real paychecks his father had ever given him. He would take the saddle now, not caring to wait to find out how all the property was divided in the settling of his father's estate.

Already he felt like a ghoul waiting around for something that should have been rightfully his, at least in part, with no strings attached. When the will was read, there would be strings. He knew it as surely as he knew that Clare Brown McBride was a bitch.

If he had a choice . . . But he didn't.

Life had a way of getting at him in ways he did not expect. Annie had shyly offered a glimpse of herself, then denied what both of them wanted. Clare brazenly displayed what she knew far too well most men would fight for. She had badly misjudged him.

As far as his relationship with Tanner was concerned, he did not care what happened between them now. His brother had already shown his opinion of him, in a way Stone could never forget.

His family could go to the devil.

At the back of the empty barn, he had to search for the saddle, brush the cobwebs aside, and set it on the ground beside his valise. There had been a bridle, too—black rawhide trimmed with silver, matching the black tooled leather of the saddle.

He rummaged through a jumble of leather and whips, and was just putting his hand on the black and silver bridle when he heard the unmistakable click of a gun trigger.

"Get your hands up," a harsh voice ordered.

Stone did as he was told.

Turning slowly, he stared at the business end of a six-shooter pointed toward his heart. Lifting his gaze past the trail-soiled duster hanging loose on the gunman, he stared into a pair of blue eyes that were startlingly familiar, the eyes of a McBride.

At last he was meeting his half-brother, Chase. He was not warmed by the encounter, considering that Sidewinder's new sheriff wanted either to shoot him or throw him in jail.

Chapter Nine

"I didn't know you'd come back," Chase said, but he didn't move the gun.

Stone lowered his arms but kept a cool eye on the trigger. It wasn't hard feelings toward a half-breed that made him do it, nor fear of the law. He would have done the same if he were facing any McBride.

"Don't worry," he said. "I'm not taking anything that belongs to you."

In what seemed almost an afterthought, Chase pulled aside the front of his duster and holstered the gun, allowing a glimpse of his badge.

"Nothing out here belongs to me," he said. "I was protecting private property." His voice was casual, but there was nothing casual in his eyes.

"I misunderstood what you were up to."

"There's a lot of that going around."

Stone studied the man called Chase McBride, trying to analyze if he felt anything for or against what he was looking at. A man did not meet a new brother every day, and this one was no infant, but six feet tall, hard-featured, and armed. Stone finally decided it was curiosity that moved him, not anything stronger, nothing warm, nothing close to familial.

"You don't look the way I imagined," he said. "Except for the eyes, of course. There's no mistaking them."

"How do I look? Whiter?"

Chase's voice remained light, but the tightness in his expression remained. Stone wondered how much taunting and prejudice the man had endured through the years.

"Maybe a little," he said, being honest, "though I can see the Indian in you all right. Older is what I was thinking. In my mind I had put you about Tanner's age. Or maybe Lauren's. I was trying to figure when Tom started catting around."

"A long time ago. From what the lawyer told me, you and I are about the same age."

The old anger, the old hurt, surged in Stone as if it were new. For the first time he took his eyes off Chase.

"I knew about the women when I was growing up. He never was one for whores. He had his standards." Stone spoke with a smirk. "So-called respectable women, those were the ones he preferred, like the wife of the man who used to run the hotel. They didn't stay around Sidewinder long."

"It's a wonder someone hasn't shot him in the back."

Stone nodded. "An angry husband, or one of the women he used. I found a letter once, from a woman who signed it Mary Raines, like otherwise he wouldn't know which Mary was writing, begging him to come see her. It was an old letter, mixed in with some old bills of sale. I don't know why he kept it, or even when it was written, but it was filled with anger. I didn't come across it until I was almost grown." He looked back at Chase. "Now I learn that when my mother got in the family way, right after they stood before the preacher, Tom went looking for his pleasure somewhere else."

"As long as we're swapping family stories, I can tell you he found an Apache squaw living at a ranch in the county."

Stone studied the hard lines of his brother's face, the high cheekbones, the sharp jaw. Chase stood with his weight pitched forward, everything about him combative. Anyone coming up against him would be a fool to arouse his anger.

Already he had proven he was not shy about pulling a gun.

He didn't worry Stone.

"I didn't think Indians liked their women called squaws," he said.

"I was saving you the trouble."

"There you go judging me again."

It was Chase's turn to study him. "When I left two weeks ago, no one seemed to think you would show up."

"Yeah, well, I kind of surprised myself. Then I got back to find there was another McBride in the bushes. A half-breed lawman. Not that you were around tending to business."

"I don't owe you an explanation."

"I'm not asking for one."

The two brothers stared at one another, neither making a sound. Chase seemed to arrive at some kind of decision. He was the first to speak.

"I escorted my wife and son to the mission where I was raised. Word got to Sidewinder that Padre Rodriguez had taken ill. He was once kind to Faith when she needed kindness very much. She wanted to do what she could to help him."

"You've got a son?"

"Luke was one of the orphans at the mission. We decided to make him ours."

"Being kind."

"Kindness had nothing to do with it."

Stone almost smiled. This new brother was demonstrating another McBride trait besides being quick to judge and slow to talk about himself: He hated admitting to anything that might be taken as a weakness.

"My wife and son are at the house resting and getting some food. I'd have joined them, only I heard someone slamming around in the barn."

"I didn't know I was supposed to be quiet. How is the padre?"

"Better. He'll live a few more years."

Despite himself, Stone thought of Tom. He didn't have anyone eager to nurse him through his illness, though Stone knew that Lauren and Tanner's wife, Callie, came over when they could, subjecting themselves to his coldness and his wife's scorn.

That was because they were family, not because they had a strong urge to make a dying man comfortable.

But then, Tom had never treated anyone with anything other than contempt. Stone would have seen the justice in the situation if he didn't see it first as pathetic.

What, he wondered, would the women think if they knew that Clare had disrobed for the male McBrides? If Tanner related the scene to the little wife, he would probably leave out the moment when the stepmother rubbed herself against him, instead concentrating on his brother's part in the proceedings.

Stone would keep the whole mess to himself. Who was he supposed to tell, Annie? He doubted that she would believe him, especially if he told her everything; and if she did, she would misunderstand, assuming that the woman had been given encouragement.

Not that his problems were any of Annie's business. She had made that abundantly clear.

Disgust and impatience took hold of him. Putting distance between himself and the Circle M, between himself and Annie and Sidewinder, was the only way he could enjoy a little peace.

Besides, he had business to tend to, business that had nothing to do with the ranch or his family or his onetime love. Slinging the bridle over his shoulder, he picked up the saddle and valise.

"If you're not going to arrest me, I'll be moving on now."

"I'm not going to arrest you. As long as you behave yourself."

If Chase was showing a little humor, Stone could not read it in his eyes. He did not know his brother well enough. He figured he never would.

He made a hasty exit. Outside, a cold wind struck him. If he were a decent kind of brother, he ought to go to the house and introduce himself to Chase's wife and son. Four years ago he would have done just that.

Instead, he headed for his horse, tethered in a patch of grass halfway to the barn. That was when he saw Clare's lackey Manuelo and the cook Tiny coming from the direction of the corral.

He waved to them and called out, "Anyone asks, tell them I've left for a few days. But I'll be back."

I have no choice.

He rode hard into town, going straight to the boardinghouse. Carmen, overripe as ever, watched from the dining room doorway as he strode up the stairs, still carrying the saddle and valise, the bridle tucked under his arm. Annie's friendly new tenant—Stone couldn't remember his name, only his slickly combed hair—watched from the room across the hallway. Neither man spoke.

Dropping the saddle and bridle under the window, he added a few belongings to the valise before snapping it closed, then grabbed a fleece-lined jacket from a hook by the door. His last act was to throw a fistful of dollars on the bed, keeping most of his winnings to himself. Surely Annie would take his generous payment as a sign that he planned to return, that she was to hold his room for him.

Or maybe she would sell the saddle and his

remaining belongings, put all the money in the bank, and consider herself well rid of a pest.

Except that he was more than that to her, and they both knew it. Only a day earlier, standing in the spot where he now stood, she hadn't objected to anything they were doing, not until long after he had unbuttoned her gown. He didn't have to concentrate much to taste her on his tongue, to feel her softness against the palm of his hand.

The image of her, the sensations, stayed with him long after he was down the stairs, out-of-doors, well on his way to Fort Worth. Gradually his thoughts turned to his destination, to the small house on the edge of the busy cow town, to the back bedroom of that house, to the person who waited for him there.

Whatever softness he retained came to him now. He had been away from her too long. He needed to return, if only for a few hours. Then he would be out on the road again, heading back with renewed purpose to the cesspit that his onetime much-loved home had become.

Clare yearned to carve out Stone McBride's liver and feed it to the dogs. How dare he reject her? Worse, Tanner had suspected that Stone had repelled her advances.

"Put your clothes on," he had ordered as soon as Stone was out of the room. Tanner had barely looked at her. He had not understood all that she had to give.

"He practically tore them off," she had said, whining but unable to sound any other way.

Tanner had not looked impressed.

"I don't care how they got off. Put them back on."

"But—"

"Now."

Reluctantly she'd picked up her gown and drawers, holding them in front of her.

"Are you going to tell Tom?"

Tanner was at the door when she'd put the question to him.

"He already thinks you're bedding me," she'd added. "Why not turn suspicion onto your brother? You don't like him. Maybe he'll be dropped from the will."

When he glanced back at her, she dropped the clothes.

"Your father understands my needs. He can't satisfy them anymore, but that doesn't mean he wants his sons to go where he has been so many times." She rested her hands on her thighs and played with herself with her thumbs. "You want to really upset him? Drop your pants. He'll smell you on me. Smell is the one sense he hasn't lost."

He'd looked at her hands, at what she was

doing. He couldn't help it. Whatever she saw in his eyes, at least it was a reaction.

He'd got out of the room fast. The fool. There she had stood, aroused, willing—hell, more than willing, feverish was more the truth—and he had left her.

But he had looked. And he would remember. Curling up on the bed, she continued what she had begun, a poor second choice to having Tanner lie on top of her and give her what they both wanted. Once again she was taking what she could. The thought of eviscerating Stone made her climax all the more intense.

What to do next, besides getting dressed, combing her hair, and going out to pretend that nothing out of the ordinary had occurred?

She fumed about the matter for a couple of days, avoiding her husband's room as much as she could, relieved that she didn't have to see Stone's grim face again, but coming up with no plan that would see her true goals reached.

No one knew them, not even Tanner.

But they were real to her, and as vital as they had ever been. She hadn't been able to cause more than a momentary trouble between Stone and Tanner. She needed to come up with something that would shake the entire family, something that would send them running from the Circle M. It wasn't enough that they hated their father or that he hated them.

Or did he? Sometimes she wasn't sure. He growled at anyone who came close, even Lauren, but he also asked Tiny how everyone was getting along. At least that was what he seemed to be asking, though he seldom let her hear every word of the conversation. How Tiny communicated, she wasn't sure, but when he left the room, usually with the window cracked and the curtains open, Tom seemed satisfied.

Three days after her humiliation in the bedroom, she grew restless enough to order a horse hitched to the carriage. A fast ride was what she needed, and clean air that did not smell of death. Wearing her best black dress and matching cloak, a feathered bonnet sitting atop her carefully arranged hair, she cracked a whip over the horse's rump and headed for town.

These were the times she liked best, when she was alone, when she could remember, when she could plan. On this morning, however, the remembering and the planning simply would not come.

As she rode through town, she slowed the horse's pace. Much to her surprise, a woman waved to her from the side of the dusty street. No one ever spoke to her; no one had ever gestured in such a manner, though they stared openly from the street and the shop windows.

Clare studied the woman a moment before realizing who she was—the proprietor of the boardinghouse—but she could not recall her name. She was tempted to ride on, away from the unimportant creature, but a voice at the back of her mind stopped her. It was a voice she always obeyed. Ever open to opportunity, she reined the horse to a halt and watched as the woman hurried close.

"Mrs. McBride," she said, "thank you for stopping. I was wondering about something and thought perhaps you might help."

There was worry in her voice. Clare studied her shrewdly. She was dressed in black, high-necked and long-sleeved, as if she would melt if light touched her skin. Her hair was pulled back and twisted into a bun that looked painfully tight. She must have seen the McBride carriage go by and run outside without bothering about a bonnet or cloak.

Her features were adequate—straight nose, full lips, and fine brown eyes. Clare had never made the mistake of undervaluing an opponent, which included all women of every age. This one might prove attractive if she ever smiled. But she was not smiling now.

Assuming an air of helpfulness, Clare nodded. "Whatever can I do? We've never met, have we?"

"I'm Annabelle Chapin. I own the boardinghouse."

"Ah, Mrs. Chapin, of course."

"Miss Chapin."

Clare smiled.

"One of my boarders has been gone for several days, and I hoped you might tell me something about him. He's your stepson Stone."

Clare lost the smile, then hurriedly pasted it back in place.

"Ah, Stone. Has that rascal neglected to pay his rent?"

"No, not at all. In fact, he's been more than generous."

"Has he?" Clare was finding it very difficult to remain sweet.

"But he left some of his belongings, and I didn't know . . . well, if anything had happened to him at the ranch."

"You know about the ranch."

"I . . . yes, I know that's where he works. Everyone knows about his father. I should be asking about him. How is Mr. McBride?"

Miss Chapin looked decidedly ill at ease. And more worried than ever. She cared for the bastard, though she did not want to admit it, probably even to herself. Women were fools to deceive themselves. That was a mistake Clare never made.

"My poor husband continues to hold on. What a brave soul he is."

The woman's eyes narrowed ever so lightly, and Clare feared she had gone too far with the saddened-wife role. She simply could not make it seem sincere.

"Is Stone staying with him?"

Clare made a hasty decision.

"No, not at all. There was a rather unpleasant scene a few days ago. He left angry. As far as I know, no one has seen him since."

Annabelle Chapin looked away hurriedly, but not before Clare could see the dark anguish in her eyes.

"He does that," she said softly.

"Does what?" Clare asked.

"Leaves when he's angry."

Clare had no idea what she was talking about, but that mattered little. Miss Chapin was upset. A woman did not get in such a state about a man she did not care for. Miss Chapin cared for Stone a great deal. And she did not want anyone to know.

When the woman looked back at her, the anguish was gone, replaced by a decided glint of anger. Clare liked the anger as well. The feelings Miss Chapin had for the man must run deep indeed. And Stone, being the private sort he was, the unbending McBride, the controlled one, would not know how to deal with affection—if, that is, he even recognized it.

Clare bit her lower lip. "I probably shouldn't tell you this," she said in a whisper, leaning halfway out of the carriage to make sure her words were heard, "but the scene I mentioned was a private one between the two of us. Very private, if you know what I mean."

"You and Stone?"

The woman sounded surprised, almost disbelieving, and Clare swallowed a sharp retort.

"Please don't reveal this to anyone, but he made what I suppose you could call advances. I hardly knew what to do, with my poor husband, Stone's father, lying in his sickbed down the hall. Naturally I rebuffed him. Just then, Tanner entered and came to my rescue. Stone left, and as far as I know, no one has seen him since."

She brushed a tear from her cheek, thinking as she did so how useful it was to be able to cry at will.

"I do hope you haven't been foolish enough to become involved with him," she said.

When at last she met the woman's eyes again, she got a shock. Annabelle Chapin was staring at her with open skepticism. The lie had been carried too far.

Clare did some fast thinking. "Has he told you much about me?"

"What would there be to tell?"

"That I married his father too quickly after he lost his first wife. Did he also tell you Tom was lonely? That he had been lonely for a long time?"

"I am not a confidante of your stepson's, Mrs. McBride. Thank you for your help."

Clare watched as Miss Chapin whirled and hurried back down the walkway toward the boardinghouse. Sitting back in the carriage, Clare took a moment to think. If Stone really had a relationship with this woman, it was one no one knew about. Annabelle Chapin wasn't a fool. She had a reputation to maintain—that of a spinster leading a respectable life. Her business, her standing in the community, would depend on it.

Clare smiled to herself. Stone, invincible Stone, uncaring and unreachable, might have a weak spot after all. If he did, it came in the form of a solemn-faced woman in an ugly dress, a woman wound as tight as the bun at the back of her neck.

McBride solidarity was fragile at best. If she were ever to shatter that solidarity completely, Annabelle Chapin might be one of the few weapons Clare had to work with.

The first thing she must do when she returned to the ranch was put Manuelo on to watching the woman closely, even if it meant his staying in town. The man could be maddeningly dense at times, but he was also ruthless and devoted to her, two traits she valued highly.

She took another look down the walkway, in time to see the Chapin woman crossing the street, straight-backed, stepping smoothly around the piles of manure in her path. Despite all that smoothness, she had a distracted air about her, as if everything she did was by rote. She also showed a frailty that Clare welcomed.

Unexpectedly, an image darkened her mind, of another time, of another woman lost to love. She herself was just a little girl, an onlooker to the woman's misery, and she was crying so hard she could not stop.

Clare shook her head. The image was absurd. She couldn't remember crying, never for real, not in all her life. Crying displayed a weakness. She was never weak.

As for the woman, she could not think about her, not now. Her mind must remain focused on the present; later she could indulge in remembrances of the past.

Snapping the whip over the rump of the carriage horse, she reined toward the road leading back to the Circle M, her frame of mind much more cheerful than it had been an hour ago when she left.

Chapter Ten

Annie yearned to get her hands around Stone McBride's throat. She had nothing erotic in mind. Violence was her only goal.

She stormed into the boardinghouse; with every determined step she was picturing her fingers pressed into the self-centered rascal's warm flesh.

How dare he be all right when she had been worrying herself sick over the past few days? The least he could have done was break a leg.

She glanced into the parlor. Robert Woodruff and Iola Simpkins sat on the sofa. Annie got the feeling they had been having a gay good time, mostly from the catlike smile on the Widow Simpkins's face as she gazed at the man.

Woodruff could not hold his smile. The instant he saw her in the hallway, he looked concerned, a small frown wrinkling his otherwise unwrinkled brow. He also looked ready to ask if anything was wrong, and if so, to spring to his feet and hurry to her rescue.

Annie did not want to be rescued. She wanted to enjoy her wrath for as long as it would last.

Before either of the cozy pair could speak, Annie whirled toward the dining room and slammed her way to the kitchen. Carmen sat on a stool by the table peeling potatoes. Josefina was washing dishes at the sink. Both stared at her, surprised. The *patróna* never made so much noise.

Annie sighed. It was another of her curses to be lonely—all right, she admitted it, she was occasionally struck by the feeling—without ever being alone.

Josefina gestured for her daughter to leave. The girl abandoned her paring knife and was out the door and gone before either woman could blink.

"Señor Stone?" Josefina asked. "You have learned something?"

There was no keeping anything from her dear friend. "He's all right."

Josefina nodded sympathetically. "For this we are sorry, *patróna*."

Dear Josefina. She always understood.

"Very sorry," Annie said.

She didn't mean it, no matter how much she wanted to, but it felt good to say it. Her coldness made it easier to cope with the worry that had driven her out of her mind. With all Stone had told her about the Circle M, she could imagine one of the brothers shooting another and then burying the evidence. Even Tom might rise from his sickbed and inflict damage on one of his boys.

With the McBrides, anything was possible. The least of their sins, but the most constant, was thoughtlessness.

Josefina stood motionless, a wet washcloth dripping into the pail of dishwater in front of her. It was clear she wanted to know more.

"He went away angry, after an argument." Annie hesitated. "The way he did with me four years ago."

Though the final argument had happened before Josefina had come to Sidewinder, she knew a little about the breakup. She had guessed a great deal more than Annie had ever openly revealed.

"Who tells you this?" Josefina asked.

"Clare McBride."

"Ahhh." The word was dragged out far too long to give Annie comfort. "The cause of this argument, was it over the care of his padre?"

"Not exactly." Annie swallowed hard. "She said she denied him what he wanted."

Another long "Ahhh," followed by, "There is no need to ask what Señor Stone wanted, or what was denied."

Annie caught the look in Josefina's eyes. "I don't believe her either, at least not everything she said."

Settling herself on the stool, she took up the abandoned paring knife and got to work on the potatoes. Clare's silky, whispery voice came back to her.

. . . he made advances.

Right away Annie had seen through the lie. Stone would never involve himself in such a way with a woman he hated so much.

Or would he? He had come back to Sidewinder declaring openly enough that he no longer loved his former betrothed, but every time she got angry with him, she found herself in his arms. What if he was always aroused by a woman in such a state?

If that were true, he must stay in a ready-for-bed condition most of the time. Without much effort, he could enrage just about any female who strayed within a mile of him.

She pictured him looking at her in the middle of his room, his incredibly blue eyes assessing her as if she were already undressed, his mouth moving in on hers. The image proved too much. Her eyes watered, and she could no longer see what she was doing.

"*Patróna*, you have cut yourself. You are bleeding on the potatoes."

Annie blinked. Red drops on white were easy to spot, even through a blur of tears. She dropped the knife and sucked her thumb.

Her first reaction was economic, as it was so often these days. "What a waste," she said as she stared down at the bowl.

"I can wash the potatoes," Josefina said. "No one will know." She grabbed the bowl before Annie could protest, set it aside, and inspected the injury. "It is not deep. I must bandage it for you."

"I'd rather suck on it." Annie attempted a smile. "I'm feeling a little childish right now." She sighed. "Why do I let myself get so upset over the man? There's nothing between us anymore."

Josefina looked at her with an all-too-knowing eye. "If this is what the *patróna* believes, then this is what must be so."

Annie hated it when her friend agreed with her in such a tone.

"He was rude not to leave a note, or a message. Someone must have been around here. Robert Woodruff, for instance. He never seems to leave, not for very long."

"Señor Woodruff does not wish to be far from someone who lives in this house."

"Mrs. Simpkins? They did seem to be

chummy in the parlor just now, but—"

Josefina muttered a few words in Spanish, a habit of hers when she wanted to call her employer *estúpido* and could think of no softer substitute word. Apparently, she did not believe in a possible liaison between the two boarding-house guests.

The smooth-talking widower and the older, giggling widow did seem an unlikely pair.

Annie sighed. It was an unwelcome habit she had formed in the past few weeks.

"I'm doing you no good in here. If I try to help, I'll bleed all over the food."

"Find Carmen. She will help me." Josefina shook her head in disgust. "Look for her outside the door, watching the men go into the saloon."

The mother proved right, but Carmen gave no argument when asked to return to the potatoes. Instead, she tossed a smile over her shoulder at one of the men and slowly went inside. The girl was a true flirt, but was she anything worse? Annie did not think so. She had the body of a woman, but she liked to play games like a child.

The real problem was that she might misjudge a man someday and be irreparably hurt.

Poor Josefina. She, too, had her woes.

Annie took a moment to glance up and down the street, not looking for Stone, of course, simply assessing the raucous, shabby town that was her home. Her one point of pride was that the boardinghouse was neither raucous nor shabby. But only because she worked hard to keep it so.

Hurrying inside, she glanced into the parlor and was relieved to find it empty. She was in no mood to hear Mrs. Simpkins's threats about moving in with her niece. Nor did she wish to speak with Robert Woodruff. The man was pleasant enough and he did tell amusing tales, but sometimes her cheeks ached from so much unaccustomed smiling.

She walked swiftly down the long hallway, went out the back, and knocked at the door of the shack that sat a few feet behind the boardinghouse.

Henry opened the door and scratched at his scraggly beard. "Something wrong?"

Henry usually thought something was wrong, probably because that was the way much in his life had gone—wrong.

"I'm in the mood to dig in the garden. It's getting far too overgrown. Could you get out the tools?"

"It looks fine to me," he said, bristling. His gray eyes squinted. "Besides, you got on fine clothes for such dirty work."

"How can you tell? All my dresses look alike."

Henry scratched harder at his beard.

"I'm sorry," Annie said. "I'm in a foul mood.

You're right, of course. I'll go get an apron and some gloves."

She turned, but not before he muttered something about feeling sorry for the weeds.

Three more days went by without any sign of improvement in her humor. The boardinghouse benefited. She dusted everything in sight, took down the draperies and beat them over the clothesline in the back, rolled up the rugs, waxed the floors, beat the rugs and put them back again, all with the help of her uncomplaining staff.

She was considering returning to the garden when she overheard Josefina and Henry talking outside the back door, in a rare conversation that was not filled with bickering.

"I'm so tired I just might fall down and break the other leg," Henry said.

"The *patróna* has much on her mind."

"Sure wish McBride would get back. She ain't happy when he's here, but without him it seems to me she's a mite worse."

"She has other worries besides Señor Stone."

Henry clucked his tongue. "We for sure ain't had much business lately."

"The winter is always slow. Christmas approaches. People stay close to their homes at such a time."

"That don't pay the bills."

"It is not for us to criticize the *patróna*."

"I ain't criticizing her. She's the bestest woman I ever knowed, though she sure don't want no one thinking it."

"Your words sounded very much like criticism."

"That ain't how I meant them."

And the two were off to arguing again.

Annie ducked into her room and closed the door. The exhaustion she had been holding off for days hit her. She felt as if the roof had caved in and all the falling debris had landed on her. Tempting though it was to throw her body on the bed, hide beneath the covers, and try to forget what she had overheard, she began instead to pace.

How selfish she was. She had been thinking only of herself, making certain she kept too busy to worry about any one particular part of her life. She had completely forgotten about Josefina and Henry. If she worked, they worked. It was the way they were.

They deserved far more than the roof over their heads and the food she was able to provide them. Money would be appreciated, too, more than the pittance she gave them when she could.

Worse was her growing debt to Hiram Wiggins. If she was going to worry about anyone, Hiram ought to be at the top of the list.

She ceased pacing and stared out the window at the next-door saloon. A long time ago, Ace Bellamy, owner of the Roundup, had stopped her on the street with a suggestion for the two of them to make extra money. Despite the practicality of his idea, she had not been interested, and she had, far too snippily, told him just that.

She wasn't snippy now. She was worried. And she was in need. She also needed to apologize to the man for her rudeness.

A new resolve struck her, but she waited until after dinner to do anything about it. Her two guests asked her to join them in the parlor, but she declined. Anyway, Mrs. Simpkins did not seem especially enthusiastic in the invitation, and Robert Woodruff far too much so.

In her room she hastily smoothed her hair into its tightest bun, seeing no need to look wanton or even feminine, threw on a cloak, more to cover anything that might be considered a womanly curve than to ward off the outside chill, and hurried down the long hall toward the front door.

Robert Woodruff stepped from the parlor directly into her path.

"Could I assist you in any way?" he asked. "If you have an errand, perhaps I could take care of it for you."

He had not, she recalled, made such an offer when she was beating draperies and rugs, and she hadn't so much as laid eyes on him when she was waxing the floor.

She forced a smile. "Thank you for the offer, but this is something I must take care of."

She got through the door fast, as much relieved that he did not follow as she was worried over what she was about to do. Dark had descended, and she took a moment to draw a breath. Music and laughter filled the night, and she could detect the scents of smoke and whiskey coming from the Roundup, a place she had always told herself was a hotbed of decadence. Her opinion had been fortified after Stone's return and his nightly visits to the place.

For some reason, she thought back to the time in the spring when the McBrides were beginning to return to the fold. Tanner had been the first to answer his father's summons, and then the woman who was to become his wife. Annie hadn't known all that was to happen, of course, when Callie Winslow took a room and promptly applied to Ace Bellamy for work in the saloon.

Annie had not been gracious to either Callie or Tanner, but she'd told herself it was because she was working very hard and hadn't the luxury of patience. Josefina, along with Carmen, was in Mexico at the time, summoned to the village of her birth to care for her dying mother. During the months the pair was gone, Annie had come to realize just how much she depended on them, not only for help but for companionship.

Adding to her distress was the certainty that she had not wanted anything to do with any McBride. By the time Lauren arrived, Josefina was back in Sidewinder, but that did not bring the complete relief Annie was expecting. Like everyone else in town, she knew that Stone had been summoned. Unlike everyone else, she was not so sure he would ignore the summons.

Her fear had been well founded. She would never forget standing in the back of Hiram's store and hearing Stone's deep, strong voice for the first time in four years.

Life had not been the same since that day, an example being her loitering out here in the dark, summoning her courage to go into a place she had long viewed with scorn.

In her heart she knew it was the laughter that offended her most. Life was serious. No one should be having such a good time.

But if they were, she might as well get some money out of it. Ace Bellamy certainly did.

When she went through the swinging doors, barely avoiding a drunken cowboy who was staggering out to the street, she got no looks of stunned surprise, no gasps, no sudden silence in the room. Instead, a couple of the women threw her a curious glance, then got back to the men they were with. For the most part, the men seemed intent on their cards, though a few kept an arm draped around a woman leaning close.

The smell of smoke and whiskey was strong, as she'd expected, but not so much that she failed to detect another odor: the scent of money, piled on the tables in amounts that to her seemed obscene. The sight was also fascinating. She could hardly look away, not until a shouting match between a couple of gamblers drew her attention to the back of the saloon.

She grew faint of heart and was about to retreat when she saw Ace Bellamy approach her from the bar.

"Miss Chapin, what an honor," he said smoothly.

A tall, sharp-featured man, he was not exactly handsome, but he was slickly turned out, his dark hair hanging straight to his white collar, a small, well-trimmed moustache arching over his smiling lips. With his high cheekbones and darkly fringed eyes, he gave the appearance of having mixed heritage. When he looked at her, he was all graciousness.

"Can I offer you a drink?" he asked. "No, I suppose not. But why don't we take one of the tables at the side and you can tell me what brings you into the Roundup."

"I'd rather stand."

"Of course," he said without a blink. "But

away from the door. We do sometimes have trouble with hasty entrances and retreats."

She let him guide her to the bar. One of the saloon women approached, a heavy-bosomed blonde with more hair than Annie had ever seen on one person before, though she was badly in need of a respectable top to her gown. Bellamy waved her away. Pouting, she leaned over the bar.

"Barney, how's about a whiskey?" she purred.

The jowly, solemn-faced bartender shifted his eyes from her bosom to his boss. Bellamy nodded, and a shot glass of liquor appeared in front of the woman. She threw it back in one swallow. With a sly look at Annie, she swerved away, hips twisting, and made a path toward the piano on the far side of the room.

Annie watched the whole thing in awe. The saloon woman might not match her boss's good manners, but she managed to make Annie feel more than a little inadequate in the woman department. It was a good thing she was not trying to play on her femininity tonight. In the Roundup she was hopelessly outclassed.

Despite the closeness of the air, she held her cloak tight to her chest. "Maybe this is an inconvenient time for us to talk. I can come back another time."

"I assure you, Miss Chapin, you have my undivided attention."

It was the encouragement she needed to get this over with. With her back to the door, ignoring the noise and the smoke and the smells, she got to the point right away.

"You mentioned once that some of your customers had requested a place to eat. We both agreed the other facilities in town were less than desirable."

"You speak politely. As I recall, I spoke of the swill offered elsewhere."

"Yes, of course."

Annie was growing more nervous by the second, as if she had a premonition that something disastrous was about to happen. The best thing she could do was hurry on and get out.

"You suggested I provide meals for these customers. For a handsome fee, you said, with you taking a share for guiding them to me."

"It seems an equitable arrangement."

"I agree. Let's talk money. I am prepared to tell you how much such a meal would cost, what I would expect to make in profit, and what I consider a fair sum for you."

"Ah, a woman after my heart. You know what you want to say."

Annie almost smiled. Efficiency did have its advantages over big breasts. Taking a deep breath, she threw figures at him, and he nodded at each one.

"Don't you need to write any of this down?" she asked.

"Where business is concerned, I have a remarkable memory. As do you." He said it admiringly, then proceeded to discuss details about when he could let her know about diners, how many there might be, suggesting they start off slowly to see how the arrangement worked.

They shook hands, and he held on. His grip had a reassuring feel to it. She made no attempt to pull away.

"I will not, I assure you, refer the more unruly customers to your establishment. Believe it or not, I do have a number of perfectly respectable patrons who find an evening of cards a pleasant diversion from the cares of the day. For instance, there's the gentleman entering now."

Annie glanced toward the door, and her heart soared. Stone stood there. He had returned. She had not realized how glorious the sight of him would be, tall and finely honed, his black coat worn over a white shirt, unbuttoned at the throat. He was hatless, his dark hair unkempt enough to make her fingers itch to ruffle it a little more.

Unfortunately, he was also glaring at her in a way that pretty much killed the glory. Her first instinct had been to rush toward him and make sure he was truly all right, but the coldness of his expression kept her in place.

"He seems disturbed by something," Bellamy said as he dropped her hand and took a step away.

Annie felt a little of her own anger. Stone had no right to look so good, or so judgmental. After all, he hadn't bothered to let her know he was leaving. Typical Stone behavior. She came close to grabbing the saloon owner's hand again.

"He's always disturbed. Pay no attention to him."

"I have dealt with McBrides before. You ask too much."

As she watched, the buxom blonde in the skimpy gown appeared at Stone's side, leaning close, pressing her breast against his arm. He looked at the woman and said something. The woman smiled.

Annie turned hollow inside. This was how she imagined him spending time at the Roundup. She held on to the bar for support. Somehow she had to get past him and out the door. Somehow she had to show him she did not care.

It was at that most unfortunate moment that one of the men at the closest table chose to stand and bellow, "Calling me a cheat is fightin' words."

Tossing the table aside, sending money and cards flying, he drew his gun. Stunned, Annie stared at the sudden violence. Bellamy jerked her to the floor as Barney came over the bar, white apron flapping, and tackled the man with the gun.

Gunfire exploded. A bullet passed over Annie's head, shattering a bottle of whiskey on the shelf behind the bar. It was all over in an instant, all but the pounding of her heart and the ringing in her ears.

The bartender stood, straightened his apron, and shook his head. "Sorry about the whiskey, Ace," he said.

"It happens," Bellamy said.

Annie blinked and tried to clear her mind. She would have thought she'd imagined the whole thing except that there was the grizzled, unkempt gunman lying spread-eagled on the floor scarcely three feet from her. He groaned once, then held still.

Bellamy helped Annie to her feet. She clung to his arm, expecting a massive brawl to break out, with women screaming, shots going wild, chaos ruling. As if he did this sort of thing every day, the gambler who had been the object of the gunman's ire righted the table and began to gather up the scattered cards and cash. Otherwise, all was quiet, everyone pretty much remaining at his business, keeping to his place.

Except for Stone, who was bearing down on her with mayhem in his eye. For a moment, she had forgotten him and the blonde.

He seemed to move in a cloud of dust, an

avenger who sent scrambling anyone who got in his way. He looked her over, as if examining her for damage. On the outside she was fine, she could have told him, but nothing inside was working right.

Without a word to either her or the saloon owner, he clamped a hand around her wrist and dragged her toward the door, barely making it around the fallen man, who, as best she could tell, was being ignored.

Coming out of her shock, she tried to dig her heels in, but her captor was too strong. She could do nothing but stumble after him, embarrassingly aware that all eyes were at last turned on her, the method of her departure apparently more interesting than the almost-gunfight.

A quick glimpse back at the saloon was all she allowed herself. Unfortunately, it included the blonde, smirking at her from across the room as the piano man beat the keys in a loud and lively tune.

Annie had time to think that, with the thoughts of murder pounding in her heart, he ought to be playing a dirge.

Chapter Eleven

Stone kept walking, skirting tables of gawking onlookers, ignoring Annie's yelps of protest as he pulled her toward the dark outside. At the swinging doors, his progress was slowed by a customer trying to enter, but he kept on going, taking Annie with him, and the man hurriedly stepped aside.

"Miss Chapin?" The query came from an astonished voice behind him.

Stone gave his captive no chance to reply, but he noticed that her protests had ceased, along with her struggles to free herself. On the street he saw Chase striding toward the saloon. Another McBride cleaning up a mess. He didn't bother to wave or acknowledge his brother's approach.

When he had Annie within the sanctity of the boardinghouse, away from public view, she renewed both her struggles and her protests. After her very public appearance in the Roundup, Annie was a little late in being concerned with proprieties. Still, he would honor that concern as best he could. Their confrontation would be in private. He glanced into the parlor. Robert Woodruff and Iola Simpkins stared back.

"Help," Annie said in what was more a squeak than a demand.

"I say—" Woodruff began.

"Oh, dear," the widow cried.

Neither showed any inclination to get up, not after they got a second look at Stone.

"Don't pay any attention to us," he said. "We're having a lovers' quarrel."

"No, we're not," Annie said in a very angry voice.

"Now, now, sugar," Stone said.

He swung toward the dining room, his hand still firm on her wrist. He did not let go until they were in the deserted kitchen, the door closed behind them. A small lamp on the table cast soft light on them both, but there was nothing soft about the light in her eyes.

"Sugar?" she hissed. "A lovers' quarrel?" She rubbed the spot where his fingers had dug in. "How dare you?"

He pushed aside the guilt he felt for hurting

her. "I dare a great deal more than that. What the hell were you doing with Ace Bellamy?"

"Nothing more than you were doing with your friend."

"What are you talking about?"

"The woman with all the hair and everything."

"She's not my friend. Don't change the subject. You almost got yourself killed. I didn't know you made a habit of hanging around saloons."

Her chin went up. She looked magnificent, glowing with righteous indignation, but that didn't keep him from wanting to throttle her.

"There's a great deal you don't know about me," she said, calmer. "As for what I was doing, that is absolutely none of your concern. Besides, I was in no danger. Barney—"

"You're on a first-name basis with the bartender?"

She ignored him. "Barney handled the disturbance well enough."

"Not quite. That bullet missed you by inches." He shuddered when he remembered the near tragedy. And he had been stuck trying to rid himself of the clinging blonde. The woman had almost got her hand snapped in two.

"The important thing is it missed me," Annie said.

She spoke sharply, but he could see the lingering horror in her eyes.

He bore in. "Shooting's not all you have to worry about in a saloon. What if someone had decided to get friendly with you in there? Or worse, later, after you were out on the street. Barney wouldn't necessarily interfere. And you wouldn't know the first thing about defending yourself."

"Don't be absurd. Of course I would."

She had an answer for everything, though not necessarily a good one. A new wave of anger struck him, this one, he suspected, coming in part from an old hurt. He wasn't thinking clearly, but the realization didn't slow him down. Neither did the niggling suspicion that he might be overreacting, making a fool of himself.

He probably was. Annie had that kind of effect on him.

"Maybe a friendly man is what you wanted," he said.

"I'd have to go elsewhere, wouldn't I? I don't see one in here."

"Then look closer. I'm about to get very friendly indeed."

Giving her no time to react, he unfastened her cloak and threw it aside, then made a quick and thorough study of what was revealed. The dress, her usual black uniform, did not disguise the slender shoulders, narrow waist, or flare of her hips. It actually accented her breasts, which were heaving in enticing indignation. To be truly prim and proper, she should be wearing a potato sack.

"You don't look armed," he said, putting a leer in his voice. "Unless there's a weapon under your petticoats." He moved close. She backed against the door. "Maybe I should check. You look angry enough to shoot."

"I can scratch and bite."

"I'm willing to bet you never have."

"Which doesn't mean I can't do it. There's a great deal I haven't done, but right now I'm willing to try several things."

"Me, too," he said, stroking her cheek. She felt warm and silken and completely desirable. Damn her.

She bit her lip. "Stay away from me."

"No."

"You've been gone for days and now you just stroll into the saloon, dislike what you see, and assault me. What were you thinking? Why do you even care?"

She asked questions he could not answer, questions he did not want to think about. She was diverting him; he must do the same to her. His choices of diversion were more pleasurable than hers.

He ran his thumb across her lips. "You

missed me. Don't deny it. I can tell."

She sighed, but it came out in a quaver. No longer was she quite so sure of herself. But then neither was he.

"Maybe your stepmother was right," she said. "You do like to have your way."

It took a half second for him to realize what she had said. He dropped his hand.

"You talked to Clare?"

Annie glared at him, but after a moment lowered her lashes. They rested above cheeks ignited to red.

"I was curious about why you were gone. She rode into town. It seemed natural—"

Stone's stomach knotted. "Nothing about Clare is natural."

"She said you made advances to her." And in a smaller voice, "I hadn't noticed before how beautiful she is. You never told me."

"What the hell difference does it make?" The real import of what she'd said hit him. "Wait a minute. I'm a little slow to think right now. She mentioned advances, did she? Of course she did. I can tell you how the conversation went."

"No, please, just let me go. Forget I mentioned her."

But Stone could not stop.

"Being the lusty beast I am, with my dying father down the hall, I grabbed her and tore off her clothes. While she was fighting back, Tanner came to her rescue. That's when I stormed out, not to be seen for days."

Annie brought her eyes back to his. "She didn't give so many details. She left me to imagine them."

"Which you did."

"I couldn't stop thinking of what she'd said. I didn't believe her. Don't look like that, I didn't. But it was a little like the way you left me. I'm talking about all those years ago. We were both angry. You didn't stay around long enough for us to calm down."

Annie had a way of turning those brown eyes of hers into pools of pain. If he wanted to get back in control, he ought to look away.

Doing what he ought to do was getting harder and harder lately.

"We keep getting back to that last night, don't we?" he said. "I don't remember it quite the way you do."

"I said it was a *little* like that time. I didn't say it was exact."

"Annie, quit twisting things to your own ends. Concentrate on right now and let the past alone." He spoke to himself as much as to her. "I needed to go to Fort Worth. When I got back, you weren't here. So I wandered next door, thinking a whiskey would taste good after the hard ride. And there you were, snuggling against Bellamy. The next thing I knew, a gun was blasting a few feet from your head."

"Don't blame me for the shooting. Besides, I wasn't snuggling." The spark was back in her voice. "And if I were, it should mean nothing to you. My relationship with Mr. Bellamy is my business and his."

"You're right." He leaned against her, pressing his body to hers, their lips only inches apart. "But I want to know anyway."

She squirmed. He moaned. She stopped the squirming.

"You've got me figured right. I was seeking companionship," she said. "And a little fun. All that music and laughter must have got to me. And Ace was very accommodating."

"You're playing with fire."

"No, I'm not. He was a perfect gentleman."

"I don't mean with him."

A long moment passed with him leaning his body into hers, feeling the softness and the peaks and valleys. Her breath grew shallow and quick. If the same tremors racing through her were also racing through him, it was a wonder the kitchen didn't ignite.

At last her eyes sought his. "We keep doing this."

"Yeah. And we keep stopping it, too. Just not for very long." He rested his arms against the door on either side of her head. "Is it companionship you want, Annie, or this?"

He ran his tongue across her lips. She trembled against him.

"Accommodate me, Annie. Show me what you mean."

"No."

She made a feeble attempt to shove him away. He took her wrists and pinned them over her head. Her breathing turned as heavy as his.

He licked her lips again. "Open for me."

"Don't—"

He took advantage and stopped her words with the deepest of kisses. The sweet taste of her ran through him like heated wine. She trembled and sucked at his tongue. He could not contain his desire.

Freeing her wrists, he dropped his hands to her waist, then to her hips and pulled her hard against him so that she could feel more completely what she was doing to him. Their bodies fit, though he cursed their clothes. As he kissed the side of her neck, she wrapped her arms around him. Her hips pulsed in a rhythm he understood, and she moaned. She, too, was about to explode.

He forced one hand between them and rubbed where he knew she would want his fingers most. So many thicknesses of clothing, but her feverish shifting grew in intensity. Holding her was like trying to contain a heat-filled storm. After only a moment, he could feel her dampness seeping through to him. He struggled with his belt, loosening his trousers, and then he tugged at her skirt, as feverish as she, as desperate, as wild.

He wasn't fast enough. A tremendous shudder ripped through her. He covered her mouth with his to swallow her cry. Wanting her, aching in a way he had never ached before, he also felt a triumph and a satisfaction because he had brought her to this.

She held herself stiffly until her cry became a whimper. For a moment she stared at him, her eyes lit by a wondrous surprise; then she fell against him, spent, the storm subsided. He held her gently in his arms and willed himself to forget his own hunger. His body was slow to react. He could have lifted her skirt and taken her there and then. But he did not. He held her and told himself it was enough.

A knock sounded at the door.

"Is anyone in there?" Robert Woodruff asked. "I was hoping for a cup of coffee. Miss Chapin? Are you all right?"

Stone wanted to shoot him through the door.

Annie stiffened. Stone was about to reply when she covered his mouth with her fingers.

"The kitchen is closed," she said in a remarkably strong voice. Stone marveled at her all the more.

"That's a shame," Woodruff said; then after a

moment, "And Mr. McBride? I didn't see him leave. I was worried about you."

"We have a back door, Mr. Woodruff. Please, I have work to do in here." Her eyes met Stone's. "I've not quite finished tidying up."

"Just as long as you're all right."

"I am. Do not concern yourself about me." The latter seemed directed mostly at Stone.

"If you're sure," Woodruff said, then reluctantly added, "Good night."

She did not respond. They listened to the sound of footsteps moving across the dining room and out into the hall. Only then did both of them begin to breathe.

Silence. The floor creaked, and the walls moved in. Once again they were alone, with only each other to hold back the world.

"Let me go," she whispered, avoiding Stone's eyes.

"Annie—"

"Let me go."

"I want to hold you."

She finally looked at him. "I'm sure you do. You're not done with me yet."

An all-too-familiar irritation stirred him at the moment he was trying hardest to be forbearing.

"That's not what I meant. This was your first time to experience such a feeling. Don't try to deny it. You need holding."

"What would you know about what I need?"

"Maybe nothing. But I knew what you needed a few minutes ago."

"You knew what I wanted. It's not the same thing. Did you have any idea of how I would feel afterwards?"

She spoke with a bitterness that burned, and he stepped away. As tough as she was trying to be, there was a vulnerability about her that twisted his gut. He wanted to help her, as much as he'd wanted to hold her, but he did not know how.

And he did not know why, except that her well-being was important to him.

"Tell me, Annie, how do you feel?"

"Used."

"We used each other." The stricken look on her face shamed him. "I'm sorry. I shouldn't have said that." Which didn't change the fact that what he said was true.

"You shouldn't have done what you did, either."

"When was I to stop? Face the truth. We have a strong desire for one another. You want me as much as I want you."

She closed her eyes. Tears beaded on her thick lashes.

"No gentleman would say such a thing."

"When a man and a woman have the urges

we do, the concepts of gentleman and lady do not exist."

"Then I will have to kill the urge." She looked at him. "Please don't touch me again. Not like that. Not in any way. Whether I should or not, I really do feel used. And dirty. I feel dirty most of all."

"I did nothing unnatural."

"You did what you had no right to do, and so did I. We are not man and wife. Such intimacy is meant for the marriage bed. Not against a kitchen door."

"Are you saying we must get married?"

"Of course not." She spoke as if she were a thousand miles away, with no chance of contact with him, and no desire to change the situation. "You haven't ruined me. At least I don't think you have. You would know more about that than I."

"I haven't ruined you. Your virginity is still intact."

"Not in my heart." She stared down at the stained front of her gown, for a moment transfixed, as if she did not comprehend what it signified. Perhaps she didn't. Perhaps she did not know what her body could do. He had once wanted to be the man to teach her. Tonight he had become, if only for a while, that man again.

"Please leave," she said.

"You have to tidy up."

"Some things don't clean as neatly as others. But I plan to try."

"Annie, if you think I understand what just happened here any better than you do, you're wrong. The way we affect one another is as confusing to me as it is to you. I would apologize, but I wouldn't know what I was apologizing for. And I can't honestly say I would do anything different."

"I'm not asking for an apology." She stepped away from the door. "Solitude, however, would be a blessing."

She spoke strongly, but he could see the white knuckles of her fists clutched at her sides.

"It's clear that you want no advice from me. Nor help. So be it. Good night, Annie. I'll try not to bother you again." He paused. "The woman at the saloon, the one with the hair and everything—I don't know her. She means nothing to me."

He left the kitchen and reached the bottom of the stairs without seeing anyone. His luck didn't hold. The back door opened, and Henry Jackson limped down the long hallway toward him at a fast clip. Sir Henry, Annie's defending knight, wore no shining armor, but he compensated for it with the hostile glint in his eye.

"I heard you brung Miz Annabelle back from the saloon."

"I don't think you plan to thank me for rescuing her."

"I plan to shoot you where it would do the most good if you've hurt her."

"Who said I hurt her?"

"The Widow Simpkins was all atwitter about the way you brung her. She come rushing out back cackling for Josefina, but she'd already gone to her room with Carmen. I said no need to bother the woman. I'd see to Miz Annabelle, and that's what I'm doing."

Eyeing the man carefully, Stone decided on a limited revelation of the truth. Annie would not appreciate his telling everything.

"She's in the kitchen, not in the best of moods, if you're tempted to check on her. She did not take kindly to my escorting her back from the Roundup before she was ready to leave. But as a shooting had just taken place only a few feet from her, it seemed to me the best thing to do."

Henry scratched at his scraggly beard. "A shooting, eh?"

"A disagreement over cards. She did not seem aware of the danger."

"Too independent, that's what she is."

"She has had to be."

Why he was coming to her defense, he had no idea, except that if anyone were to criticize her in any way, he preferred to be the one to do it.

A twinkle sparked in Henry's eyes. "Was the widow right? Did you really drag her back like she said?"

"That's one way of describing it. You could also say I rescued her from harm."

"Good thing I didn't see it. I might'a misunderstood and had to fight you."

"Yes, it's a very good thing."

The two men stared at one another. Then, shaking his head, Henry limped back down the hall, leaving Stone to hurry up to his room. He would like to draw the curtains and sleep for a week, forgetting all about Annie, Clare, Tom, Tanner . . . even Fort Worth, for a while. He could manage most of the forgetting, except where Annie was concerned. The problem was, he had taken with him the taste of her on his tongue and the scent of her in his nostrils. Worst of all, he remembered exactly how she had felt in his arms.

Why do you even care?

He hadn't been able to answer her when she'd put the question to him, and he couldn't answer it now.

He truly meant he would not bother her again . . . at least he would try. But *she* would bother *him*. She always had. He was beginning to think she always would.

* * *

Outside the boardinghouse, Robert Woodruff stood in the shadows and stared at the glow of his cigar. That his landlady and her lover had been doing obscene things in the kitchen did not bother him. It was clear they did not like one another, though they could not keep their hands to themselves.

Their attraction was not a problem for someone as experienced as himself. The kind of lust that dwelt inside Miss Annabelle Chapin could be transferred to another man—one more kindly, more thoughtful, more solicitous. When the occasion arose, he could be all three, to a degree that sometimes surprised even himself.

If he found she liked a little roughness, he could give her that, too.

It was irritating to bide his time by entertaining the foolish widow. But he always liked to have a contingency plan. If Miss Chapin did not succumb to his charms, Mrs. Simpkins most definitely would.

In the meantime, he would seek out a woman at one of the saloons. Not the Roundup this time, not with the sometimes surprising Annabelle having decided to visit there. If he asked around discreetly—he could be very discreet when necessary—he would find out why.

Flicking the cigar into the street, he went whistling down the walkway. Not much longer, he told himself. If necessary, he would remove

Stone McBride from the scene. He was not a man given to violence, but he could force himself to it if no other method would do.

Actually, he rather liked the idea. Miss Chapin would need a strong pair of arms to get over her grief. She was, after all, only a woman. Long ago he had learned that all women were fools.

Chapter Twelve

Annie stripped and bathed herself, using the bucket of water Henry left every evening beside her bed, then washed every stitch of clothing she had been wearing. She wrung the clothes so tightly they were close to dry, then strung them about the room.

Donning an unadorned flannel nightgown, she crawled beneath the covers. In the dark her clothes hung around her, shadowy reminders of her weakness. With a cold wind rattling the window, she did not sleep; she didn't even try. Instead, she lay still as a post and remembered. Included in that remembering was everything each of them had said, everything each of them had done.

What she could not recall with much exactness was the feeling he had aroused in her at her most wanton moment. Such a time was to be experienced only with the senses, not recalled in the mind. But she remembered the intensity of the moment, the joy that was at once a shock and a revelation.

The difference between their previous kisses and the touches of last night was the difference between a warm summer and a glorious burst of spring. She could become obsessed with that spring; she feared she already was.

Annie knew only one way to clear her mind, and that was to sweat. The next day dawned drearily gray. With the floors and windows already cleaned during previous bouts of worry, she polished silver, emptied drawers and cabinets, washed their contents and stored them carefully back again, asking for no help, barely aware of Josefina, Carmen, and Henry as they went about their usual chores.

Annie's boardinghouse might not be the busiest one in Texas, but it had to be the most pristine.

Three men referred to her by Ace Bellamy joined Woodruff and the widow at the dinner table. Annie had not seen Stone all day, and she did not see him that night. The next morning dawned bright and brisk, inspiring her to take her profits from the extra customers and march to the general store.

This was her first time to venture out since Stone had dragged her from the Roundup. She hadn't thought much about how people might talk; Stone has occupied most of her thoughts. Was it her imagination that everyone on the busy street was staring at her as she hurried along? Abe Cochran from the stagecoach office had recognized her when she'd made her dramatic and much-regretted exit. She remembered the startled look on his face as Stone had pulled her past him.

Abe was a garrulous man. He had probably told everyone in town.

By the time she got to the store, she was in a truly defensive mood. Without ceremony, she laid the money on the counter in front of Hiram Wiggins.

"It's the best I can do. But it's a start," she said in a more militant tone than she had intended. The proprietor had been kind to her, and she was grateful. She softened her words with a smile.

"Annabelle," Wiggins said, "you look at me like that and I could almost forget the rest of the debt."

Annie's cheeks immediately burned. The man had never been so complimentary. Had the news of the saloon encounter changed his attitude toward her? Worse, could it be that what she had experienced with Stone in the kitchen showed on her face or in her eyes?

She hadn't been violated, of that she was sure, but she had been reached. It was the word she had chosen to describe what Stone had done.

She looked down and traced a ridge in the worn countertop.

"I'll pay you more when I can. But I have some extra meals to prepare and I'll be needing more supplies within the next few days. I'll pay for what I get, but it may be a while before I can give you extra money again."

He peered at her closely over the top of his spectacles. "I've been meaning to tell you something, Annabelle Chapin. It's time I did. I haven't forgotten how your mother sold me this place when your father was not long in his grave. She gave me a fair price when anyone could see I wanted it more than just about anything and would have paid more."

Annie tried to interrupt him, but he hurried on.

"There you were, two women alone with that rascally little brother of yours. Then and there I vowed to help you when I could. I'm glad I can do just that. I'm not pushing you for your money. You know I trust you."

His kindness made her want to cry. She also wanted to hug him, but such a display of affection would put an end to whatever favorable reputation she had left. Besides, it was not how an independent businesswoman should react.

"I need to be worthy of that trust," she said. "And the only way to do that is with cash."

"You're harsh on yourself."

Not nearly harsh enough.

"Miz Chapin, good to see you again."

Annie looked at the coveralls-clad man walking toward her across the store, his work boots falling heavily on the wooden floor. For the life of her, she could not recall his name.

Wiggins must have sensed her problem.

"Lester Thompson," he said loud and clear, "I didn't see you come in."

"Don't know how you missed me. The wife says with these boots of mine I could wake the dead just by walking close to a grave."

He smiled at Annie. The teeth he exposed were mottled, but the smile was so genuine, she felt teary-eyed all over again. She was in a maudlin mood today, when she wasn't being irritable, and all because of unexpected shows of friendliness.

"Don't know if you remember," the farmer went on, "but I was here the day Stone McBride got back into town."

"I remember."

"Hope everything's going all right with his family. It's hard when a pa dies, especially when the dying takes so long."

Annie had no idea how to respond, so she nodded mutely.

Thompson went on to recall when his own father "passed," as he put it, and then his mother a few years later. He was about to launch into a similar report on his wife and her parents when Bill Hanes walked in with a friendly greeting and, naturally enough, a mention of Stone.

Annie immediately took it as a sign that he, too, had heard about her exit from the saloon.

"Haven't seen him lately," he said. "I need to get out to the ranch tomorrow morning and make sure everything's all right." His eyes narrowed ever so slightly, not enough so that she could accuse him of prying, but it warned her that he was about to tread on delicate ground.

"Someone was saying they saw you talking to Clare McBride the other day."

Both his choice of topic and his curiosity surprised her. She had been thinking so much about her encounter with Stone, she'd forgotten about Clare. What if she told Hanes everything the woman had said? The details ought to give him something to think about. And poor Lester Thompson, an innocent bystander, would probably be so shocked he would never speak to her again.

Hiram Wiggins would no doubt try to say something nice about the wicked stepmother.

Annie almost wished she could hear him try.

Annie had a curiosity of her own, and she faced Hanes with what she hoped looked like sincerity.

"I had never met her. Her stepson has mentioned her—"

Hanes snorted, but she hurried on.

"Since he's staying at the boardinghouse, it seemed time to introduce myself to her. Besides"—she thought carefully over exactly what she wanted to say—"he had been gone for a few days and I wanted to make sure he still wanted a room. She said he had gone to Fort Worth."

Actually, Clare had said no such thing. Stone had mentioned the town while he had her trapped in the kitchen. She saw no need to be completely accurate. She wished only that she were better at being sly.

"I haven't talked with him about the trip," she added. "Do you know if he will be going there often?" *And why he made the long ride?* "I don't want to charge him for meals he does not eat."

She caught the twinkle in the lawyer's eye. She wasn't fooling him one bit.

"Stone keeps his business to himself, I fear, though I have told him I represent the entire family, not just Tom."

"I see."

And she did. Stone kept his business not just from her but from everyone, although when he got her alone, everything else about him was offered willingly.

"Fort Worth was where my letter caught up with him," Hanes said. "He'd been living there, or at least passing some time."

"Had he?" she said casually, as if she didn't care. In truth, her heart was pounding. Had he been living there alone?

Of course he had, she told herself. He'd told her that in so many words. But that didn't mean she ought to believe him. He had also told her the saloon blonde was not his friend. He hadn't said they hadn't or wouldn't enjoy another kind of relationship.

She was about to leave when Doc Pierce entered the store.

"Miss Chapin," he said with a nod, then, "Bill, I thought I saw you come in here."

"Needed to pick up some supplies. Cigars and such."

Wiggins set a heavy package on the counter. She could hear the whiskey sloshing about inside.

"I rode out to the ranch," the doctor said. "This seemed as good a time as any to report. Tom's about the same, maybe a little weaker. It's hard to say. He gives me hell—oops, sorry, Annabelle—he complains when I poke around and listen to his chest. I figure as long as he's grumbling he's doing well enough."

Annie wanted to ask if he had seen Stone. But of course she couldn't. Besides, the lawyer did it for her, although she could have taken issue with his phrasing.

"Miss Chapin was just asking about Stone. Did you run into him by any chance?"

"Matter of fact, I saw him as I was leaving. He asked about his pa, and I told him he ought to go in and see for himself. I know there's bad blood out there, but—"

Hanes cleared his throat and glanced at the farmer Lester Thompson.

"Everybody in the county knows it, Bill. I'll bet even Annabelle here might have heard a rumor or two."

Annie tried to look innocent and ignorant at the same time, but all she could think of was Clare's ugly insinuations. *Bad blood* scarcely described the way things were at the Circle M.

"I try not to listen to gossip," she said, and felt like the biggest hypocrite in the world. She had hung on the woman's every word.

Suddenly the store was suffocatingly close. Making her good-byes, she hurried to the street and practically ran toward the sanctuary of the boardinghouse, looking neither to the right nor left. All was quiet inside. Mrs. Simpkins must be in her room for her afternoon nap, and Robert Woodruff had said he would be taking his daily walk. Josefina and Carmen were out in the back doing the laundry over a big tin washtub. Henry had promised to work in the garden, assuring one and all that he wouldn't harvest anything unless he got a second opinion as to what should be picked.

She ought to get right to work in the kitchen, but she needed a few minutes alone in her room. She started to unlock the door, but the knob turned easily in her hand. Strange. She always kept her bedroom locked, since it also served as her office and sometimes she kept varying amounts of money inside.

With so much going on in her life, she had probably forgotten her usual precaution.

She stepped inside. With the curtains drawn, the room was dark, but she immediately sensed that something was wrong. It was her last clear thought, for suddenly her head exploded and she sank into a mindless dark.

"Patróna."

The urgent whisper came to Annie through a fog so thick it obscured sound as well as light.

She felt lost, unable to imagine where she was. She stirred. Her head pounded. She was lying in bed, but that was about all she knew. She wanted to rub the ache, but someone was holding her hands. She opened her eyes to flickering lamplight, then closed them against the stabbing pain.

"Josefina?" she managed. "What happened?"

The answer was a rush of Spanish, and then an order for Carmen to fetch a damp cloth and a glass of water.

Annie flexed a few muscles to make sure the rest of her body was all right; then, with her head protesting the slightest movement, she held very still. "What happened?" she repeated, this time a little more querulous.

"Thanks be to God," Josefina said. "You will live."

"Of course I'll live." But with a thousand hammers working on her skull, she wasn't sure she wanted to. "Did I slip and fall? The last thing I remember is coming into the room and then . . . nothing."

"The door was open. Henry found you and called to me. He has gone for the sheriff."

That meant dealing with another McBride. "Surely there's no need for that."

"*Madre de Dios, patróna*, you did not fall."

"Then how—"

Josefina's answer was forestalled by the arrival of a crowd—Carmen with the water, Sheriff McBride, Doc Pierce, and a woman and child who looked vaguely familiar to her. The doctor shooed them all back into the hall, shut the door, and sat at the side of the bed.

"I understand someone hit you."

"That's absurd. Who—"

"Hush."

He lifted her gingerly, just enough for his fingers to probe the back of her head, then laid her back again. She bit her lip to keep from crying out.

"Yep," he said. "It feels like that's what happened all right." He ran his hands over her body. "Nothing else hurts? Don't answer. You'd be letting me know soon enough if it did."

He patted her hand, then stood and went to the door. "We'll need some ice." That was all she heard before he went into the hall and closed the door, leaving her alone. She could recall nothing more than she had already told Josefina, except the feeling of unease she had experienced about the unlocked door. The moment she walked into the room she had felt that something was wrong.

She forced herself to her elbows and, when the room stopped spinning, looked around. The drawers of her bureau were open, the papers on her desk disarranged, there were even clothes on the floor, something she would never allow.

Someone had been through her personal belongings. She rested again on the pillow, tears of anger burning her eyes.

The door opened. "You can talk to her a minute," she heard Doc Pierce say, "but she needs rest. Don't upset her more'n she already is."

Heavy-booted footsteps crossed the room to

her bedside. She looked up, following a line of dark trousers, leather jacket, a dark shirt open at the throat. It took a while to get to the grim face. The sharp features, high cheekbones, and copper skin did not draw her attention so much as the startling blue eyes. She and the man had never formally been introduced, but she recognized him right away. The last time she had seen him, he was hurrying toward the Roundup, at the same time as his brother was dragging her away.

"Sheriff McBride," she said.

He set aside the hat he was holding in his hand. "Sorry to make your acquaintance under such circumstances." He looked around the room. "I'd guess you don't normally leave the place like this."

"No, I don't."

"You wouldn't know if anything's missing, would you?"

"I keep nothing of value in here. Except for money sometimes. I had it with me today."

"That's something a thief wouldn't necessarily know. What about jewelry?"

"Nothing of any value. I'm a simple woman, Sheriff."

He studied her. "Now, I don't know about that," he said, proving that the color of his eyes did not lie: He was definitely a McBride.

"Have any strangers come in here lately?"

She started to say no, then thought about the dinner guests of the previous night. She told him as much as she knew about them, stressing that they had seemed very polite, though he seemed unimpressed with that bit of information.

"I'll talk with Bellamy," he said. "What about guests?"

"Only two besides your brother. They've been staying here awhile."

"I'll want to talk to them, too."

Doc Pierce stuck his head in the door. "The ice is here. Time to leave."

Chase McBride nodded. "My wife came with me. She wants to help."

"I don't need hovering over," Annie said. She tried to sit up. Again the room whirled. She lay back down.

"You need some hovering," Pierce said. "I watched over your father and mother both when they were ailing. You know I'm not one to raise alarms when it's not necessary. Can't tell if you've got a concussion. Somebody needs to be around to watch you, make sure you get enough liquids and some food down you."

"Josefina can do all that."

"You've got more company coming for dinner from the saloon. The women already got things worked out, though it took some talking on both sides. Josefina and Carmen will see to the cooking. Mrs. McBride will stay as long as she's needed. The boy Luke will send for me if you fall asleep and have a hard time waking up."

"He'll send for me, too, if you think of something I need to know," Chase McBride said.

The doctor shifted her to her side and pressed the towel-wrapped ice against the back of her head. "Let it stay there for a while. It should bring the swelling down. But I'd suggest you take those blasted pins out of your hair. You've got it pulled so tight, I don't know why your eyes aren't squinting."

Annie concentrated on tolerating the ice. The men left. Josefina came in to cluck over her and was replaced by her temporary nurse, Faith McBride. She was tall and willowy, her coloring as fair as her husband's was dark. She was the vaguely familiar woman Annie had not been able to identify.

In the few months since she had come to town as the wife of the new sheriff, Annie had seen her occasionally on the street or in the general store. They had nodded, but neither had introduced herself. Annie figured that they were alike, neither opening up easily to new friendships.

And now here she was in Annie's bedroom, standing while Annie lay in bed.

"You don't want me here, do you?" Faith McBride said.

"I'm not one for letting strangers get close."

A dark memory clouded the woman's face. "Neither was I. Chase changed my mind."

She began to straighten the room, closing drawers, picking up clothes.

"You don't have to do that," Annie said.

"I know. But the mess will bother you every time you see it. If I touch anything you don't want bothered, let me know. If I put something in the wrong place, tell me that, too."

Each kept to her private thoughts until the room was presentable again, Annie was in her nightgown, hair loose and softly brushed, the covers pulled over her, a fresh towel of ice against the back of her head. Busy with the room, Faith let Annie do the most personal parts of the undressing. She seemed to sense how much Annie hated being out of control.

Annie slept, she had no idea how long, and when she awoke, the ice was gone and a bowl of steaming soup rested on the bedside table. She forced herself to sit up and feed herself. Faith McBride sat in a chair a few feet away and watched.

"My brother-in-law caused quite a ruckus a short while ago. I'm surprised you didn't hear him."

"Stone?"

"He insisted on looking in to make sure you

were breathing. Then he went to find Chase. He did not look pleased."

"He seldom does."

"It must be a family trait."

Annie found herself warming to the woman. "Smiling comes hard to him," she said, then hoped it did not reveal too much about how close she and Stone had been.

"It used to be that way with my husband. I guess he still seems unsmiling to others. When he's alone with me and Luke, he's different. Callie says the same about Tanner."

Annie couldn't imagine why the woman was telling her all this. But she didn't ask her to stop.

"Tom is the only one who does not seem softened by his wife," Faith added. "But then, that's understandable."

Annie found herself smiling. "You must have spent time around Clare McBride."

"I shouldn't be talking. But it's no secret how the McBride children feel about their stepmother. And that includes Lauren." She hesitated. "It's none of my business, but it seems that marriage has done all of them more good than anything else they've ever done. Stone needs a good woman, too."

At last Faith had got to the point. Annie should have seen it coming. Unable to swallow another spoonful, she set the soup aside, letting the action pass for a response.

A knock sounded at the door. Faith stood and straightened the bedcovers, then, in a gesture that was uncomfortably personal, did the same for Annie's hair, making sure the long locks fell smoothly across her shoulders.

Soup bowl in hand, she walked to the door and opened it. Stone walked inside. Before Annie could protest, Faith left and the two were alone.

He looked at her for a long time before crossing the room and stopping beside her bed. She could not bring herself to look up at him. But neither could she concentrate on anything other than his presence.

"You look pale," he said.

She would have preferred something of a kinder nature, especially after all the care Faith had taken with her. At least he did not begin by railing at her for letting herself be assaulted.

"Come back later," she said. "I'll try to get some color in my cheeks."

"I didn't mean it as a criticism."

She sighed. This was Stone she was dealing with. He had never been much for sweet talk, even when they were in love.

"I know you didn't," she said. "You're right. I'm probably the color of these sheets."

He pulled the chair Faith had been using closer to the bed and sat. His nearness made her all too aware of her nakedness beneath the plain nightgown. She shouldn't be thinking of such a thing, but at the moment she could think of nothing else.

Nervous, she fingered her hair. She knew he watched everything she did.

"Doc says you'll be up and about tomorrow," he said. "I disagree."

Of course he did. Didn't he always?

Her head throbbed. "Why is that?" she asked.

"You need rest. You work too hard."

"No, I don't. I'm in bed because apparently someone hit me on the head."

"I didn't know that was what it took to get you there."

She looked up at him, startled. His lips twitched. In another man it would have been an outright laugh.

"You're teasing me?"

"Bad timing, I know. Doc told me I was not to upset you."

You upset me just by being on the same earth.

"Everyone is mollycoddling me," she said.

"Let 'em."

There fell between them a silence that was not entirely uncomfortable.

"Chase said you didn't see who did this to you," Stone said.

"I didn't know I had been hit until everyone started telling me so. One minute I was standing, feeling fine, and the next thing I knew I was lying here with the worst headache of my life."

"So you have no idea who was waiting for you when you walked inside."

"I'm not sure anyone was waiting. I rather guess the thief was interrupted. Otherwise he would have already been gone."

"Maybe."

"Have you considered the irony of my being hurt in my bedroom instead of the saloon?"

"I was waiting for you to point that out. Yes, I've considered it. Trouble can come anywhere."

Another silence. She closed her eyes.

"You're tired," he said.

"A little."

"Then I've stayed too long."

He touched her hand. His warmth shivered through her.

"He's a dead man," Stone said.

Annie's eyes flew open. "What are you talking about?"

"The man that did this won't have a chance to hurt you again."

He stood. She thought he was going to lean down and kiss her. Instead, he just looked at her, then walked out the door, closing it softly behind him, leaving her to stare after him and wonder what it was that had just taken place between them.

By the time sleep came, she still had not come up with an answer. But she felt curiously comforted. The pain was not so severe as it had been before.

Chapter Thirteen

Stone spent the next week shaving time off his work at the ranch and his much-needed gambling so that he could watch over Annie. Not close, where she could see him and complain about mollycoddling, but nearby, where he could make sure no one hurt her again.

He spotted nothing suspicious, but he couldn't shake the feeling that danger was still hanging around. He had meant what he said about the culprit being a dead man. He had never so much as shot at anyone in his life, though he had found himself in a few barroom brawls. Now he was wearing his gun. He wouldn't hesitate to use it.

Chase hadn't come up with a clue about who might have struck her. The two diners who had come over from the Roundup both had alibis; the others who came, two or three a night, didn't take kindly to his sitting at the table questioning them.

They ate their food, paid, but did not linger, though Stone suspected they would have liked a cigar in the parlor and a chance to visit with their hostess.

He wouldn't have minded the same. But that wasn't his purpose. Besides, Woodruff stuck to her more closely than flies on a pie. He gave off the heat and the smell of a man who was courting, looking for a wife to replace the one who had died.

Annie was no replacement. The man she married ought to look upon her as his first and only love.

At least that was Stone's opinion. He would have passed it on to her, but ever since the shooting in the saloon and whatever it was that had followed in the kitchen, she hadn't shown an interest in anything he thought.

By the time Christmas came, he was in as foul a mood as he had ever been. Lauren had made the rounds of most of the McBrides, sending word to him through Faith, insisting on a family gathering at the Circle M. His sister was letting her heart rule her brain, wishing things into existence, things that could never be.

Still, he would be there. He wanted to take

Annie with him. To keep an eye on her, he told himself, but he wasn't sure his reason was that simple.

They were standing in the parlor when he asked her. The time was Christmas Eve. Dinner was long past. Behind her was the six-foot evergreen tree Henry had cut and helped to decorate, along with everyone else in the boardinghouse except Stone. Candles around the room cast a soft glow over everything, and a stack of mesquite logs was crackling in the fireplace.

From the strands of berries and popcorn on the tree and the ribbon-wrapped branches of holly on the mantel to the tin holders under the candles, everything had a warm, homey look to it, and that included Annie. Though she was wearing black, her hair was down, and the long, wheat-colored strands picked up a sheen from all the light. She'd lost weight since the assault, but the loss gave her a fragile demeanor that was both enticing and deceptive.

He found out the deceptive part as soon as he mentioned Christmas at the ranch.

"Don't be ridiculous," she said, as strong as ever. "I'm not a McBride."

"Doc Pierce and Bill Hanes will be there."

"Good for them. But I have people here who need a holiday meal. Even the deputy sheriff is dropping by, although I suspect he's as much here to watch over me as he is to eat." She took a deep breath. "Besides, this is where my life is. It's where I belong."

"Are you sure, Annie? Are you sure for all time?"

He hadn't planned to ask such a thing. He hadn't realized he was thinking it. But her response was important to him, as important as anything in his life.

She looked toward the hearth, her eyes deeper and darker than he had ever seen them.

"We're talking about one day, Stone. Just one day."

"You haven't answered me."

Her gaze returned to him. He could not read her thoughts.

"I'm not sure what the question meant. The best I can say is that now and for any future I can imagine, the place where I live is the place I will always live, and the work I do is the work I will always do. I am able to take care of myself far better than you think I can. I always will."

She spoke of the future with a certainty that he envied. There was so much in his life that was unsettled, so much he could not predict. All he knew was that he wanted her with him when he faced the Christmas gathering. It wasn't fair to subject her to what would probably be a volatile afternoon. But he wanted her there, nevertheless.

He wasn't much concerned with fairness right now, a fact she would willingly point out if he gave her the chance. And he sure as hell did not care for the talk about caring for herself.

He sensed a presence behind him. Whatever argument he might have put to her was lost as he turned to the hallway. Robert Woodruff looked back at him with what could only be described as a triumphant smile on his face. The smile did not last long. Stone doubted if Annie noticed it.

Stone did not like Woodruff. He never had. The man smiled too much. Stone had learned early in life never to trust people like that. Either they were simpleminded or they were devious. One thing Woodruff had never seemed was dumb.

Was he the kind of man Annie found appealing? If so, Stone did not know her very well.

He spared one last, long look at her, then left without ceremony, thinking tonight would be a good time to head for the Roundup. Even before he stepped inside, he could tell the place was rowdier than ever, as if the fifty or so people crowded inside could use loud laughter and drunkenness to make up for having no place else to go on Christmas Eve.

Stone wasn't judging anyone. He was here, too.

In the midst of all the noise, he couldn't concentrate on his cards. He wasn't interested in the women, nor in the whiskey, either. Rather than risk losing what he'd won on earlier nights, he returned to the darkened boardinghouse.

All the candles in the parlor had been snuffed, but he could smell the melted tallow, and also the odors of cinnamon and vanilla from the baking that had gone on in the kitchen all day. They were the smells of Christmases past. He didn't dwell on the memories long.

In his room he stripped quickly, without bothering to light the lamp, and crawled beneath the covers. The bed beside him shifted and a soft giggle sounded.

He jumped out of the bed fast and lit the bedside lamp. Carmen, black hair spread across the white pillowcase, smiled up at him.

"What the hell are you doing here?" he growled.

Her gaze traveled down. "Oh," she said, then whispered something in Spanish he could not translate. He didn't have to. The surprised and approving look in her eyes reminded him that he was naked, a circumstance she liked far too much.

He grabbed the top cover and wrapped it around his middle, leaving only a thin sheet to cover her. He couldn't have been more stunned or more threatened if he had found a lit stick of dynamite lying in his bed.

"Carmen," he said, his voice raspy, "answer me right now. What do you think you're doing?"

She licked her lips. "This is Christmas, is it not? I bring you a present. It is the most valuable thing I have to give."

He didn't think she was talking about wool-lined gloves.

She sat up, and the sheet dropped to her waist. He jumped back, then realized she was dressed in her usual blouse and skirt.

"But I have a problem," she said. "I did not know how you would want your present wrapped."

There was something so innocent about her sitting there, fully clothed, lips pouting, eyes shining, that he thought about pulling up a chair and explaining how she was too young and needed to save her valuable gift for a man she truly loved, that he was not the one for her, that she would hurt those who loved her without bringing any happiness to herself. But he would be blabbering out reasons she wouldn't even hear.

Or, taking a more easily understood route, he could pick her up and throw her out in the hall. Carmen would not like that, not at all. The comparison to dynamite came back. She was burning, all right, and if he didn't handle her right, she was likely to explode.

And what would her mama think? Castration,

that's what she would be thinking. She would be going for the kitchen knives.

Stone rubbed his throbbing temple.

"Look," he said, "I'm flattered. I really am."

The light began to dim in her eyes.

"But there's someone else in my life right now." He was not really lying. "It wouldn't be right to hurt her or you."

"Then be gentle. No one need ever know."

He blew out an exasperated breath of air. "I don't mean physically hurt. Besides, you couldn't keep a secret like this, and you know it."

"I am not a child," she said, her tone challenging him to prove otherwise.

She tugged her blouse down a couple of inches, then ruffled her thick hair. With her fine, dark features and shapely body, she truly was beautiful. All he could think of was how another man might use her and ruin her life. With a start, he realized it was a consideration that might occur to a father. Over the past few years, he really had changed.

She got out of the bed and walked toward him, her bare feet silent on the carpet. He gripped the cover as his head continued to throb.

"Are you afraid of me?" she asked. "I will not bite. Unless you want me to. It is possible men like such things."

He gave up trying to reason with her. She saw this as a game. And she was pursuing this seduction with a stubbornness that would do a mule proud.

"I'm not afraid. I'm just not interested."

She stopped. "*Una mentira*."

"No, it's not a lie, Carmen. You have much to offer a man, a young man who will love you and give you his name."

"Young men bore me."

"How many do you know?"

"A thousand."

For all her boldness in watching the men passing by on the street, the ones going in and out of the saloon, he doubted she knew more than a few, of any age—certainly none of them in any physical sense of the word.

But she was proud. He could see it in the tilt of her head and the straightness of her spine.

Dynamite.

"You'd better leave before someone finds out you're here."

Her eyes sparkled with tears. "That is all you have to say? Leave?"

"This will be our secret."

She waved a hand in the air. "You think I will tell?" Then the Spanish came at him so fast and furious he could translate only a few words, but they were enough to tell him she had terrible revenge in mind for various parts of his anatomy.

She came toward him, skirt swishing. He got out of her way, and she slammed her way into the hall. He didn't look after her. Instead, he made certain the door was locked, a useless gesture since she must have had a key to get inside.

He sat on the side of the bed and rubbed his head. Women. He didn't understand them, no matter their age.

Tonight Annie and Carmen. Tomorrow Clare. If it hadn't involved getting dressed again, he would go next door and order some of that whiskey he had turned down less than an hour ago.

Chapter Fourteen

Stone went down early on Christmas morning, before breakfast, hoping to avoid any human contact. He wasn't handling such things very well lately. Thinking of all that lay ahead of him, he doubted that today would be any different.

All was quiet, but he noticed that the table was already set in the dining room. Beside each plate was a wrapped package. There was one for him. Annie must have laid everything out last night.

He opened the gift. It was a crimson hand-knit woolen scarf, long and thick and warm. It would come in handy on the winter days ahead while he was riding the range. He would use it today on his journey out to the ranch.

He had bought her something, too, but he

hardly considered it a suitable Christmas gift. Still, he hurried back to his room, took the purchase out of the drawer beside his bed, and returned to the dining room, where he wrapped it in the same paper she had used.

He put it at the place where she usually sat. He didn't need to enclose a card. She would know who had bought it. Who else but him would give a woman like Annie a gun?

She had another one, or so he had been told. But it was probably bulky. This one was small enough to fit into a pocket or a purse. She could carry it with her when he wasn't around.

As for the card, what would he have written on it? *Peace and goodwill to men* hardly seemed an appropriate sentiment, despite the holiday.

Shoot any bastard who tries to harm you would be more to the point.

Hearing someone stirring in the kitchen, he left quickly, got his horse from the livery, and rode hard through the crisp Christmas morning. He was the last to arrive at the ranch house. Most of the others had gone out the day before, but he figured a few hours under the same roof with Clare was all he could stand.

As he reined toward the house, Jeb waved to him from the corral. Beside him was the cowhand Zeke. A third party, a towheaded boy, was straddling the fence, staring at the horses milling about. The boy must be Luke, Chase's adopted son. Returning the wave, Stone considered joining them. But that was the coward's way of getting through the day. Sooner or later he would have to go inside.

When he did, the women—all but the ought-to-be hostess—were bustling about the kitchen, testing the patience of the cook Tiny. The men—all but the dying host—were drinking brandy around the tree in the parlor. He had a bad moment when he recognized the ribbons and small carved figures on the tree as the ones his mother had used.

He caught Tanner's eye. They shared a moment of understanding. Somehow the presence of the decorations seemed wrong in this house where she had been so quickly replaced.

Like his younger brother, the others in the room—Chase, Lauren's husband, Garrett, Doc Pierce, and Bill Hanes—were standing around swirling glasses of brandy. It was the lawyer who offered him a drink. Stone took it readily, postponing for a short while the visit to his father.

"Where was I?" Hanes said. "I forgot what I was talking about."

"The snowstorm of seventy-eight," Doc Pierce said.

"Oh, yes. Stone, I was telling the others how bad it was here. Right at Christmastime, too. If we get snow in this part of the state, it normally doesn't come until January or February. But this storm came down on us with a vengeance. First it rained, then it froze, and as a final insult, down came the snow on top of all that ice."

His gaze went around the room; he settled it on Stone.

"Put some people out of business. I tried to get out to the ranch, but the ice stopped me. None of you McBride boys were around, of course. Lassiter here and the doc, they can tell you how it was. Bad, real bad."

Stone got the idea that Hanes was trying to tell him something. He figured he knew what it was. Tom had had a hard time during and after the storm, and so had the ranch hands. Stone should have been around to help with the work.

The lawyer's ploy had little effect. Stone had enough troubles without taking on an extra load of guilt.

But he did start thinking about Tom. Setting aside his glass, he excused himself, nodded to the women in the kitchen, and went upstairs. He found Clare standing outside the closed door to the sickroom. It was the first time he had seen her in private since she had displayed her unwanted wares.

She was dressed in red, a matching ribbon entwined in her upswept hair. As usual, she had taken great care with her appearance, as if any man in the house other than maybe Tanner would be interested. Only her narrowed eyes acknowledged his presence.

He nodded. He couldn't bring himself to offer a merry Christmas, but he did have a greeting, lest she believe her stepson did not think of her.

"Glad to see you've got your clothes on," he said. "It's gotten a little cold since that norther blew in earlier in the week."

The sound she made was very much like that of a hissing cat.

"How's Tom?" he said.

"See for yourself."

She whirled from him and started down the stairs. He watched as she straightened her skirt, licked her lips, and put on what he assumed was her happy face before she joined the family in the parlor. He knew whom she was trying to impress. His little brother had better beware.

When he looked at the closed door, he was surprised by the feeling of sadness that overcame him. This house had sometimes been a joyous one, especially at the holiday season, despite its unloving patriarch. Emily had seen that such was so. Somehow Tom had usually managed to behave himself until after the start of a new year.

During some of those times, Stone had allowed himself to believe they were a real family, two sons and a daughter devoted to their mother, working together to make the land and the people who lived on it thrive. Tanner had been wild, true enough, given to shirking duties and twisting the truth, mostly in jest—no real harm in him. Or so Stone had thought.

And Lauren? She had been pampered, enthralled by the brashness of one of her brothers, irritated by the strong ruling hand of the other. But he had had to do what he could to give her guidance. Emily hadn't done so. She'd hated to criticize anyone. She had wanted all to be well.

Had everything been a sham? They had been divided far too easily. Because of Clare, of course, but she was not entirely to blame.

Neither was Tom.

And what in the devil was he doing worrying about matters that were long past, matters he could do nothing about?

He went inside the sickroom and closed the door. The window was open a crack. Lauren or Callie, or maybe both, had been up here to make sure the patient got fresh air.

His father was propped up in the bed. He looked about the way Stone remembered him—pale, his features gaunt, his hair long and gray and thinning. Tom gave every sign he was sleeping. Then he opened his eyes and stared at his firstborn son.

"Glad to see you finally made it," he said.

"And a merry Christmas to you, too," Stone said.

Tom grunted.

"How are you feeling?" Stone asked.

"No worse than usual."

"And no better."

"I'm still dying, if that's what you're worried about."

Stone ignored the sharpness. He had expected nothing less.

"Would you like to go downstairs? It's too quiet up here. I could carry you. We'll make a bed on the sofa."

"Wouldn't that be like throwing a smelly old skunk into the party?"

Stone studied his father long and hard. He looked shrunken, his nightshirt too big for his fleshless body, folds of gray skin circling his neck. It was the eyes that got him most, eyes that were shrunken, defiant, and at the same time lost. For the first time, Stone understood the loneliness of the man. It mattered not how he had come to this condition. He was here. And Stone couldn't look away.

He glanced at the gnarled hands lying on top of the covers. "Your nails need cutting."

Tom's mouth twitched. "Leave 'em be."

Stone ignored him. He went to the bureau where his mother used to keep her sewing supplies and found the small scissors he was looking for. Pulling a chair to the bed, he took one of his father's hands in his. He was surprised at the warmth of the wrinkled skin. He had expected it to be cold and clammy.

"Don't fight me," he said. "I'll cut you."

"You'd like that, wouldn't you?"

"It would make my day."

He worked quickly. Tom did not try to pull away.

"You don't like being cared for," Stone said, more an observation than a question.

"It's a damned poor way to end one's life. I'd rather a horse had thrown me years ago."

"I wouldn't like it either."

"So maybe we aren't too different after all."

Stone wanted to argue. He and his father had little in common and never had. But it was an issue he didn't much want to argue over, not today.

"You feel like talking?" he asked.

"What d'you want me to say? I'm leaving everything to you?"

Stone almost gave up. In memory of Emily McBride, he persevered.

"I've been doing a lot of riding around, looking things over, seeing things that need to be done."

"Not 'til I'm gone. You're not in charge yet."

"What was this land like when you first came here? Sometimes it seems crowded now, with so many ranches, so many farms in the county. It used to take a week to get to a neighbor. The way the roads are now, Lauren's not even a half-day's ride away."

Tom closed his eyes. For a moment Stone thought he had gone to sleep. When he finally spoke, his voice was low. Stone had to lean close to hear.

"Grass," Tom said. "You never seen such grass. Not everywhere, of course. Too much limestone breaking through the dirt. But it was growing wild right around here, and it trailed on down south. It'd tickle the belly of a horse, it was so high. Calves, hell, you could lose 'em in it if you weren't real careful."

He fell silent, and Stone let him gather his thoughts.

"Most of it's gone now. Too much grazing, too much plowing under. When I was a boy, I used to think it looked like a green sea, and the hawks flying over, they were gulls like they have down at the coast."

He fell silent as he stared in the direction of the window, stared with a lost look, as if a bird might fly in at any minute.

" 'Course I knew they were just looking for kill. But ain't that what gulls do? Look for fishes in the water and critters in the sand?"

"There have always been predators," Stone said.

"Always will be, too. A man has to be careful. Women, too."

Father and son looked at one another. Stone got the idea that Tom was trying to tell him something, wanting his thoughts to be read without putting them into words. Like Hanes downstairs, he was saying more than he appeared to be.

A fit of coughing ended the moment. Tom choked on phlegm. Stone sat his father up, held him until the choking stopped, then went out to call for Doc Pierce.

Pierce came immediately and ordered quiet for his patient, pretty much accusing Stone of getting Tom upset. Evicted from his kitchen, Tiny came up to sit with him.

Stone was left with the task of going downstairs and sharing what was left of the holiday with the rest of the McBrides and their spouses. Unfortunately, that included the stepmother and stepmother-in-law to the brood. With the boy Luke now part of the family, she was also the resident grandmother, a fact no one seemed brave enough to point out.

Lauren was bright and beautiful, Callie and Faith equally so, but the conversation was strained. If it hadn't been for Luke talking about how Jeb was going to teach him to rope a calf, not much genuine enthusiasm would have been evident at the table.

The reason was clear. As long as Clare was

swishing around in blood-red taffeta, peace and goodwill did not stand a chance at the Circle M.

Stone did not ride back to Sidewinder until the next day shortly after dawn. Christmas night he stayed with the ranch hands, who had their own celebration in the bunkhouse, courtesy of the McBride women. Chase and his family stayed at the main house. Everyone else had gone soon after dinner was cleared away.

For a while Stone rode alongside Chase's wagon, but he couldn't rid himself of the feeling that he ought to hurry up, that he was needed in town. Never a man given to act on instinct, he could not make the feeling of dread go away.

At last he acted upon it. Making his excuses to Faith and the boy, glancing at Chase, wondering if he ought to put his worry into words, he spurred his horse on ahead of the wagon and rode hard the rest of the way.

His boots had no sooner hit the ground in front of the boardinghouse than Annie came rushing outside. Her hair was disheveled, her eyes wide as she reached out for him.

"You're here. Thank God," she cried.

He took her hands. They were cold as ice.

"What happened?" he snapped, cursing himself because he had left her.

"Carmen's gone. He took her."

The words came out a sob. In the background he could hear Josefina crying.

"Who? When?"

"Woodruff." Annie was breathing so hard and so fast he could barely catch the name. She seemed unaware of the crowd gathering around them.

Ace Bellamy came over from the saloon.

"I offered to help. She wanted you."

Stone held her for a minute. As far as he could tell, she was all right. Except for the panic. He wanted to absorb it into himself, to suck it from her and give her a moment's calm.

But she was having none of the comfort he offered. She pushed him away.

"You have to get him, Stone." She brushed away tears. "He'll hurt her."

"I'll get him. Now tell me what happened." He looked around the street. "We'll talk inside."

His aim was to get her into the parlor. They got no farther than the front hall. Pulling free, she began to pace, her trembling hands squeezed in front of her. Josefina stood in the background, red-eyed as she leaned against Henry. Neither spoke. They both stared at him.

"Take it slow, Annie," he said. "I need to know everything."

She nodded, but she did not slow down.

"He asked me to marry him. I almost laughed, he took me so by surprise." She blinked and looked at Stone. "I had no idea he had anything like that in mind. I don't know him. I'm not sure I even like him." She covered her mouth with a curled hand. "He turned mean. He said he'd wasted weeks on me. That he would make me pay."

"When was this?"

"Last night. This morning his room was empty."

"He has *mi niña*," Josefina said with a sob, but she seemed to lack the strength to tell him more, and he looked to Annie.

"Carmen was different yesterday. Sullen and quiet. Something happened to her, but she wouldn't tell us what it was. She must have left with him during the night. Some of her clothes are missing, as well as a few coins she had been saving for a new dress."

Stone let out a long, slow breath. Damn it. He blamed himself.

"Do you have any idea where they were headed?" he asked.

Annie shook her head.

Henry spoke up. "He always talked about moving on west. He mentioned the New Mexico Territory, said it was a place that'd always interested him."

"What's the deputy doing?"

"He's sending out telegrams to the counties between here and El Paso, alerting the sheriffs.

The Rangers, too. He said that's what Chase would be doing."

Stone thought a minute.

"You got some coffee?"

Annie looked at him as if he spoke another language.

"I'd like a cup, and something to eat." He looked at Josefina. "You help her, will you? I'll need it fast."

He wanted to hold Annie again. Instead, he nodded toward the kitchen and repeated, "Fast."

While the two women went into the kitchen, he went outside to talk to Bellamy. He found him near the boardinghouse door.

"Ask around the saloon. See if anyone saw a man and a girl leave during the night."

"I already have. No one claimed to have seen a thing."

"Ask again. Make 'em believe you really want to know. And spread the word down the street. If anyone's passed out, slap 'em awake."

Bellamy nodded brusquely and returned to the Roundup.

Stone glanced around the crowd, giving anyone who wanted to do so a chance to speak up.

"Never liked that man," one said. "He was too clean."

"The poor girl. Knew she'd get in trouble one day."

Stone glared at the latter speaker. He shut up and slunk away.

Stone went back to Annie, accepting the hot coffee and plate of cold meat and potatoes without a word. He would have a hard time swallowing any of it, but the preparation had given her something to do. She needed to contribute, too.

By the time he was saddling a fresh mount, provided by the livery, Chase was riding up. He listened to what had happened without breaking in.

"I'll check with the deputy," he said when Stone had finished, "then ride with you. Two sets of eyes are better than one. Besides, I'm an Indian, in case you forgot. I know how to track."

Within minutes the two men were ready to ride. Bellamy gave them the direction.

"They're headed west, on the old Goodnight-Loving Trail. You were right. I had to slap an old fellow to make him listen. He passed them sometime around midnight. He was coming into town."

Woodruff had a long head start. It would be a difficult ride. There was no telling how long the girl would last.

Annie stood on the walkway watching, listening. Stone went to tell her good-bye, to give her a final reassurance that he was far from feeling.

"I should have shot him," she said.

He didn't understand her at first.

"That gun you gave me. When he came on so strong, I should have pulled it out and shot him between the eyes."

He took her face between his hands.

"Don't worry. I'll do it for you."

He kissed her quickly, then turned to Chase.

"Let's ride."

Chapter Fifteen

"Do you whine all the time?"

"I'm tired and sore and I'm hungry." The girl's voice trembled, the tremble more evident with each word.

" 'I'm tired and sore and I'm hungry,' " he mimicked her. "Good God, you'd better be good tonight. You'd better make this worth my while."

A sniff. "I don't know what you're talking about."

A leer. "You will." He fondled his pistol, then waved it in her direction across the campfire. "I can give you either end of this, you know. The handle hits real hard. And the barrel . . . it has its uses, too."

Another sniff. "I want to go back," she said,

not understanding what he meant. "I won't tell anyone anything. I promise."

He laughed. It was an ugly sound.

"Not yet. I haven't given you what you want. You were begging for it in Sidewinder. You need to beg for it now."

A small voice. "I don't want . . . it anymore."

"How do you know? You've never had it. At least that's what you claimed. You'd better not have lied."

A flare of temper. "I am not the liar here, señor." And then, when the gun waved in her direction, more softly, "I want to go home."

The firelight flickered across his stubbled face, and his hair hung lank across his forehead.

"I don't care."

She began to cry quietly.

"I took you for a screamer," he said. "I like screamers. You'll do that for me, too."

Huddled by the fire, clad in only a blouse and skirt and soft-soled shoes, she stared at him through her tears. Cicadas chirped in the surrounding dark, and silent eyes watched.

"You will die for this," she said, showing a little spirit.

"You've got me real scared."

He set the gun aside, stood, and began to unfasten his trousers. "Let's get this over with. Get over here on the blanket. I'll give you something to cry about."

"Brave talk." This voice was deep, steady, sure, and came from the dark behind the man.

The click of a trigger sounded over the crackling of the fire. From the opposite side of the crude camp, Stone watched as Sheriff Chase McBride pressed the barrel of his gun against Robert Woodruff's neck.

Stone walked out of the woods where he had been watching the runaway pair, doing what Chase had requested, holding off on killing the man. They had been one day and part of the night on the trail. Light from the fire had drawn them to their quarry. Whatever patience Stone possessed had been long used up.

Chase hadn't wanted to rush them. "Woodruff's armed," he had said.

"He's not going to shoot her. He's not done with her yet."

"He could be provoked. Do it my way."

Stone had let silence be his answer. While his brother had circled around the camp to come at Woodruff from behind, he'd kept his own gun aimed at the scoundrel's heart. He didn't move it now.

Still huddled on the ground, Carmen looked up at him. Her tear-stained face broke into a smile. Heedless of his pistol, she launched herself at him, throwing her arms around his middle, holding on and trembling. He holstered the gun and stared at Woodruff over her bent head.

"If you need to shoot him," he said to Chase, " 'cause he's trying to get away, no one's going to report anything different."

Woodruff slowly raised his hands. "You wouldn't shoot an unarmed man."

"How do we know you haven't got another weapon somewhere on you?" Stone said. "You look like the kind to wear a gun strapped to his leg."

"Search me. You won't find one," Woodruff said. "Besides, I haven't broken any law. She came on her own. She wanted a man. Believe me, she was begging for it."

"Yeah," Stone said. "I heard her begging all right."

Chase trailed the barrel of his gun up and down Woodruff's neck.

"Are you claiming that everything that's happened is the fault of this child?" Chase shook his head. "I've got a feeling about you, Robert. Instinct tells me this is not the first time you've done something like this."

Woodruff sneered. "Is that the Indian in you talking?"

"No. It's an instinct I developed while I was a Ranger."

Woodruff's sneer died. "A Texas Ranger?"

"No other kind means anything right now."

Woodruff's eyes darted back and forth. Stone could almost hear him calculating.

"Try to run," Stone said; then to his brother, "That'd be fair, wouldn't it? Shooting him while he's trying to escape, I mean. We do want to treat the man fair, especially if it's the last thing he'll ever know."

"I should have killed you when I had the chance," Woodruff said, his small, dark eyes on Stone.

"What you should have done was ride right on through Sidewinder weeks ago. But then, you're not very smart, are you?"

Stone could see the rage building in the man; then suddenly he seemed to cave in on himself. The fight went out of him like air from a balloon. He didn't look dapper anymore. In his stained dark suit, he looked trail-dirty, unshaven, beaten. Best of all, to Stone's way of thinking, he had lost his smile.

While Chase bound Woodruff's hands behind his back, Stone led the girl toward the horses at the far edge of the trees.

"I've got food and water," he said. "Your mother packed them for us."

Carmen buried her face in her hands. "I cannot show myself to her again. I am a disgrace. She will never forgive me."

"You didn't see her face as we were riding after you. She'll forgive you. She already has."

The girl shook her head as the tears returned.

"What you have to do is forgive yourself," Stone said.

She looked up at him. "I was angry. I hated you. I hated everyone. The man . . . he was angry, too. He said we could get back at everyone. And we would have a time of much pleasure. It was what I wanted more than anything." She stared blankly into the dark. "I am so ashamed."

"When we get you back to town—"

"No!" She pulled away from him. Her eyes were red and wild. "I will not go back with you. I will kill myself first. It is the only way I can know honor again."

"You're too young to talk of such things."

She brushed back her tangled hair and stared proudly at him. "I am not a child, though you think me so. When my father died, I swore on his grave that I would help my mother. That I would never dishonor his name. I have broken that vow. *Mi madre* will love me and she will say she forgives, but she will know what I have done."

Stone started to protest, then looked long and hard at the girl. He saw in the face looking up at him, he heard in the voice, not the selfishness of a child but the beginning strength of womanhood.

What he was supposed to do about it, he had

no idea. Of late, his record with women was none too good.

"If you will permit me to interrupt, I believe I have an idea."

Stone looked past her to his brother. Chase stood with his back to the light, one hand firmly gripping the arm of his prisoner. Slump-shouldered, Woodruff stared at the ground.

"Interrupt as much as you want," Stone said. "I need all the help I can get right now."

"You are a proud man. Does it pain you to say such words to me?"

"Why should it? Because you're part Comanche?"

"No, I don't believe that worries you. But something else does. Whether either of us wants to admit it, I am a McBride."

Chase's words took him by surprise. He gave as honest an answer as he could.

"I wouldn't ask for Tanner's help, that's for sure. Or even Lauren's, though that would probably be a mistake, since this is a woman thing we're dealing with right now. But I'm asking you. It's probably because we don't have a past—at least not one that we share."

"It's a strange blessing."

"What is?"

"This respect because we don't know each other well."

"Blessing seems a strange word to use."

"Maybe, but then I'm not a total savage. I was raised by a padre, don't forget."

A whimper from the girl brought Stone's attention back to her. He unwrapped the provisions the women had sent with him, then the four of them went back to the fire, Woodruff bound by one hand to a tree at the edge of the clearing so that he could eat, Carmen choosing a place away from everyone at the far edge of the light, consuming little for all her professed hunger of a half hour ago.

The brothers sat and talked. Mostly Chase talked, and Stone did the listening. Neither included Carmen in the discussion, but she was listening so intently she scarcely breathed.

At last Chase said, "Do you think the señorita will agree?"

Before Stone could respond, she spoke up. "The señorita agrees. What you suggest is better than taking the knife to my wrists."

It was a point neither man could refute.

Two days of waiting, pacing, consoling an inconsolable Josefina, staring at glowing coals in the fireplace when she ought to be getting rest, keeping Henry busy so that he wouldn't pace alongside her—all of this had Annie about out of her mind.

On a late afternoon when she heard horses stop in front of the boardinghouse, she dashed outside. In the gathering twilight, Chase and Stone dismounted. They were alone.

Behind her Josefina began to wail. Annie's heart turned to ice.

"You didn't find them," she said. "Or you were too late. Otherwise you wouldn't be here so soon."

Stone started for her. She brushed at her eyes as she looked him over, joyous because he was uninjured, ashamed of that joy. "Someone's hurt . . . or worse. Carmen—"

She could barely whisper the name.

Out on the street, a crowd began to gather. Ignoring them, she watched Stone's face, searching for confirmation of her worst fears.

"Everything's fine," Chase said loudly over her head to the crowd. "We found them. Everything's been taken care of. Now go on about your business."

A few muttered protests were hurled back at him, and no one moved. He looked around at the men and women, one by one.

"I said go about your business. We found them. They're all right."

Annie swayed, and Stone took her by the shoulders.

"Is that true?" she said. "How can that be? They're not here."

"It's true," he said.

"Thanks be to God," Josefina cried and bowed

her head as she made the sign of the cross.

Slowly, reluctantly, the onlookers began to disperse, and Annie wondered if they were disappointed because bodies had not been brought in.

"You need me here?" Chase asked.

Stone shook his head. "Go on to your work."

"I'm going to my family."

Annie wanted to scream. They spoke so matter-of-factly while she could barely breathe. She most certainly could not let go of her fears, not so quickly, no matter what Stone said.

Too much remained unanswered.

Without another word, Chase mounted and was gone.

Stone took Annie's arm. The warmth of his hand, the upright strength of him, even the solemn face shadowed by bristles should have encouraged her. But something was wrong. Carmen should be here, burying herself in her mother's arms. And Woodruff's dead body should be thrown over his saddle, proof that the law really did rule in Sidewinder.

Stone led her inside. They did not stop until the parlor. Josefina and Henry stood in the doorway, a thousand questions in the mother's eyes.

Stone gestured for Annie to sit, but she could not. She faced him in front of the dying fire.

"He did not harm her," Stone said.

"Do not lie, Señor Stone," Josefina said. "I am

not a fool. They have been gone too long. And she is not with you."

"He did not harm her," Stone repeated. "But she feels she has harmed herself. She feels she has dishonored you."

"I am a mother. I care only for my daughter's safety."

"She is safe."

Annie could be silent no longer. "Where?" she said. "There is no place safer for her than here."

"She is with Padre Rodriguez at San Raphael Mission. It is where Chase was raised."

"I will go to her," Josefina said. "She needs me."

Stone stared at Annie. "She needs time to heal," he said.

"And Woodruff?" Annie asked.

"I thought you might be asking that. We turned him over to the Rangers. They'd been looking for him, too, along with a whole string of sheriffs. His real name, it seems, is Roger Woods, although sometimes he calls himself Ralph Wright. There are warrants out for his arrest. He makes a habit of ingratiating himself with widows or single women, marrying them, then disappearing with their money."

"And I was his next victim," Annie said.

"You didn't make a very good one."

"No," she said. "I didn't."

She could have told him why. She could

never have given herself to the scoundrel. Someone else already occupied her heart.

She looked down. The truth was something she would keep to herself.

"This mission," Josefina said. "Is it far away?"

"A two-day ride," Stone said.

"I know right where it's at," Henry said. "It'll take us probably three days in the wagon."

"Us?" Josefina asked.

"You ain't going alone. And Mr. McBride here just come back. You got somebody else in mind besides me?"

The mother turned her warm brown eyes to Annie. *"Patróna?"*

"Both of you can go, of course," Annie said. "But are you sure this is wise?"

"I must know that she is all right. I speak of her heart and her soul. If she chooses to remain with the padre, I will not protest. But I must let her know I love her."

"She knows," Stone said.

"She must be told again," Josefina said. "I thank you for what you have done. You are a brave and good man. But I must hold *mi niña* in my arms before I can rest."

Brushing a tear from her cheek, she left and hurried up the stairs.

Henry cleared his throat. "I'd best go see about getting a wagon. She'll be wanting to leave early." He started to leave, then turned back. "While I'm at it, Mr. McBride, I'll take care of that horse of yours, too. We're all grateful for what you and your brother done."

And then Annie and Stone were alone. She wanted to touch his hands, his face, to bury herself in his arms. And she would. But not yet.

"Provisions must be prepared for them," she said.

"I'll help," said Iola Simpkins from the doorway where Josefina had been standing.

"Mrs. Simpkins," Annie said, "that won't be necessary."

"Oh, yes, it is." The widow sniffed. "That rascal had the nerve to sweet-talk me as if I didn't have any better sense than to believe what he said. Oh, I listened, all right, and I passed some pleasant hours with him. But my late husband taught me to be careful of things and people that look too good. On Christmas he finally got around to asking me about how well off I was—put it plain, too, didn't try to put any sugar on it. I let him know real fast that Mr. Hanes was handling things for me. There's no way I could get at what little money I have without going through him."

So saying, she turned and headed for the kitchen.

Annie stared after her.

"I had her figured all wrong," Stone said.

Annie turned her attention to him. The

widow wasn't the only woman he did not understand.

"You look exhausted," she said. "Go on up. Someone will bring you some food in a while."

"That's all right," he said, running a hand through his hair. "I'm not hungry."

You will be for what I bring.

Waving aside his protest, she hurried around him and made for the kitchen. She was so filled with certainty concerning her purpose, she almost exploded from it. Her heart was pounding so hard, she feared that anyone getting close could hear it.

Stone especially. She planned to get very close to him. Exhausted as he was, he would not have the strength to push her away.

Chapter Sixteen

Annie knocked on the door to Stone's room, opened it before she could change her mind, and slipped inside. All was dark and, at first, silent. After a moment she could hear his breathing. Not only was he here, he was already in bed.

Her breath caught. Too much soul-searching had gone on out in the hall for her to quit now. She refused to retreat.

Knowing the room well, she walked to the far side of the bed, turned back the covers, and lay down beside him. She didn't touch him. Simply being there, with the covers pulled to her chin, was as far as courage and love could take her. The next move was up to him.

Nevertheless, she took the trouble to feather

her hair around her on the pillow, moving swiftly and, she hoped, without sound. Stone did like her hair to be loose. It was the one thing he liked most of all.

He lay so still, she feared he was asleep, in which case she would have to figure out a way to wake him up.

The pace of his breathing quickened, and she took heart.

"Aren't you going to ask who's in bed with you?" she said, shattering the silence with her whisper. "Unless it doesn't matter."

"It matters. And I know who's in the bed."

His voice was deep and low, but he might as well have responded with a trumpet fanfare, considering the way it destroyed her calm.

"I do have one question, however," he added.

Her heart pounded.

"Are you still wearing that black dress?"

She tried to make out his profile in the dark, but he was all shadow and little substance, a disembodied voice.

"I imagined a dozen things you might say, but that wasn't one of them." She did not try to hide her pique.

"You didn't answer the question."

"No, I'm not wearing the black dress. I'm not even wearing shoes. If you must know what I replaced the dress with, you'll have to find out for yourself."

"I plan to."

He packed a great deal of meaning in those three words. Annie's heart swelled, and every muscle in her body tightened. Never had lying in bed required so much physical exertion. She almost feared whatever lay ahead. She hadn't gotten much sleep in the last few days. But then, neither had he.

"You are not going to ask why I'm here," she said in a half question, half command.

"If it's just for talk, I'll have to change your mind."

"It's just for talk," she lied.

Was that a chuckle she heard? Impossible. Not coming from Stone.

Beneath the covers his hand rested on her belly, and she almost flew out of the bed. He was substance, all right. With his heat and solid presence, he was the stuff of life.

"I guess I'm not dreaming," he said.

"You're not dreaming," she managed to get out. "I'm real enough."

"Oh, yes." His voice was ripe with meaning. "I hope you're sure about this, Annie. It's too late to turn back."

"Even if I change my mind and ask to leave?"

"Even then."

She closed her eyes and felt the blood coursing through her, every nerve ending tingling from her head to her toes.

"It's a good thing I'm sure," she said.

"A very good thing."

His hand moved to her breast. Through the thin nightgown she could feel its warmth. She had never felt anything so good. Well, almost nothing. She knew something of the sensations that lay ahead for her, that lay ahead for them both. The knowledge fired her as much as his hand.

During his interminable absence of the past two days, she had finally admitted the truth. She loved him, more than she had loved him when they were betrothed, more than she thought it possible to love. Her love was so vast, all of Texas could not contain it. It leapt into the sky and circled the moon. The mere thought of him melted her bones.

Right now she loved him so much she wanted to cry. But he would ask why the tears, and she would have to lie. To hold the tears at bay, she turned and curled herself against him. He was naked. She almost jumped back. Almost.

Her fingers itched. She did not know where to put them. Several places on the expanse of warm, muscled flesh tempted her. Already at the limits of her boldness, she chose his chest.

"Make love to me, Stone."

She barely got the words out before his mouth came down on hers. When his tongue slipped between her lips, coherent thought fled, and she gave herself up to sensation—a thousand pinpricks of pleasure in every part of her body and a great joy that settled in her soul.

Her discontented hands went to his neck and into his hair as she pressed herself against him. She wanted to find a way inside his skin, as he was already inside her. She burned, oh how she burned for more kisses, more touches, more of everything—all of her burning having begun with no more than the touching of tongues.

He broke the kiss. Her protest came out a gasp. But he was not done. With a few deft, impatient movements, he managed to throw back the covers and remove her gown, then toss it aside. His hungry hands discovered that she was now as naked as he, and he moaned.

She shivered at the sound.

"Are you cold?" he asked against the side of her neck.

"I'm on fire."

He blew into her unbound hair. "Annie," he said, running his tongue around the edge of her ear, "dearest Annie."

She let herself believe that at the moment she truly was his dearest. She let herself believe she was loved.

Tonight he would be giving her what he could. She would give him the same. With her, that would mean giving him everything.

She began by trailing her hands over his

shoulders and down his strong, taut back, explorations she had imagined in her most wanton moments of reverie. Nothing had prepared her for the feel of him, the smoothness, the hardness, the heat.

He rippled under her touch. In return, the tips of his fingers stroked her throat and made their way down to her breasts, playing with the aroused tips. She threw back her head and gave herself to him with an ardor that was as consuming as she had known it would be.

He was here, he was safe, and for a while he was hers. The darkness caressed them as they caressed one another. She had never known such happiness.

While his lips paid homage to her breasts, his hand trailed down her side, to her back, and lower until he was holding the fullness of her buttocks in his palm. She buried her face in the crook of his shoulder. It seemed the most natural thing in the world to rest her leg over his hip, an act that put the most intimate parts of their bodies dangerously close together.

"Too fast," he said, and eased her away until she lay on her back beside him. Blushing, she had no time to protest anything he did, for his hands and his lips were on her in an instant, doing their magical things.

What a relief it was to give herself completely to him, letting him make the decisions as to what he would kiss, where he would stroke. He chose unerringly. Under his tender assault, she found that her greatest difficulty lay in lying still enough to give him access. Her sighs, her cries, her frantic hands gave him encouragement.

"I've wanted you so long," he whispered. "You are beautiful."

He made her feel beautiful, in the dark. Beautiful and wanton and no longer alone.

Her juices flowed shamelessly. When she thought she would go mad, he positioned himself on top of her. She parted her legs and felt the hard tip of his sex press against her. Propping his weight on his elbows, he kissed her eyes.

"I'll try to be gentle," he whispered.

The tip touched her body in a probing movement that was far too tentative to satisfy the insistent throbbing that had taken control of her. She was not fragile. She would not break.

Impatient, she thrust her hips upward and he was inside her. His mouth covered hers, and he swallowed the small cry she could not contain.

For one delicious moment, neither of them moved. It was as if he realized the profound importance of what he had done, of what she had begged him to do by coming to him in the middle of the night.

The moment proved the calm before the storm. When the tempest broke, she was swept into a different kind of dark, this one velvet and swirling as his body pounded against hers. He seemed weightless as she held him tightly, fearful she might tumble from him into the void.

At last came explosions that shook them both. They seemed to last forever, yet were fading far too soon. Neither broke the embrace. She pulsed everywhere and wondered if it was the same for him. How strange it was to be joined in this most intimate way, yet know little about whether the joy invading her also invaded him.

All she knew was that he held her in an unbreakable embrace, each breath as ragged as hers, his body rent with matching shudders that had not quite been spent.

Gradually the passion subsided, and she waited for the regret she had feared would strike. It did not come. Instead, and far worse, was his shift away from her. She was struck not only with a sense of abandonment but with the realization that she had no idea what would take place now.

Certainly there would be no declarations of love . . . unless he made his own avowal first, and convincingly enough so that she knew he was not simply being kind. He had risked his life for Carmen, or so his reasoning might go; the least he could do was accommodate Annie when she forced herself on him.

Except for the slowing of their breathing, all was quiet.

A new terror struck, worse than the awkwardness she was feeling. What if he thanked her? He might do so, for accommodating him. Nothing could be more humiliating. She could never face him again. Her imagination raced faster than her heart. She could almost hear the words. She poised, ready to flee.

To her great relief, he rested his arm over her middle and pulled her close to him. In the chill of night, with no sheet to cover them, they shared the warmth of each other's body.

She took a deep breath, more nervous than she'd been out in the hall.

"I guess that's that," she said.

"Annie—" he said.

They spoke at the same time. She wanted the mattress to swallow her.

"That's that?" He sounded incredulous. "Did you really say 'that's that'?"

"I was trying to be honest. I'm not exactly experienced in this kind of thing." Her voice grew small. "Maybe neither of us should do any talking."

He pulled the covers up and returned his arm to its resting place around her middle. The weight had a comfortable feel to it, as if he wanted to keep her beside him forever. It was a fanciful thought. Despite the tension between them and her uncertainty about what to do next, she smiled to herself in the dark. Stone had that kind of effect on her.

"I'm never to say anything?" he asked.

"Not right away." She meant it with all her heart. Whatever he said would take her smile away.

"Good. Because I don't have any idea what to tell you or ask you. Except that what we have done means more to me than you can know."

He couldn't let things be. She should have known he couldn't. The trouble was, his soft words raised more questions than they answered. How was she supposed to respond?

I love you and I always will.

Too much.

It means a lot to me, too. You made me feel good.

Too little.

She settled on a portion of the truth, starting slowly, building as she went.

"While you were gone, I was terrified about what would happen when you finally found them. I had to keep up a brave front, for Josefina mostly, but for myself, too. And when you came back, I was so relieved I wanted to cry. But that didn't seem the right reaction."

"This did."

"Yes. We've been . . . teasing each other, though that's not the right word. Whatever we've been doing, it wasn't satisfactory to either one of us."

"And this was."

"It was satisfactory to me." She could have laughed at the inadequacy of her statement. But laughter might free other emotions; she could easily break into sobs.

"To me, too." He held her closer to him. "You don't know how much."

So tell me.

She did not say the words. Whatever he was holding back was something she did not want to know about, not tonight, not right away.

In the following silence, she imagined she could still feel him inside her, still thrill to the memory of everything. Hers was a selfish pleasure, and she knew it. The fears of the past few days returned. The harshness of reality tarnished her joy.

"It wouldn't have been this way for Carmen," she said.

Stone let out a long, slow breath of air.

"No, it wouldn't have been the same. She left with him willingly enough, but by the time we found her, she'd long since decided she wanted to return home."

"What made her leave? I know she was restless, but running away doesn't seem like the kind of thing she would do. She didn't leave a note, of course. Even if she'd wanted to, she can't read or write."

"Padre Rodriguez will take care of that."

Annie could not let up. "Did she give any hint about her reason? Robert Woodruff, or whatever he calls himself, is hardly the answer to a young girl's dreams."

Stone didn't answer.

"You know something," she said.

"It's not anything I ever planned to reveal."

"Please. I have to know. She was my responsibility as much as anyone's."

She spoke with earnestness. She could almost forget they were lying in bed without a stitch of clothes between them.

Almost.

She concentrated on Carmen.

"You want me to say I won't tell anyone? That I'll never mention to Josefina whatever it is you tell me? You ought to know I won't, not if it would hurt her."

"It might." He hesitated. "The truth is, on Christmas Eve night Carmen came to me."

"What does that mean, she came to you?"

"She came to my room while I was at the saloon. When I got back, she was in my bed."

Annie's stomach knotted.

"You have a very busy bed."

"I knew I shouldn't have told you."

"I'm sorry, I just . . . please, go on."

"The bed's not so busy. I got out of it fast. And I told her to leave. After a show of temper, she did."

Annie could imagine the scene . . . the young girl presenting herself in all her vulnerability, her dreams and awakening passion as fervid as they were fragile.

And what had she gotten in return? Rejection of the cruelest kind.

"It wasn't just temper, Stone. She was hurt and humiliated." Annie knew the feelings well.

"That's why I didn't tell anyone."

"And then after Christmas you got back from the ranch and learned she had run off with someone else."

"Someone who had been rebuffed himself."

"By me. I guess we share in the guilt."

"You should have accepted Woodruff's proposal?"

"I should never have encouraged him."

"Why did you?"

To make you jealous.

She shrugged and kept her silence.

"Carmen's wounds are already healing," Stone said. "Quit laying blame."

"I can't."

"You need distracting." He put his hand on her breast.

Her breath caught. "You've already done that."

"I'm doing it again."

Already her insides were beginning to boil.

"I hadn't considered doing anything twice."

"But you had considered it once."

"I'm in a poor position to deny it."

A sudden thought struck.

"When you asked me if I was in my black gown . . . that's how Carmen came to you, wasn't it? She was in bed, but she was still dressed."

"You're hard to distract."

Humiliation struck her anew. She wanted to hide her face in her hands. She wanted to get up and run. She had thought that in stealing into his room, she was being original. She wasn't even first.

But his hand moved from her breast to very, very low on her abdomen. She changed her mind about running. A team of oxen could not have dragged her from the bed.

She covered his hand with hers. He had a strong hand with long, wonderfully supple fingers. She freed the fingers lest he think she was trying to keep him from his goal.

This time the lovemaking was slow and languorous. When he kissed her, which he did with expert thoroughness, it was as if her body had been dipped in honey and he was licking the sweetness from her skin.

As slow as they both were in the beginning,

the end came far too fast, the ecstasy spent all too soon, and she was left once again in his arms knowing not what to say.

This time she chose not to linger. Easing from the covers, she found her nightgown and slipped it over her head. Much to her dismay, he leaned over and lit the bedside lamp.

She tried to smooth her tangled hair, then pressed her fingers against her swollen lips, not because she was ashamed but because of the look in his eye as he studied her. How easy it would be to crawl back beside him and do what they had been doing until dawn broke and they were forced to face a new day.

She chose a more difficult path. She headed toward the door. He started to get out of the bed. She raised a hand and he stopped, for which she was grateful. It was difficult enough to look at his bare chest and arms, provocatively revealed above the waist-high covers. If he stood, she would see everything.

His everything would be a sight to behold.

She blinked away the image.

"I'm going to keep what happened to myself," she said.

"I planned to hurry next door and tell everyone in the saloon."

"They'll never believe it."

"They will if I throw in some details."

"You wouldn't."

"No, Annie, I wouldn't."

Under the warmth of his gaze, she almost melted to the floor. Leaving the room was proving almost as difficult as entering it had been.

"It was hard for you to come here," he said.

"It was harder to stay away. I guess I'm heir to a lot of human frailty. I'm not as strong as I thought."

"Frail is the last thing I think of when I think of you."

What's the first?

She almost asked him, but he spoke before she could.

"There's one thing more. It's a compliment of sorts. I hadn't decided to tell you."

Her heart fluttered. "But now you will."

"Now I will. Before we left him with the Rangers, Woodruff confessed you were the only woman he'd ever been tempted to take with him."

The fluttering stopped.

"That's a compliment?"

"I said of sorts."

"So you did." She made her voice light. "I guess it's a good thing you didn't keep your vow."

He looked truly puzzled, and more than a little worried. He was probably thinking of vows they had made to each other long ago.

She hurried on. "I meant the one about killing

the man who attacked me in my room. It's enough that he will be spending a long time in jail."

He frowned.

"What's wrong?" she asked. "He is in jail, isn't he? The Rangers aren't about to let him out."

"He's in jail, all right. It's just that he's not the one who struck you."

She shook her head in puzzlement. "What are you talking about?"

"I asked him about it. I asked him really hard. He looked truly surprised. He said he had no reason to search your room, not after you had let me know you were such a success. And he never struck you. He would have been afraid of hitting you too hard and ending all his plans early. Besides, as I said, he cared for you in his own way."

"And you believed him?"

"I believed him."

Chilled, she rubbed her arms. "But that means—"

"It means that whoever did it is still running free."

"I thought it was over."

"Some things are. Some things aren't."

"Whoever it was wouldn't dare attack me again."

"I was thinking of us."

The floor moved under her. She gripped the

doorknob so tightly she almost broke it off.

"And which category did you put us in?"

"Whatever is going on between us, it's not done. You know it as well as I. But I don't want you roaming around the boardinghouse in the middle of the night. Next time, Annie, I'll come to you."

Chapter Seventeen

What they were doing was wrong. Stone knew it, and so should Annie. But over the next two nights, after long hours spent at the ranch moving the cattle from pasture to pasture, arguing with Tanner over the stock or the feed or whatever subject came up, riding the line mending fences, then coming back to town for an hour at the saloon, he could do only one thing.

He went to her room, took her in his arms, and found a release he could find nowhere else.

She was in his blood. Wrong as it was, he could not deny the truth.

She ought to lock her door. She ought to tell him to go to hell and be fast about it. He would be going there soon enough, if for no other reason than what he was doing to her.

But she did not turn him away. He found her soft and gentle, then feisty, a different woman each time he was alone with her. Even in the dark of night she spilled sunlight across the room, brought warmth to the cold air, and, most miraculous of all, brought a momentary peace to his soul.

The first time he'd gone to her, the night after she'd come to his bed, she did not respond to his knock. Not right away. When she finally opened the door, she backed up to stand in the middle of the room in her plain white nightgown, her hair down, a youthful, innocent look about her that twisted his heart.

For a moment she was the sixteen-year-old girl he had first seen working in her father's store. In those days she'd worn her honey-colored hair unpinned, and there had been a coltish way about her as she moved around the counters straightening goods, filling orders her father gave to her. She was shy, barely able to lift her deep brown eyes to him, but he'd caught her watching when she thought he was occupied elsewhere.

He had got the idea that if he spoke to her or, God forbid, touched her, she would flutter away like a butterfly. He had been very young himself, a loner even in those days, but old enough and needful enough to know when something special presented itself to him.

Looking at her in the boardinghouse bedroom, he felt the same way. And then he saw her eyes. Years after that first meeting and the hundred meetings that followed, the eyes had slowly lost their shyness. Tonight they challenged him. They did not shift away.

"I thought you weren't going to let me in," he said.

"So did I."

"You wanted only one night?" he asked, giving her a chance to answer yes and turn him away. He did not ask himself if he had the strength to leave.

"I thought once was all I needed." She glanced at the floor, then back at him. "I was wrong. Is that what you want me to say? I'm saying it. Once was not enough." She turned from him. "Now please get undressed. It's late and with Josefina gone, I have to get up early."

Her brusqueness stung.

"All caught up in the throes of passion, are you?" he asked.

Then he saw the clenched fists at her sides and sensed the trembling beneath the thin gown. Cursing himself for the fool he was, he hurried to her and kissed the side of her neck.

"I'll leave," he said. "You're right. It's late. I probably woke you."

"You didn't wake me."

He put his arms around her and pulled her

back against him. She dragged his hands up to cover her breasts. She did not have to drag hard.

She sighed, her body soft and yielding against his palms. "Annie," he whispered into her hair, "I've been thinking about you all day. About what might happen between us." He ran his thumbs across the tips of her breasts. "About this."

"Me, too," she said, so softly he could barely hear her.

He took everything from there, at least most everything. While he was taking off his clothes, not being very neat about it but fast, very fast, she went over and turned down the bedroom lamp, leaving only the uneven light from the fireplace to cast a glow over the room. He got no more than a quick glimpse of her slender figure as she eased out of her gown and slipped beneath the covers.

He joined her and let his hands discover what his eyes could not see. All the harshness of the day faded—the hard work, the tense arguing, the loneliness of the ride, the too-familiar pressures in the saloon—all of it was gone when he ran his fingers across her smooth skin, when he felt her muscles tighten in response, when he heard the soft sigh that whispered from her sweet lips.

Covering her mouth with his, he swallowed

the sigh. He could not get enough of touching her, kissing her, exploring the subtle curves of her body so different from his. He was a rascal, the true bastard of the family for being here. She was the angel, encouraging him with tentative touches on his chest, his stomach, his thighs.

"Let me guide you," he said when he could no longer stand the tension. He put her hand on his sex.

"Oh," she said, but she did not pull away. After a moment she required no more guiding. Her fingers took on a will of their own. She hesitated only when he began his own exploration of her. A cry sounded in her throat; then her legs parted and he was inside her.

This was his true coming home, the only one that mattered.

They climaxed far too quickly. He held on to her tightly, unable to think about anything except the places where their flesh touched. When she eased from beneath him, he wrapped an arm around her waist as if, like a butterfly, she might flutter away. Slowly the passion faded. She stroked his arm for a moment, then with a catch in her voice asked that he leave. Summoning the little reason left to him, he admitted she was right to ask. Staying the night would have been another wrong, hinting as it did of a permanence he could not offer.

Still, he kept her in his embrace.

She drew a half dozen breaths. "I have to think," she said. "I can't do that with you in my bed."

"That's as good a reason for me to stay as any."

"Please," she said.

He could not deny her. Dressing almost as hurriedly as he had undressed, though with far less eagerness, he leaned down to kiss her, then went slowly to his room, where he fell into bed and slept a dreamless sleep.

The next day went much the same as the one before, but when he knocked at her door shortly after midnight, she opened it right away and was in his arms in an instant, her hands tearing at his clothes, her lips ravaging his.

She almost knocked him over. He recovered fast, but not so fast that he didn't let her continue to undress him. When they were both naked, they fell on the bed, sparing no time to crawl beneath the covers. She wrapped her arms and legs around him, stroked his hair and face, ran her hands across his body everywhere she could reach.

Inflamed, he tormented her with kisses, using his tongue in the places he had learned aroused her most. She responded with all the ardor he could have wished for. She burned the cares of the day from him, the troubles of the past, the worries about what all the tomorrows might hold. When at last they were spent, they eased beneath the covers. Neither spoke, but he could feel a growing tension in her, a gradual withdrawing that was more of the mind than the body.

She had to be asking herself a thousand questions, most of them about where this lovemaking would lead. Nothing he could say would give either of them satisfaction; nothing would be the complete truth.

She pulled away and stared up at the ceiling. "I don't know what made me do that."

"Do what?" he asked, feeling stupid.

"Throw myself at you. I didn't know I was going to do anything like that at all. But then the door opened. . . ."

Her voice trailed off. He wanted to give her a reason she could accept, but the truth was, he had been as surprised as she.

"Whatever it was, I hope it happens again," he said.

Her lips curled into a small smile. "I'm sure you do." The smile died. "I'm not promising it will happen again."

"Are you promising it won't?"

"I'm like you, Stone. I'm not promising anything."

With that, she turned her back to him and

pulled the cover high, so that all he could see was a tangle of glorious hair.

He took it as a good night. Like before, he slid from the bed, dressed, and went to his room.

On the third night he came in the boardinghouse exhausted, thinking he ought to go to his room, telling himself he should, then moving without will along the dark hallway toward the door of her room.

He knocked and entered. She sat at her desk on the far side of the fireplace, a wrapper over her nightgown, her hair long and flowing.

"I thought I would go over some papers until you got here," she said, almost defensively, as if he expected her to throw herself at him every night.

"I can leave," he said.

"You've said that before."

"And meant it." He added, more honestly, "Almost."

"I wanted you to go. Almost."

They looked at one another for a minute. She turned from him. "I'm almost done."

He watched awhile as she bent to her work; then he moved slowly to the bed and undressed, lay down and awaited her. The next thing he knew, she was shaking him. He awoke to darkness and the feel of her hand on his arm.

"It's almost dawn," she said. "You need to leave."

He sat up and shook his head. "I really fell asleep, didn't I?"

"You really did." Dressed in one of her black dresses, she was kneeling beside him on top of the covers.

"I'm sorry," he said.

"There's no need to apologize. You were exhausted. You can't keep up this pace."

He tried to smile. "Sure I can."

"No, you can't."

"I want to. I need to."

"Need is a strong word. You need to see that your horse is cared for each night. You need air and water. You don't need to take care of me."

She spoke simply, bluntly, once again the practical Annie.

"They're hardly equal," he said. "Besides, whatever we're doing, I thought it was by mutual agreement."

"And so it is." She looked away. "Please get dressed. I'll meet you in the kitchen. It's cold outside and there's a threat of freezing rain. You'll need some hot food before you set out."

Ah, yes, practical Annie.

When she was gone, he hastily pulled on the shirt and suit he wore for gambling, then hurried upstairs for his ranching work clothes. He felt like an actor, playing parts, wearing costumes for each of his roles. The role he felt most comfortable in was the one with Annie, when he wore nothing at all.

Downstairs he found a plate of hot biscuits, ham and eggs, along with a cup of steaming coffee. Annie stood by the stove and watched as he ate.

"What's it like at the ranch?" she asked. "You never say anymore. It's not my business, but I can't help wondering."

"The same as always."

"That's no answer."

He put down the cup. "No, it's not. The truth is, the ranch is getting in my blood again. I didn't think it would, but I can't keep from caring."

"And Tanner?"

"He cares, too, but whenever we try to talk about anything, we end up in an argument. Chase shows up on occasion. He would rather boil in oil than admit it, but I think he likes the place, too. And Lauren, of course. She shows up to care for Tom—she and Callie and sometimes Faith."

"How is Tom?"

"Worse. And eternal. Lauren thinks he's hanging on for some reason, but she doesn't know what it is."

Annie took a deep breath and looked away from him. "Have any of you discussed what you'll do when he's gone? What you'll do about Clare?"

"Buy her out, I hope. We haven't discussed it, but I feel sure that's what everyone will want, including her. She can't care about staying out there. I can't imagine why she hasn't already left."

She nodded, glanced at him, then looked away again.

"What about you? Will you let the rest of them buy you out? Will you be leaving after your father dies?"

Annie concentrated on the heat waves rising from the stove. She prayed the questions sounded casual. Stone must not know that her future depended upon what he said.

He took an eternity to answer.

"It's what I planned when I decided to return."

"Of course. The Circle M is no longer your home."

"No, it's not. At least not the way it is now."

Which sounded as if it could be, if the situation altered enough. He was cruel to hold out hope with such a statement. She could not let herself be fooled into believing he wanted any kind of permanent relationship with her. And if he did, that relationship did not include a sharing of vows, a ring, a sharing of love.

She took his plate. "More coffee?"

"No, thanks."

"It's almost light. Remember to wear that woolen scarf." She cursed herself for sounding too much like a wife. But she could not help herself. No matter how he viewed her, she was wed to him in a way that was as strong as any vow.

Only not legal. Not recognized by anyone but her.

He had secrets. But so did she. After a flurry of dinner guests from the Roundup, business had slowed again. She had only one paying guest other than the widow Simpkins, a preacher who was visiting Sidewinder's lone church. He wouldn't be here long. The papers she had been studying when Stone arrived last night were bills from the general store and from the stable where Henry had rented the carriage to take Josefina to the mission.

She also owed the farmer Lester Thompson for the ham and beef he had supplied her last week. She tried to keep that bill current, since she knew he needed the money. In the wintertime, life was hard on a farm.

Somehow she would survive. She always had. The trouble was that since Stone's return, her life had changed. She was living by new rules, new precepts, new dreams. If her lover could be called a dream. Gladly and sadly, she knew he was far too real to be considered anything insubstantial.

An ice storm struck late in the day, and she wasn't surprised when Stone did not return to the boardinghouse. He showed up the next day to tell her he would be spending occasional nights at the ranch, bunking down with the foreman and the few hands still working at the Circle M. If her lovemaking was a little frantic that night, he did not seem to notice. And he was loving, oh so very loving as only he could be, as if he actually cared for her, which she supposed he did. But not in the way she wanted. Not in the way that said he would give up everything for her.

A week later, when Henry and Josefina returned, it was with news that Carmen was doing well at the mission with Padre Rodriguez, that he was teaching her to read and to care for the children he took in.

"She is contented, *patróna*. The shame no longer burns her heart."

As happy as Annie was with Josefina's news, it was Henry she wished most of all to speak to.

"Do you know how to play cards?" she asked when the two of them were alone in the parlor.

On the journey he had shaved his beard, making him look years younger. Even his hair was trimmed. Annie felt as if she were speaking to a stranger.

But it was Henry's familiar crackly voice that answered. "I play right well enough. Won a pot or two in my time."

"Could you teach me?"

He scratched at his face, and she got the feeling he missed his beard.

"Any fool can learn cards," he said, then grimaced. "That didn't come out right."

"Don't worry. Can any fool play well enough to win?"

"You're speaking of yourself."

"I have a good head for figures."

"And you don't get all idgety-fidgety the way some women do."

Annie supposed that was a compliment, and she nodded.

Henry's eyes narrowed. "What you got in mind?"

She waved a hand airily. "Nothing in particular. Passing the time, maybe. The winter evenings around here can be long and dull."

He gave no sign that he saw through her lie.

And so the nightly lessons began. They used the dining room table. Sometimes Josefina and the preacher sat in, but she was a poor player, never remembering whether a flush beat a straight or that three-of-a-kind beat two pairs. Too, she had a strange way of looking at Henry from time to time, as if she was afraid of something he might say or do. Annie gave it little thought. She had never been able to figure out the relationship between those two.

Surprisingly, the preacher proved to be the best player at the table, though he was given to talking about the cards as the devil's instrument and declined to make even the mock bets that took place between Annie and Henry.

By the time Stone arrived, the cards were put away and Annie was waiting in her room. More and more he was giving signs of a growing exhaustion and a restlessness that eased only after they began making love. She never tired of his body, of the sleek, warm skin, the hard muscles, the skill of his hands and lips.

He never spent the night, not after that one time when he had fallen asleep. She had passed much of that night watching him, loving him, feeling her heart break a little more. By the time dawn came, she had returned to her usual self-control.

But the loving and the hurting did not stop.

Neither did the worry. Hence the cards.

On a particularly bitter evening when she felt certain he would stay at the ranch, she dressed in her most severe gown and covering cloak, pinned back her hair so tightly her lips flattened, and without a word to anyone at the boardinghouse strode next door.

Ace Bellamy was standing close to the swinging doors. His eyes widened slightly, but otherwise he showed no surprise to see her.

"Miss Chapin," he said with a slight bow. "What brings you out on this cold night?"

Clutching her purse to her, she glanced around the smokey room at the tables, at the men, at the money stacked in front of them.

"I've come to play poker," she said with a lift of her chin. "Could you please arrange a game for me?"

Chapter Eighteen

"I ain't playin' with no woman."

Annie stared down at the man. She couldn't see much of his face, covered as it was with hair, but his eyes were small and dark and beady. The rest of him was big, especially the hands spread on the table. Between the hands lay a stack of coins and bills.

"It would be humiliating to lose to me, I know," she said with a smile.

"Ain't no way I'm gonna lose."

She looked at the man sitting across the table from him. Smaller and less hairy, he looked not one whit cleaner. He certainly didn't look friendlier.

"You're losing to me, Budge," the second man said.

"Not fer long," Budge said.

Ace Bellamy looked from man to man. "Are you sure this is the table you want?" he asked Annie.

"Oh, yes," she said. She did not add that it was the table with the most money showing. She also did not mention that if she didn't sit down soon, she would lose the rest of her fast-disappearing nerve and bolt for the door.

Bellamy turned to the gamblers. "Budge," he said, then to the second man, "Finch, I didn't take you two for cowards. I guess I was wrong."

Budge came halfway out of his chair. "Nobody ever called me a coward."

Finch gave a more dramatic response. He drew his gun and set it on the table beside the deck of cards. "Same here."

"Settle down," Bellamy said. "Neither of you is a coward in the usual sense. But it takes a truly brave man to do something no one else is willing to do. In this case, take on the lady here."

Annie didn't know if she was supposed to smile, curtsy, or snarl. She chose to look at Bellamy.

The two gamblers stared at one another.

"Oh, hell, I will if you will," Budge said. Finch nodded in return.

And so that was how Annie found herself sitting at the table with two strangers, neither of whom did more than growl and look away, as if she would disappear if they didn't acknowledge her.

She emptied her purse on the section of table in front of her, stifling a sigh as she stared at the bulk of her savings. The amount wasn't huge, just over twenty dollars, but it was a fortune to her.

"Should we cut for deal?" she asked a little too brightly.

Finch passed her the cards. Trying to remember everything Henry had taught her, she began to shuffle them.

Suddenly she became aware of the silence in the rest of the saloon. No talk, no laughter, not even a tinkling piano to break the quiet. She was equally aware of the man who was now standing opposite her, close, far too close to the table. His hands hung loose at his sides as her gaze slowly traveled past the dark suit coat and paisley vest, the white collar, the strong, bristle-shadowed jaw, the straight nose, the startling blue eyes of Stone McBride.

The cards shot out of her hands and spilled across the money. Cheeks burning, she gathered them up.

Stone pulled back the remaining chair and sat. "Deal me in." He glanced at the two men. "Anyone got a problem with that?"

They shook their heads.

Annie was not so compliant. "I do. This is a private game."

He took off his hat and rested it on his knee, then ran a hand through his dark hair. "There's no such thing in a public place."

She glanced at Budge and Finch. They seemed glad of the company.

With her mind racing through all that Henry had taught her, she set the deck of cards in the middle of the table. Stone won the cut. "Ante up," he said and began to deal. "A dime will get you in."

Annie found the proper coin. Imitating the men, she tossed it out. She knew Stone saw her trembling hand. He gazed at her with a questioning look in his eye.

"Keep dealing," she said. "Let's get on with the game."

Annie slammed the front door to the boardinghouse, almost catching Stone with the edge.

"You let me win," she said.

"Prove it," he answered, close on her heels.

"I could have taken Budge and Finch on my own."

"I don't doubt it."

"You cheated."

"No, you were dealt good hands, fair and square. Beginner's luck, it's called. I've never seen another player quite such a beginner as you."

"I knew the game."

"True."

"I could even tell when those two men were bluffing."

"Most of the time."

She forced herself to look at him, something she had rarely done when he was sitting across the poker table from her. He'd loosened his string tie and opened the collar of his shirt. She was startlingly aware of his leathery skin, his lean features, the contrast of his sinfully blue eyes.

"They quit early," she said.

"That they did."

"Which left only you and me. That was when I really began to win. You cheated."

He did not answer, and she became aware of onlookers, Henry and Josefina watching her from the dining room, Mrs. Simpkins and the preacher from the parlor.

Waving her hands in disgust, she hurried down the hall and into her room. Stone followed.

She whirled on him as he slammed the door closed behind him. "The preacher will know you're here."

"Tell me to leave."

"Leave."

"No. I wanted to see if you would say it."

Annie wanted to slap him. She also wanted to throw herself in his arms. She was truly pitiful.

"I doubled my money," she said. "I'm sure half of my winnings are yours."

"Keep it all. You earned it."

"You don't sound proud of me."

"I'm not. You've got your money. Don't go in the Roundup again."

It was then that she saw the set of his mouth and the tightness of his jaw. Only then did she realize how angry he was. He hid it well, the way he hid all his feelings, but she could sense it building in him like heat.

She refused to be intimidated. "I'll go if I want to."

"If you want to gamble, gamble with me here."

Didn't he know she did that every night?

"I'm trying to take care of myself," she said, to herself as much as to him. "Whatever method I choose is my business." She was very much aware of the careful way he was assessing her, and she almost faltered. Still, she wasn't done. "I don't tell you what to do at the ranch. You don't tell me what to do in town."

His eyes narrowed. "What if I told you to take your clothes off?"

She stared at him in disbelief. "That's crudely put."

He took off his coat and tossed it aside. The vest and tie followed.

"I'm feeling crude right now."

"I would rather be sweet-talked."

"No, you wouldn't. Not tonight."

Damn him, he had started the heat churning deep in her belly, and she could feel the swell of her breasts. She was like the chickens who came running when they heard the sound of their food being scattered on the ground.

She turned her back to him and heard his boots hit the floor as he tossed them aside.

"Don't get undressed, then," he said. "We can do this any way you want."

She wrung her hands, a habit she had picked up since he'd returned. "You make what we do sound like something that needs to be taken care of, like washing or eating or going to the store."

"It's a lot more than that and you know it."

She knew it, all right. But how much did he understand?

He stepped close and unpinned her hair so quickly she had no chance to stop him. When he eased the cloak from her shoulders, she did not try to still his hands, not when they stroked across her shoulders and down to her breasts, nor when they began to tug upward at her skirt, lifting it so that he could reach underneath and unfasten her petticoat and drop it to the floor.

Next came her drawers. By then she could barely stand.

Beneath her skirt his hand roamed until it found its mark between her legs.

"You're ready for me, Annie." His voice was husky. His hand was sweet.

She leaned back against him. "Sometimes I hate you."

"Sometimes I hate myself."

"No," she said. "Don't ever do that, not because of me." His fingers shifted back and forth and she gasped. "Please don't stop."

He didn't, not until he had her panting and close to tears from the pure joy of his touch. When he took his hand away and turned her to face him, she cried out in protest. But he knew what he was doing. Unfastening his trousers, he turned her back to the wall and lifted her skirt.

"As you can see, dear Annie, I'm ready for you."

She parted her legs enough to allow him entrance. He lifted her, and as if she did such things every night, she wrapped her legs around him and held on tight as he plunged deep inside her. His thrusts were quick, sure, as sweet as his fingers had been. She cried out. He covered her mouth with his, and with the room whirling around her, he brought her to ecstasy.

Burying her head in the crook of his shoulder, she let the thrills slowly subside. Slowly, very, very slowly, the room took its rightful stationary place around her and the world returned to insinuate itself between the two of them.

Holding on to him, she tried to pretend they had made love on a cloud, the two of them apart from any ordinary existence, the passion they shared unique to only them. But it was like fighting against time. The truth moved inexorably on. He had made naked those parts of them that mattered the most and had taken her against her bedroom wall.

No cloud, no special existence.

But there had been passion. For her, it was unique.

As was the embarrassment.

He lowered her to the floor, and her dress fell modestly around her, but beneath its folds she still tingled with wicked pleasure. Bending her head, she watched as he fastened his trousers, catching only a glimpse of his limp sex. Somehow that glimpse seemed more intimate than anything they had done, giving her a view of his vulnerability. Fool that she was, she loved him all the more. And she drew a small sense of triumph from the realization that she could change his body as much as he could change hers.

He cupped her face and slanted soft kisses

across her lips. "Annie," he whispered.

She turned her face from him. "Please, don't say anything."

As always, she lived in fear that he might apologize. It was why she was frequently so brusque with him when their lovemaking was done. Oh, how she would have cherished the luxury of tenderness. But that would tell him how she felt. And he might feel obligated to do something out of a sense of honor, something foolish like asking her to be his wife.

He feathered her hair around her face. "You used to wear it down."

"That was a long time ago."

"It was the first thing I noticed about you. Your hair and the shyness in your eyes."

She swallowed the lump in her throat. "Both have changed, haven't they? My eyes and my hair."

"Have you changed inside?"

His voice was thick, almost tentative. Was he asking if she still loved him? Surely not. Not even he could be so thoughtless. Not even he could be so cruel.

"We've both changed, and you know it. Now please, you truly must leave. It's late."

He stepped away, and she eased from the wall to stand at the foot of her bed, his boots and her undergarments lying on the floor as testimony to what they had done. His coat and vest, tossed more vigorously aside, had made it to the chair beside her desk.

He sat on the chair to pull on his boots, but folded the coat and vest over his arm. His shirt was wrinkled where she had clung to him. Otherwise, he appeared as if nothing had happened between them. Did his intimate parts ache the way hers did? Did the traces of passion linger still?

"Good night," she said, desperate to clear her mind.

He paused at the door. "I've decided to go to Fort Worth. I'll be gone a while."

"Thank you for telling me."

"When I get back, we need to talk."

Here came the honor. She wanted to scream.

"If you think it's necessary," she said.

"Oh, it's very necessary, Annie. And long overdue."

He hurried over to kiss her, this time more passionately than she'd expected. Then he was gone, leaving her leaning against the bedpost, unable to stop the tears.

Listening to his footsteps in the hallway, she locked the door and brushed the tears away. At the desk, she emptied the money out of her purse and counted it hurriedly. Forty-two dollars and fifty cents. It was enough to pay the farmer and the stable and most of her debt to the store. Certain as she was that Stone had let her win, she could not refuse to use her ill-gotten gains. He might be honorable, but such nobility was something she could not afford.

Setting the money aside, she picked up the letter she had received last week, the one from her brother Sam, who wrote from his home in Albuquerque, telling of the store he had opened, one much like their father had owned, telling her of his plans and hopes. She had not known how to respond. Now she did.

Picking up the pen, dipping it in ink, she hurriedly began to write.

Chapter Nineteen

Clare stroked the wispy gray hair away from her husband's forehead, then, with a shudder, wiped her fingers on her gown.

"You feel warm," she said.

He stared up at her. His eyes had lost most of the blue that had once been his best feature. Now they were dark, hinting of gray like everything else about him. They reminded her of iron nails.

"Don't fret too much," he growled. "I don't have much time left. Where are the boys?"

He meant his sons. They were hardly boys. Especially not Tanner. He was all man.

"Stone's gone again," she said. She knew it hurt Tom, though he would never let anyone know. In some areas she could read him very well.

"Who knows where Chase is?" she added. "Doing something lawful, I'm sure. And Tanner"—she could barely say his name without a tremor—"he's somewhere out on the range."

Tom never had to ask about Lauren or the wives. They made frequent appearances at the house, nosing around, giving orders about his care. Today Clare was spared their presence. It was one of the few things for which she could be grateful.

Would Tom never die? Sometimes she thought he would outlive her, or if not that, she wouldn't last long after he was gone. It was a stupid thought. The weaker he got, the stronger she became.

The door opened and Tiny came in. Immediately he went to open the window to let in the cold outside air. She rubbed her arms. No matter how good the air was for Tom—something she very much doubted—she hated the cold. It reminded her of the days when she'd been poor, when she and her mother had been unable to afford heat.

Visions of her mother flashed unwanted in her mind. She had to get away from them. She had to get away from Tom.

Without a word, she hurried to the hall and down to her room, closing the door firmly behind her, turning the key as if she could lock out memories.

In a fury, she threw herself on the bed and pounded her fists on the mattress. Why didn't he die? Why didn't his "boys" have the big explosion that was building? Why didn't some desperado shoot Chase? Why didn't Stone stay away?

Chase didn't really worry her. He was an Indian and in her mind of no consequence. Neither was Lauren. She was a woman, weak the way most women were, not at all like the stepmother she detested.

Clare's triumph was that they all hated her. Not in the way she hated them, of course. They didn't know that kind of hate.

Once Tom was dead, she knew they would not hang around the place the way they did now. Except Tanner, of course. She wanted to pool her share of the Circle M with him and buy out the others. Stone would agree. Manuelo had reported that Stone gambled every night for money. Why he did so, Manuelo had been unable to find out. She really didn't care, though she suspected the reason lay in Fort Worth.

Once Stone sold out, so would everyone else, leaving her and Tanner in sole possession of the ranch. They would of necessity be thrown together. She could convince him to give in to the urges she knew he was fighting. He was, after all, his father's son. She had caught Tom. She would catch Tanner.

If only the visions would go away.

In the stillness of the room she heard a crying woman, a mewling, pitiful creature, and, more softly, a crying child. She saw shadows and tired eyes and felt a hunger in her belly that never went away.

Too, there were men, strangers who stopped the crying for a while. Oh, how she had hated those men. She hated them still.

She pushed away from the bed and sat at its edge. This was getting her nowhere. Self-pity never did. She needed a ride into town. With no one in the house except the pathetic cook, she had no one to torment. And she did like to torment the McBrides.

Or one of their lovers. Manuelo had told her that Stone and Annabelle Chapin had such a relationship. Manuelo made a very good spy.

She had only one quarrel with him. When the Chapin woman had returned unexpectedly to her room, he should have hit her harder. With her death, Stone's departure would have been all the more assured.

Dressing hurriedly in her riding clothes, taking great care with her hair and the feathered bonnet that matched her velvet riding cloak, she hurried down to find one of the hands and order the carriage. She didn't bother to tell Tom she was leaving. She never did.

And he didn't seem to care, not anymore. She wasn't concerned, as long as he did not change his will.

She found the ride into Sidewinder invigorating, as much for the freedom she felt as for the purpose she had decided on for the trip. Subtlety, she decided, was out. Besides, it was one thing she had never been much good at.

Reining the carriage horse to a halt in front of the boardinghouse, she set the brake and climbed to the ground. On the walkway, she was very much aware of the stares of two men at the front of the next-door saloon. They weren't just staring, they were gaping. She licked her lips, glad to know she had not lost her touch.

The men were fools, of course, but still they were men.

The door to the boardinghouse was unlocked, and she strode inside. The entryway was wide, its rug clean but worn. To her left, the dining room was empty. To her right, in the parlor, she found her prey. Annabelle Chapin wore a scarf over her pinned-back hair and an apron over her dark dress. She was rubbing a cloth over a breakfront behind the sofa. When she saw her visitor, Clare could have sworn she stiffened.

Clare smiled. She liked to put people on the defensive.

"Miss Chapin," she said sweetly, "have I caught you at an awkward time?"

The woman set the dusting cloth aside. "Not at all, Mrs. McBride. Please come in."

The invitation was said through pinched lips, but still it was said, and Clare strode into the parlor. A movement in the dining room caught her eye. It was a Mexican woman, a servant obviously, with a rather thin, gaunt man at her side.

Clare touched her brow with the tips of her gloves. "It's been a long ride. Do you think I might have some tea?"

Annabelle Chapin nodded and looked past her toward the servant. The woman nodded and disappeared through a door at the back of the room. The man held his place.

"I really do need to speak to you in private," Clare said, looking pointedly at him.

He growled and limped down the long hallway.

"Might I sit?" Clare asked. Really, the woman had no manners.

She took the proffered chair. "And may I call you Annabelle? I feel I know you so well."

Annabelle took off her scarf and apron, smoothed her hair, and took another chair.

"How is that? We met only the one time."

"Yes, but sometimes men are not discreet."

Did the woman pale? Yes, definitely yes.

"I speak of my stepson, of course," she went on. "Stone. But of course you know him well."

"He rents a room here."

"Is that all he rents?"

The question brought Annabelle half out of her chair, and Clare motioned her back.

"Pardon me, that was crude. And cruel, too. But I thought you should know—"

Josefina chose that moment to bring in the tray. Two cups, a teapot, and a plate of small cakes were placed on the table between the chairs, along with sugar and cream. Why, the servant seemed almost civilized.

"That will be all," Annabelle said.

With a grimace of displeasure, the servant left, and Annabelle poured the tea. Pulling off her gloves, Clare doctored her tea heavily with cream and sugar and took a sip. Passable. She set down the cup.

"Look, Mrs. McBride," Annabelle said, "if you're going to tell me more innuendos and rumors, the way you did last time, I really don't want to hear them."

"You offend me. I felt there were some things you needed to know. I swear on the grave of my mother that what I tell you is the truth."

Silently she sent a wish that her late mother would understand the false vow. Her mother had been foolish and weak, but she had never been unkind.

Ignoring her own cup of tea, Annabelle stared at her.

"Very well. What is it that I absolutely must know?"

"He won't marry you."

Hurt flashed in the woman's eyes. Whatever skills Annie possessed, and Clare assumed that several made their appearance in bed, hiding her feelings from another woman was not one of them.

"I assume you're speaking again of Stone," Annie said. "I did not realize he had taken you into his confidence."

"Oh, he hasn't. But I hear him talking to Jeb. The foreman, you know. He's been there forever, and Stone and he are quite close."

"And he's told this foreman he wishes to remain single? Not that I care, you understand."

Her denial came too late.

"Men take women for granted, you know. Especially a man who is already getting what he wants."

That brought Annabelle to her feet.

"You go too far, Mrs. McBride. I must ask you to leave."

"Everyone knows what I'm talking about. Everyone at the ranch, that is. I'm surprised the scandal hasn't spread to town."

It was, of course, a complete lie. If not for Manuelo, Clare herself would not have known the truth, no matter how much she suspected it.

Pulling on her gloves, she stood. "I regret if anything I have said offended you. But I do believe in knowing the truth. A woman is so helpless when she's deceived."

Reticule in hand, she walked to the door that led outside. Annabelle followed. Good. Clare had saved the best for last.

"How long has he been gone from here? Two weeks? A little more, I believe. Quite a while for a man supposedly watching over his dying father. Too long. In truth, he returned to the Circle M two days ago. I asked him when he planned to return to you. As usual, he gave me no civilized answer. But I have observed him carefully. Though his father is rallying once again, your lover seems in no hurry to get back to your bed."

Annie stared at the closed door. The woman had been lying. She had to be. But she was clever, playing on her latest victim's vulnerability. Where Stone was concerned, Annie was truly unprotected. All the reasoning in the world would not ease the hurt in her heart.

Behind her, Josefina let out a spate of Spanish that sounded none too complimentary about Clare McBride. Whatever she said, Annie agreed.

But what if this time Clare hadn't lied? Stone had been gone an eternity. He might have returned. If he had, he would go to the ranch to see his father. Perhaps, weary from his journey, he had decided to stay. But that would have meant giving up his nightly visits to her. He enjoyed them. She was not so foolish as to believe otherwise.

He was also giving up his visits to the saloon. Perhaps he had gambled in Fort Worth, got his fill of it . . . and of other things she did not want to contemplate.

If Clare had wanted to destroy her, she had chosen her poison well.

Annie returned slowly to the parlor, stared at the cold tea, looked at her scarf and apron, found herself unable to get back to work. It was a condition new to her. She could always work. If only her head would stop pounding so.

She looked at Josefina. "I need to lie down a while."

"The woman lies."

"Probably. Still, I'm suddenly very tired."

"Henry will help me with the dinner. Do not be concerned, *patróna*."

"Henry's been a lot of help to you lately, since your return."

"He is not all bad."

It was quite a concession. Annie attempted a smile.

"Go," Josefina said, shooing her down the hallway. "Later, I will make fresh tea and bring it to your room."

For a change, Annie let herself be cosseted, from the nap time to the tea to the dinner brought to her on a tray. Giving in to indolence, she did not come out of her room again until early the next morning. She came out with a new resolve, probably one she would regret. But lying around feeling sorry for herself was doing little good.

She started the biscuits. When Henry came in with the morning's supply of eggs, she asked him to go to the livery and rent her a horse and buggy or whatever conveyance was available. She would need it for only the one day. She would also need directions to the Circle M Ranch.

Wrapping herself in her warm woolen cloak and putting on a serviceable bonnet, nothing fancy and feathered like Clare McBride's, she ignored Josefina's protests and started on the two-hour journey, cracking the whip over the horse's rump.

Although not inexperienced with handling such an animal, the task did require her constant attention, along with the directions passed on to her through Henry, and she had little time to consider what she would do when she actually arrived at her destination.

The house was as Stone had described it, long ago when he had expected her to live there as his wife. Two-storied and shingled, it was far grander than other ranch houses she had seen on the trips she had taken with her father to deliver goods from the store. Of course it was grander. It had been built by Tom McBride.

She did not let the size of it worry her. It was the people inside that counted. They were terrifying enough.

A man came from the barn and offered to care for her horse. She started to ask about Stone, then stopped herself. Thanking the man, she knocked at the door. No one answered.

"Go on in," the ranch hand called out. "Doc Pierce came by earlier. There's a bunch of the family in there. Probably upstairs with Mr. Tom."

"Is Mr. McBride all right?"

"He's holding on. At least he was when Doc left. That's one tough old man."

Annie watched as he led her horse and buggy away. A bunch of them, he had said. That had to include Stone. Her heart ached so much she grew dizzy. He had returned. Clare had not lied. Much as she wanted to turn and run, she had come too far to back down now, and she did as she was instructed. She entered the lair of the McBrides. A short, slight man wearing an apron stood in the doorway at the far end of the parlor.

"Oh, I'm sorry." She took a step backward. "I thought no one heard my knock."

Smiling, he gestured toward the stairs.

"I should go on up?"

He nodded. This had to be Tiny, the mute cook Stone had mentioned. She wanted to return his smile, but she found it impossible. She hadn't the strength.

Going in front of her, he led her upstairs to a closed door. Behind it, she could hear voices. Before she could summon her courage, Tiny opened the door and stepped aside. Clearly, she was on her own to announce herself.

She walked into the room. At first no one looked at her. She recognized Chase and Tanner and their wives, and Lauren, of course. They were standing around, looking a little awkward, she thought. Clare had placed herself at the far side of the bed, as if she were hovering over her dying husband. Perhaps the ranch hand had been wrong. Perhaps Tom McBride was already gone. She almost panicked.

Then Tom McBride spoke.

"Come on in. Might as well. Everyone else has."

His voice was surprisingly strong for a man so wan and thin he looked as if he couldn't lift his head.

Everyone turned to her. Stone was not among

them. She glanced at Clare, who gave her a triumphant smile.

"I thought . . ." Annie began, then said, "I'm sorry for the intrusion," and turned to leave.

"No." Lauren was the first to reach her. "How thoughtful of you to visit my father."

"That's not why she's here," Clare said.

"That's enough, Clare," Lauren said. "Of course it is."

But Clare was not done. "She came looking for Stone."

Annie felt the floor shift under her.

"Shut up, Clare," Tanner said sharply. Callie rested a hand on his arm.

"I speak only the truth," Clare said. "Ask her."

"That's not necessary," Annie managed. "I'm sure you don't care why I'm here."

"Oh, but they do."

Faith came to her. "Are you feeling all right? It's a long ride out here."

"I'm feeling fine." It was a lie, but Annie was feeling a surge of irritation at having been taken in so easily.

She looked around the room, at everyone, even Lauren's husband, whom she had not seen at first. He was a handsome man, like the others, and the women were all so pretty. That included even Clare. Annie felt out of place, but not because of the way she looked.

"What a big family you are." If she sounded

simpleminded, she did not care. They did not know that a big family was what she had always wanted.

"There's a lot of us," Tanner said.

Chase shrugged. The women smiled.

"There's nothing more important than family," Annie said.

Lauren looked at her husband. "You're right."

"I don't mean husbands and wives, not entirely. Fathers matter, and mothers, and sisters and brothers, not because they always get along. They matter because they share a kinship that no one else does." She looked at Chase. "Even those who think they don't belong."

She felt a growing anger, mixed with frustration. It gave her the courage to go on.

"Stone doesn't talk much, but what he says lets me know you don't agree. Your affections lie outside one another." Her eyes blurred, but she was too wrought up to care. "What a waste."

She looked at Tom. He was smiling at her. Smiling. She couldn't believe it. Stone said he never showed pleasure at anything.

The shock of the smile brought her back to herself. "I'm sorry. I've been rude. I don't know what came over me." She looked quickly around the room. "Please pardon me. Or don't. I may have been rude, but I have not been wrong."

She hurried from the room and down the stairs. She could hear someone coming down behind her. She looked up to see Lauren.

"Please," Annie said, "I really want to go. You've been nothing but kind to me, and so has everyone else. I wish you could be as kind to each other."

Without waiting for a reply, she hurried outside. She felt guilty about taking the horse from his rest, but the ranch hand assured her the animal was fit enough for the ride back to town. Still, she made the journey slowly. She had much to think of, and nothing to regret.

By the time she was back at the livery, turning over the horse and buggy to the stable hand, assuring him she would send his money right away, she knew what she had to do. She had people to talk to, schedules to check, everything important, each detail deciding the rest of her life.

The one person she could not allow herself to think of was the man she loved.

Chapter Twenty

Stone was digging deeper and deeper the hole that was his new life since he had returned to West Texas. What he was doing was crazy. He knew it, and so would everyone else when they found out the complete truth. Still, he knew he could not turn back. Once he had determined his course, he had no choice but to follow it.

First came the essential long stop at his sister's ranch, the San Reanido. He swallowed his disappointment that she wasn't there. In coming to her as he was, he was judging her character and her heart, and he needed to find out if he was right. After he talked to the housekeeper Mrs. Shaughnessy and Mrs. Whitlow, the cook, and he was assured that for the time being at least all would be well, he debated whether to ride into town or go to the Circle M.

As much as Annie called to him, he should find out if all was well with Tom, or as well as things could be. And he needed to find his sister before she returned home. He made it to the porch at the Circle M. There he saw Lauren and Tanner talking, with Clare standing nearby. Dismounting, he walked slowly toward them, going over in his mind what he would say.

"He's still alive, if that's what you're checking on," Tanner said.

Jolted from his thoughts, Stone looked at his brother. As always, though they stood close, a thousand miles separated them, a thousand differences, a thousand angers over matters as serious as their mother's death, as trivial as the time of day.

"That's what I wanted to know, all right," Stone said. "There's no fooling you."

"You two, don't you ever let up?" Lauren said.

"Apparently not," Stone said.

"Annabelle Chapin was right," Tanner said.

"What the hell are you talking about?"

"Tanner." Lauren spoke sharply. "Now is not the time to discuss this."

"Discuss what?" Stone asked.

"Tell him," Clare said from the side. "Let him know she came out here looking for him."

"And I wonder why she did so, since she's never been out here before," Lauren said, her eyes flashing at her stepmother. "Papa said you went into town yesterday. It's my guess you stopped by the boardinghouse."

"One grows lonesome out here," Clare purred, her eyes on Tanner.

Stone looked at Lauren. "Annie was here?"

"You're a cold bastard, you know that?" Tanner said. "You're doing wrong by that woman."

Stone's temper snapped. Maybe he was hurting Annie, maybe he wasn't, but no way was it his little brother's place to tell him.

"You'd be a fine judge about doing wrong."

Tanner straightened. "And just what do you mean by that?"

"Let it go," Stone said, and tried to pass him. "Lauren, I need to talk to you inside."

Tanner stepped in front of him. "No, I won't let it go. I'm not going to spend the rest of my life being accused of something I didn't do."

"The proof is in the McBride graveyard," Stone said.

He waved toward Clare, who stood there in her fancy gown with her fancy hairdo, a smile on her face, enjoying the scene, enjoying the trouble. "She's the result," he said in disgust. "She has her charms, I guess, at least for some men. Maybe you've found a way to ease your grief."

"What's that supposed to mean?"

"Take it any way you want."

Stone again tried to pass him. Tanner pushed him back.

"Let's get this settled once and for all," Tanner said.

"Get out of my way," Stone said.

Stone wasn't quite sure who pushed whom or who swung the first blow, but the next thing he knew, the two of them were flailing away at one another. All the anger of the past years came out in an explosion of fury, his passivity burned away in the heat of the fight.

He didn't try to aim. Most of his swings went wild. He took a fist to the eye and landed a blow on Tanner's jaw. The next thing he knew, they were rolling on the ground, kicking and punching like a couple of kids, not thinking, just feeling the burn of anger. Then the deluge came, and they found themselves sputtering and fighting for air.

He looked up to find Lauren standing over them with an upturned bucket over their heads.

"There," she said, setting the bucket aside. "Maybe that will cool you down."

Stone sat up and slung his wet hair out of his face. Reason was slow in returning, but when it did it came sharp as a whip. What in hell did he think he was doing?

He took a few deep breaths, then rubbed his eyes and looked at his brother. Tanner was staring at him with a sheepish grin.

"Did we just do what I think we did?" Tanner asked.

Stone shook his injured fist. "You've got a hard jaw."

"You're gonna have a dandy eye."

All the anger went out of him. "I never thought it would come to this."

"You should have," Tanner said, then raised his hands. "No offense intended. But I told you Annabelle was right."

"Are you going to tell me in what way, or am I supposed to guess?"

Lauren spoke up. "She said we weren't much of a family. She said family was more important than just about anything—"

"And we didn't have the sense to know it," Tanner said.

"Annie said that?"

"She didn't put it that way," Lauren said, "but that was pretty much what she meant."

Stone scratched his bristled jaw, staying away from anywhere close to his eye.

"Believe it or not," he said, "I've been thinking the same thing lately."

"Prove it," Tanner said.

Stone took a long, hard look at his brother, remembering the way he had appeared when he was a little boy, remembering how different they had been from one another, remembering his own fruitless efforts to change Tanner. Instead of anger or disgust or frustration, for a change he felt only regret.

"You want me to prove it? I take it you have a way in mind."

"You can start by trusting me. I fixed that wagon wheel. I fixed it right."

"That wheel was the part that gave," Stone said. "I felt it. I couldn't be wrong about that."

"I'm not saying you were." Tanner ran a hand through his damp hair. "I've had five years to go over what must have gone wrong. Someone tampered with it later, sometime during the night. That's the only thing I can figure."

Stone glanced at Clare. He'd got the feeling she had kept smiling during the brief fight. She wasn't smiling now.

"Don't look at me," she snapped. "I wasn't anywhere near this place. Besides, I wouldn't know what to do with your old wagon."

Stone looked back at his brother. Once again the years of Tanner's wildness came back, of his riding off when he was supposed to be tending to chores, of his rebellion against anything his older brother told him to do. But the wildness, the rebelliousness, had always been openly exhibited. As far as Stone knew, Tanner had never sneaked around. He had never lied.

Stone pulled himself to his feet and extended Tanner a hand. After a moment's hesitation, his brother took it. They continued to clasp hands even after they were standing and looking at one another.

"It could be I was wrong," Stone said.

"It's a possibility," Tanner said.

"For heaven's sake," Lauren said with a stomp of her foot, "can't you tell him you believe him?"

Stone shrugged. "I was afraid I would choke on the words."

"Try very hard," Lauren said.

He looked at Tanner. "Okay, I believe you. You fixed the wheel."

A weight lifted from him as he said the words. They dropped hands.

"While you're at it," Tanner said, "admit I'm right about buying a breeding bull before spring."

"If we can get the money out of Bill Hayes."

"And about not raising sheep."

"You're pushing your luck. Sheep and cattle can go together. We've got rangeland that'll work for both."

"Where exactly would that be?"

Stone was ready with an answer, but Lauren interrupted him.

"Let's take this family business a little slower, shall we? One of these days we're going to confess how much we love one another, but maybe not today. For now, I'll be content if we don't kill another McBride."

"Is Clare included in that?" Stone asked.

Clare answered for them. "No," she cried out. And then she gave another cry, this one raw and guttural, more like the wail of an injured animal than any sound a human might make. "Damn you all to hell." Whirling, she hurried into the house and slammed the door behind her.

No one spoke for a minute. Something was happening to the woman they had all hated for so long, something ugly, something that would not go away.

Tanner broke the tension.

"Looks like she's safe for another day," he said, grinning.

"Yeah," Stone said, "so it does." He looked at Lauren. "We've got some talking to do ourselves, little sister. I've done something you may not like. Then again, maybe it'll be the best thing that ever happened for the two of us. Let's take a walk, just you and me. I want you far away from anyone when you find out what's waiting for you at home. In case you want to scream."

Stone spent that night and much of the following day at the San Reanido. He hated to leave, but he needed to see Annie. He had a great deal to tell her. All of it was long overdue.

A few snow flurries were falling by the time he got to Sidewinder. Snow wasn't a common thing in this part of Texas, but neither was it a rarity. With Annie's scarlet woolen scarf wrapped around his neck, he went into the boardinghouse. Henry and Josefina met him in the front hall.

"She ain't here," Henry said.

"What do you mean, she's not here? Don't tell me she's gambling again."

"No, Señor Stone," Josefina said. "The *patróna* is no longer in the town."

A cold, hard knot formed in Stone's belly. "So where is she? The snow's beginning to come down pretty thick, and it'll be dark soon."

The two looked at one another.

"She didn't say nothing about not telling," Henry said.

"This is true," Josefina said.

"Where is she?" Stone asked, losing his patience.

"She left for New Mexico on the morning stage," Henry said.

Of all the things they could have told him, this was the most far-fetched. "What's she doing going to New Mexico?"

"Her brother is there," Josefina said. "The *patróna* said it was time she was with family."

"You got to remember, sweetie," Henry said, patting her shoulder, "she ain't the *patróna* no more."

"One of you care to tell me what's going on?"

Henry scratched at his beardless face. "Me and Josefina here got ourselves hitched when we was out at the mission. The good padre was glad enough to take care of things, seeing as how the two of us was traveling together."

Josefina's cheeks turned a rosy red. "When we told the . . . when we told Señorita Annabelle, she said she was very happy. She said we had solved a problem for her."

"She gave us the boardinghouse," Henry said. "Well, not exactly gave it. Tried to, but we're gonna be paying her when we can. That lawyer Hanes drew up the papers all legal like. Did it last night. Didn't seem too happy about it, but Miss Annabelle wasn't taking no argument from him. You know what she's like when she makes up her mind."

Stone knew.

"Her brother wrote her a few weeks back asking her to join him," Henry added. "That's what she decided to do."

"Because he was family," Stone said.

"This is the reason she gave," Josefina said. "But, of course, this is not the only thing that made her leave."

Her dark eyes stared accusingly at Stone.

Stone didn't try to argue. He had driven her away. By being slow and stupid and not trusting her, the same way he had refused to trust Tanner.

He couldn't do much about the stupid, but the slow could be fixed once he stopped standing around gawking.

"Pack some food," he said. "Pack a lot of it, enough for two. I'll be at the stable for a time getting me a fresh horse. Have it ready when I get back."

"Why d'you need a fresh horse?" Henry asked.

Josefina smiled patiently at her husband. "Señor Stone is going to bring Señorita Annabelle home."

"I'm going to try." He looked past the couple, down the long hall to the bedroom where they had made love. "At least I'll give her a few options she did not know she had."

Chapter Twenty-one

Annie sat in the crowded coach between two oversized men who showed no inclination to give her a fair share of the space on the narrow seat. She had to keep her arms folded across her chest and her chin lifted so that she could breathe.

Not that the air was anything special. With the snow coming down outside, the curtains had been drawn tight against the outside cold, but the only thing they cut out was freshness. Not one of the six other passengers, with the possible exception of the pinch-faced woman opposite her, showed any sign of having bathed in the past month.

Because of the snow, the going was slow. That didn't keep the coach from rocking back and forth and up and down and every which way that could make the journey unbearable. And the squeaking was louder than the howling of the wind—she had never heard so much noise. This was her first ride on such a conveyance. She wondered why anyone ever went anywhere if it involved dealing with the overland line.

Probably because, like her, they were desperate.

"Where'd you say you were headed, little lady?"

Annie glanced sideways at the man on her left. Ever since they'd left Sidewinder, he'd been trying to find out her destination. At first, in an attempt to imitate Tiny, she had answered him with vague gestures. But then the heavy-booted man on the opposite seat had brought his foot down on hers. Taken by surprise, she had cried out, pretty much giving the lie to her muteness.

The second time he asked, she'd answered, "West," without going into details. And now he was querying her again.

"She said west," the man to her right boomed. "That's all she's a-gonna tell you. She's a right smart one, she is."

"Now see here, I don't mean nothing by asking."

"Hell if you don't, pardon the expression, ladies."

As the men continued to argue, Annie closed her eyes and tried to picture her brother when he was a little boy. She could have done a better job if the top of her head didn't feel like it was about to come off.

Why such throbbing should remind her of Stone, she did not know, but his was the image that kept popping into her mind. She had a thousand of them—Stone staring down at her at the Roundup, Stone arguing with her over her saloon dinner guests, Stone watching her while they made love.

Annie's cheeks burned. Some images were not to be borne while squeezed in between two strangers.

The picture that stayed with her most was the last one that occurred, when he had stood in the doorway of her bedroom, his coat and vest thrown over his arm, his shirt wrinkled where she had been clutching at him like the sex-crazed woman she was.

When I get back, we need to talk.

How like him to torment her by throwing out such a statement without explanation. Over the next weeks she had decided on the nature of that talk. She had asked him what he planned to do after his father died. His lack of an answer was answer enough. He was going to tell her that his plans did not include her, that he held her in great affection but they both knew that what they were sharing was too hot to last.

He was right. She would get over him. She figured it would take seventy years, but she would.

She would have distractions he did not know about. In addition to his store, her brother had also mentioned he had a wife and son. They were ready to welcome her, too.

A son. Two years old, Sam had written. Annie was ready to be the best aunt in the world.

"We're slowing down," the woman opposite her shrieked. "We're stopping. Something's wrong. I knew it. I just knew it."

Both the sullen youth beside the woman and the one squeezed onto the floor between everyone's feet let out a disgusted sigh.

"When are we gonna get there?" the one on the floor asked.

The woman's husband, sprawled out by the door, taking up his manly share of the space, said his first words of the journey. "Hush yer mouth."

When the coach came to a complete halt, the rider who'd been up top beside the driver came to the door.

"There's an inn directly ahead where we'll be pulling up for the night."

"It's about time," the pinch-faced woman said.

"We ain't there yet, ma'am. With this snow,

we'll never make it over the hill to get to it. We need you folks to get out and stretch your legs. We'll still be moving slow. You can catch up with us over the rise."

Everyone groaned and began complaining—everyone but Annie. The father and the two youths were the first to scramble out. The large man who had defended her went next, but he stood by the door, arm extended, to help the mother and Annie down onto the hard, crusty ground.

Annie felt a little like a grape that had just burst its skin, free of constraint but more than a little exposed. Wrapping her cloak tightly around her, she looked at the landscape. The sun should be directly ahead, but with the clouds and the swirling snow, all she could make out was the dark outline of distant mountains.

With one of the stagecoach men waving a lantern aloft and leading the way, she fell into line and began to trudge up the hill. The coach creaked and swayed on ahead.

"Annie."

She shook her head. The wind was playing tricks on her mind. She was actually hearing Stone's voice.

"Annie, stop."

This time the voice was louder. Several of the

passengers began to look around into the gloom.

"Who's Annie?" one of the youths asked.

She tried to look as ignorant as everyone else. But it proved difficult when Stone appeared out of the twilight directly beside her. Everyone came to a halt—everyone but the man with the lantern. And, of course, the coach went on moving.

"Hurry up, folks," came from the front. "We've gotta keep moving, otherwise we'll freeze."

"Everything all right, miss?" asked the large man who had been her defender.

"Yes, go on. I'll catch up."

"No, she won't," Stone said.

"Yes, I will," she said, but after the man got a good look at her would-be captor, he was already scurrying after the light.

She forced herself to look at Stone. She could make out his features far too well, right now the most prominent ones being his firm jaw and determined lips. Her heart gave a little twist. Her anger helped her ignore her heart.

"What are you doing here?" she asked.

"Seems to me it ought to be obvious."

"It isn't. Go away. I have no intention of going back to Sidewinder. I've severed all ties with the place."

"Not quite all."

"I'm trying."

"You're running. That's not the same thing."

"Don't tell me what I'm doing. You don't know everything."

"Neither do you."

The snow caught in his lashes. She had an absurd urge to blow the tiny crystals away. And wouldn't that be a stupid thing to do?

She turned to hurry toward her fellow passengers. He grabbed her. As easily as if he were lifting a sack of potatoes, he tossed her over his shoulder and took off toward his horse.

"Put me down," she ordered.

"In due time."

"This is ridiculous. Just about everything I own is on that stagecoach."

"No, it's not. I climbed on top while it was slowing down. Your valise is tied to my saddle. The horse is waiting down the road a ways."

She considered fighting him, but that would make the situation more undignified than it already was. Besides, she wouldn't win, not by trying to match his strength. She held her protest until he got to the horse and set her on the ground.

"This is wrong, Stone, and you know it. I've written my brother. He and his family are expecting me."

"Is that why you're leaving? For family?"

If only the reason were so simple. And yet he

was right. She could never have a family with him, and she wanted one very, very much.

"I've already told you. I've made plans."

"Without talking to me."

"Since I had no idea when you would show up, yes, I made them without you. Give up some of that McBride pride. You are not involved."

"Sweetheart, I gave up that pride a long time ago."

Taking her by surprise, he swung her sideways onto the saddle and pulled himself up behind her, then nestled her against him, her legs dangling to one side.

"I figured we'd be warmer this way," he said.

He was right about that. Already she could feel the shift of his thighs under her. Reining the horse around, he dug in his heels and directed the animal away from New Mexico.

"You're not going to the inn?" she asked. "Even you ought to admit we can't keep riding like this for long."

"The inn's too crowded for what I have in mind."

A shudder went through her, unfortunately not one of revulsion.

"What's that?" she asked. "Freezing to death?"

"I doubt we'll freeze." He hugged her close. "Trust me, Annie. I'll take care of you."

With a sigh, she slumped against him. Of

course he'd take care of her, in his own way. They weren't done with whatever it was they did to one another. Lovemaking didn't seem like the proper word since love wasn't involved, not one that was shared.

His idea of providing care was an abandoned way station a mile or so back down the road. In the gathering dark, it didn't look like much from the outside, but inside there was already a fire going. Its light bounced from wall to wall, making the place look almost cozy, if she could ignore the cobwebs in the corner and the scurrying sound of mice.

"I've been following you a while," he said. "It seemed smart to start the fire. Someone had thoughtfully left a stack of wood."

She drew closer to the warm blaze. "You were sure of yourself."

"I'm bigger and stronger than you."

"Brute force will win the day, is that it?"

"I didn't have to use much of it."

"I was cold."

"Not for long," he said.

Too cowardly to look into his eyes, she continued to study the fire. He went out but returned shortly to set a bedroll and her valise on the floor. Out again, he came back with the saddle.

"Is the horse coming, too?" she asked.

"I found a stand of trees that'll protect him

from the wind. The snow's about stopped. He's out there munching on oats, thinking he never had life so good."

"I wish I could say the same."

"I wish you would."

He spread the bedroll in front of the fire and took out a brown package she took to be food.

"Courtesy of the bride and groom," he said.

"Josefina and Henry?" She came close to smiling. "I still can't believe they're married. I didn't think they even liked each other."

"You think maybe that's a requisite for marriage?"

She almost looked at him.

"No, I do not." And then, with a sigh, "Life is strange."

"It's unpredictable, Annie. When I get you back, please keep that in mind."

She didn't ask him what he meant. When he handed her a chunk of bread wrapped around a slice of beef and cheese, she devoured it hungrily, shifting from foot to foot in front of the fire. He ate, too, but he did it while watching her. As hungry as she was, she could barely swallow.

They drank water from the same canteen. Why the simplest acts between them seemed so intimate, she had no idea. No more than she could understand why the water tasted like him.

They saved most of the food for the rest of the journey, which should take all the next day if the weather was kind and they weren't heading into a driving wind. When the package was tucked away, safe from any hungry critters that might visit during the night, he took off his coat and scarf, then sat on the bench that was the cabin's lone piece of furniture to tug off his boots. She couldn't keep from watching everything he did.

"Are you warm enough yet?" he asked.

He had no idea.

Reluctantly she loosened her death grip on the cloak and rested it on the bench beside his coat.

He stared at her. An eternity passed before he spoke.

"I haven't seen you in ruffles in a long time."

She studied her hands, for some reason feeling defensive. "I bought the gown while you were gone."

"Why?"

Because I wanted to look pretty for you when you returned and it fit so nicely and flattered my figure and the lace along the rounded neck made me feel womanly.

"I was getting tired of plain black. Besides, if I was going back to the saloon, I needed some new clothes."

"Like hell you were going back."

Of course she wasn't. She had used up all her nerve the first time, but he didn't have to know it.

She turned her back while he finished undressing. She didn't look at him, even after he had crawled between the covers of the bedroll.

"You'll have to sleep with me," he said.

"I know it. But we don't have to do anything."

"I won't if you won't."

She could hear the mockery in his voice, and she forced herself to truly look at him for the first time since they had come into the light.

"What happened to your eye?"

"I ran into a door."

Kneeling beside the bedroll, she gingerly touched the purple and yellow bruise. "No, you didn't."

"I ran into a fist."

"That sounds more like it." She wanted to ask if some husband in Fort Worth had taken offense at his behavior, but somehow she didn't think it was so. Besides, with him lying naked beneath the blanket and the wind howling around them outside, this did not seem the time to be sassy.

But she could not keep from asking, "Whose?"

"I'll tell you about it later," he said, then added huskily, "Not now."

He was right. Not now. Hurriedly she took off

her gown and petticoat, then climbed beneath the blanket beside him. The fire toasted one side of her and he toasted the other. This wasn't supposed to happen again. She was done with passion.

Yes, and summertime would greet them in the morn.

All right, she told herself, she could let go of her anger for a few hours. She should look on what was happening as a way of saying goodbye.

Awkwardly, she eased out of her undergarments. He held the blanket up to give her as much room as he could. But he was also watching what she did. With an insouciance that was totally outside her nature, she tossed the garments over her head.

"I'll have to check for mice in the morning," she said.

"I'll do it."

"You're such a gentleman."

"I do my best."

He leaned over her and encircled one of her nipples with his lips. Her back arched and she sighed. His best was incredibly fine. One more time, she told herself; one more time. What could it hurt?

With that thought skittering briefly through her mind, she gave herself up to all the good that was about to come. While he was kissing and sucking and doing wondrous things with his lips and tongue, she ran her hand down the length of him, stopping at his thigh. He had very touchable thighs, not entirely because of what nestled between them.

"Are you hurt anywhere else other than the eye?" she asked.

"I'm hurting, but it's nothing you can't fix."

When she touched the part she figured he meant, he abandoned her breasts and put his mouth on hers. While his tongue probed in and out, driving her wild with its rough texture, they each assaulted the other, hands gone crazy with the need to touch everywhere at once. When she rubbed her fingers across his chest, his heart slammed against the tips. Knowing she was helpless where he was concerned, she felt wonderfully powerful to have caused such fierceness.

Annie forgot how to think. Emotions ruled, all of them concentrated where their bodies touched. The two of them, always so much in control, always reserved, knew no boundaries when they were like this. He whispered her name again and again, and words of such sweet tenderness they made her want to weep.

He kissed her throat. "You're beautiful."

She ran her tongue around his ear. "So are you."

He held her tight. "I want you inside me."

She laughed against the side of his neck. "I don't think that's the way it works."

"I'm jealous. I like your body better than mine."

"Use it. It's yours." It was the closest she could come to telling him of her love.

He ran his hand along her inner thigh. "I will, sweetheart, I will."

And then, when he was kissing her eyes and stroking her hair. "You're like springtime. You're everything fresh and good."

And later, as he was about to plunge inside her: "You make me complete, Annie. Don't you know that? You make me complete."

The firelight flickered across his face. Did he know what he said? He couldn't. Passion controlled him, and a need as strong as her own.

At this sweetest of moments, he was being cruel. Not intentionally—he was never that. He was cruel by holding out hope. As their bodies joined, she let herself believe him. And then, once again, she forgot how to think and gave herself up to love.

They fell asleep wrapped in each other's arms. Sometime before dawn, they awoke. He got out of the bedroll long enough to throw more logs on the fire, then crawled back beside her and they made love again, quickly, without much stroking and only a little kissing. But she was ready for him, and he was ready for her.

When they again woke, sunlight was streaming in through the dirty windows. The storm had passed. She looked outside at a wonderland of white, though the snow was a bare dusting on the ground. The storm, it seemed, had been one more of fury than substance—which, if she thought about it, was symbolic of what had passed between them during the night.

Neither spoke as they got ready to begin the long day's ride. She ought to be telling him she needed to catch up with the stagecoach. She ought to say that, no matter his reason for taking her back to town, she would eventually go away again. It would be kinder if he let her go now.

But he wasn't kind. And she found she could not tell him good-bye, not just yet, no matter her private avowal of last night. How much easier it had been to leave when he wasn't around.

They began their journey under a clear sky, with a brisk wind blowing at their backs. Sunlight reflected blindingly off the patches of snow, and she let herself close her eyes and rest her body against his. He was a source of warmth in so many ways, and for a while she let herself feel safe. She refused to look upon this journey as a retreat, although that was what it was. She refused to consider it as a return to all she had decided to reject.

With the wind helping them along, they made good time. Late in the day, when it seemed to her sleep-fuzzy mind that they should be nearing Sidewinder, she looked up to find herself on a stretch of narrow lane she had never seen before.

"Where are we?"

"Lauren's place is just over the hill. The San Reanido."

"You're taking me to your sister?"

"Sort of."

She sat up as straight as she could. "Stone, what's going on?"

"I told you we needed to talk. I've decided to show you instead."

He spoke with such seriousness, she felt hollow inside. Something was worrying him, something that had affected him more than she would have thought possible.

"I'd rather talk," she said.

"It's too late for just words."

He waited a long time to explain what he meant, never once slowing the gait of the horse. He waited until they were at the top of the rise. Before them, nestled in trees, waited the beautiful white ranch house that was the Lassiter home. With its white columns across a front portico, it looked more like a plantation house than anything one would find in this part of Texas. She'd heard about how Garrett Lassiter's father had built it for his mother, to remind her of their former Virginia home, but she'd had no idea it was so magnificent.

The house meant little to her now.

She stared at Stone, dread spreading through her like a disease.

"I did something a long time ago, Annie," he said. "While I was gone."

Suddenly she wanted to cover her ears and hide her eyes, to beg Stone to take her away and she would never question anything about him again. He could use her as he chose, could come and go at will, as long as he did not talk.

But an air of determination had settled on him, and she knew he would not veer from his chosen course.

"I wasn't exactly honest with you when you asked about what I'd been doing during those years before I returned." He looked into the distance, past the house, then turned his gaze to her. The bruise around his eye made him seem vulnerable, yet she knew that when he spoke, she would be the one to be hurt.

"I got married," he said. "It's time you knew all the truth."

Chapter Twenty-two

Stone lifted Annie down from the horse, treating her as delicately as he could. She was wooden in his arms. When he set her on the ground, she pulled away from him. Hours on horseback had left her wobbly, but she refused his help as she walked up the steps and stopped at the Lassiter front door.

He lifted the heavy brass knocker and let it fall. The sound echoed across the veranda like a gunshot. When he opened the door, she followed his gesture and walked inside. Lauren was standing in the doorway to the parlor. She smiled at Annie, then turned to Stone.

"Have you told her?"

"Yes," said Annie.

"No," said Stone.

Lauren shook her head. "So which is it? I swear, you may be my brother, Stone McBride, but sometimes I think you had no raising at all."

"Your temper's true to your red hair," Stone said. "Give me a minute to explain."

"Not just yet." Lauren hurried over to take Annie's hand. "You're freezing. Let me get you some tea."

"Later," Stone said.

Lauren rolled her eyes.

"Isn't there someone here I'm supposed to meet?" Annie said, directing her question to Lauren.

"She's upstairs. Come on. I'll show you the way. But first, let me take your cloak and hat."

Moving stiffly, Annie handed them over and lifted her skirt to follow Lauren up the winding stairs. Setting his coat and hat aside, Stone followed. He watched Annie's straight back grow more rigid with each step. When they stopped at one of the bedroom doors, he stepped in front of the women.

"Thanks for all your help," he told Lauren, "but I'll take over from here."

She looked from him to Annie and back to him, a softness coming into her blue eyes. "I guess it's better if you do. Be sure to call if you change your mind about wanting me to help."

When they were alone, he took Annie's hand and held it between both of his. "I'm not married now. I never would have betrayed you like that. Or betrayed a wife, no matter how much my affections were engaged elsewhere."

"Then what—"

A small cry came from behind the door. With a prayer that everything would turn out as he hoped, he took Annie inside. The woman he'd brought with him from Fort Worth was opening the curtains to let in the day's remaining light. A mound of pillows lay in a wide circle on top of the lace-covered bed. From the middle of the mound came another small cry.

The woman hurried toward the sound. "She's just waking up from her nap."

Stone stopped her with a raised hand. Short and bosomy, a widow whose children were grown and gone, she was wonderfully patient and caring, but sometimes she took on too much responsibility. He understood it was because he was usually gone, but he was here now.

Striding quickly to the bed, he picked up his daughter and kissed her forehead. A sense of rightness flooded through him, the way it always did when he held the fragile person he had helped bring into the world.

At last he turned to Annie.

"This is Emily," he said. "She's not quite two yet. She's mine, all mine, as much as a McBride will allow herself."

Stone held his breath. Annie's eyes were blurred with tears. She did not speak right away. He felt as if all eternity lay in the next few minutes.

"You have a child?" she said.

"She's got my eyes." His voice was shaky. He wondered if Annie could tell. "You can't see them in this light, but she's definitely a McBride."

He looked down and stroked the dark, wispy hair away from the child's delicate face. She looked up at him. "Hi, Daddy."

She spoke clearly enough to be understood. Most of what she said—and she was beginning to say a great deal—was close to unintelligible. He figured that once he was around her all the time, he would begin to decipher her chatter.

She squirmed in his arms. He set her down. Her white gown settled around her, its hem brushing the thick carpet.

"She hasn't got her shoes on." The nursemaid was being a busybody again. If he was being honest with himself, it was why he liked her. She genuinely cared for the child.

Annie knelt and held out her arms. Emily chewed on a finger and stared wide-eyed at the strange lady.

"Hello," Annie said. "My name is Annie. Isn't yours Emily?"

The child nodded. Then she grinned and

added, "Emily McBride," or something that sounded reasonably close.

"Do you know how to shake hands?" Annie asked.

Slowly Emily nodded. Annie held out her hand. She held it steady, which Stone took as a good sign. Unsteadily, Emily went over to her and with great solemnity brushed her small hand against Annie's.

"She's not walking very well yet," Stone said, then with fatherly pride added, "but she will."

"She's come a long way," the nursemaid said. "We're right proud of that little tyke."

Annie lifted her eyes to Stone. "She's come a long way?"

He came over and lifted his daughter into his arms, gave her a big swing, and was rewarded with a laugh.

"Careful," the nursemaid said. "She's delicate, you know."

"Oh, I know." It was one of the things that never completely left his mind.

He handed his daughter over to the woman, then looked at Annie.

"I've shown you what I wanted you to see. Now I think it's time to talk."

"Past time," she said.

He took her into the hallway. "There's a sitting room down here we can use."

The room was small and quiet and heavily

furnished. He turned up a lamp and faced her.

"Please, sit."

Her eyes were bright and unblinking. "If you don't mind, I'd rather stand."

He took a deep breath. "I wasn't a saint while I was gone."

"I never thought you were."

A knock at the door interrupted his reply. The housekeeper, Mrs. Shaughnessy, came in bearing a tray.

"Mrs. Lassiter thought you'd be wanting some refreshments after the long ride."

Stone buried his irritation. "Thank her for us. We'll be down before long."

Maybe they'd be down right away, if the tightness in Annie's expression was any indication of her patience.

"Where were we?" he asked when they were once again alone.

"Discussing your lack of sainthood."

"Oh, yeah. During the first part of those years, I did some heavy drinking and carousing. The truth was, and I see it now, I was trying to forget you. Trying to forget the last argument we had." He ran a hand through his hair. "Trying to forget a lot of things."

Annie swayed. He hurried to her.

"I think I will sit, if you don't mind."

When she was settled, he poured her a cup of tea. She took it, but she did not take a sip. Instead, she stared at it, as if any tea leaves present could tell her what he was about to say.

There was nothing left for him to do but plunge ahead. He felt as if he were walking on eggs. But that wasn't a good comparison. Eggs could be replaced. Annie's opinion of him was priceless.

"I tried cowboying for a while, but that didn't seem right when the land I was working wasn't the Circle M. So I turned to gambling. I managed to support myself. It was how I figured to spend the rest of my life. I would be one of the loners that hang around a saloon, then move on when the cards turn on him. And then I took up with Doris. She worked in one of the saloons."

He watched Annie's face as he talked, holding nothing back, hoping he could get an idea of how she was taking things. She looked at the tea for a while longer, then stared out the window at the dying day. She scarcely blinked. The tears he had seen in her eyes when she looked at his daughter were long gone. But the brightness was still there, and so was the tension.

"We weren't together but a few times; then she suddenly disappeared. I didn't ask what had happened to her. She wasn't the staying-around kind, or so I thought. The cards had been falling right and I'd been generous with her. I figured she was doing fine."

He took a deep breath. "There's no whiskey on that tray, is there?"

"No. I could use a little myself."

"We'll just have to go at this sober, won't we?"

"It's how I go at everything else."

She looked so beautiful in her wrinkled ruffled dress, with her buttery hair in a tangle, slight bruises under her eyes from lack of sleep. He wanted to take her in his arms, not to kiss her or paw at her, but just to hold her and do the talking with her body next to his. But that wasn't the hand he'd been dealt today. It wasn't the hand he had dealt himself.

"We had told each other there were no strings attached. Nothing special going on between us, and for me it was the truth. There was someone else on my mind. Someone I figured had already bound herself to another man."

Annie kept on staring out the window.

"I'm not trying to spare myself here. I gave her no more thought. Then the doctor in town came to my table one night and ordered me to come with him. It seems Doris had been living on what I had given her. She was expecting our child and she didn't want me to know. The baby was coming early. The doc thought I ought to be there, to see what I had done. Whatever you're thinking about telling me, he did so for you."

Annie turned her eyes to him. "Emily."

Stone nodded. "I went to the room where Doris had been staying. I went with a preacher. The last thing I wanted was to be like my father, using women and pushing them aside. She didn't want to marry me, but in the end she agreed. For our baby, she said. The baby came early, but the mother didn't make it."

Annie closed her eyes. He could see the tears on her lashes. He felt she was crying for them both.

"Emily was so tiny. And she was having a hard time breathing. Holding on to life was proving hard. Doc brought in a wet nurse. Somehow we made it through the next few months. And then the first year was past and she was getting stronger, looking every day more and more like the woman she's named after. But she still needed constant care. The wet nurse was good, but she had children of her own, raising them without a man, and she needed to be paid."

"So you continued to gamble."

He laughed bitterly. "Just when I needed them the most, the cards turned on me. I was close to busted when the letter came from Bill Hanes. I didn't want to come back. I didn't want to face you after all that I had said. But I had no choice. I'd already changed the wet nurse for Mrs. Wilcox. She's the woman down the way. She needed paying, too. And there would be other expenses I couldn't even figure on. I had to have my share of the inheritance. I didn't come back because the ranch was calling me. I didn't come back because I needed to see my family again. And I damned sure didn't come back to say good-bye to Tom. Money brought me here."

Annie hugged herself. "Of course," she said. "It makes sense."

"You brought me, too," he said.

"Don't lie now. I couldn't take it."

"I'm not lying. I didn't know how much power you had over me. And still have. When I saw you in the store, I began to understand."

He took a step toward her. She held up a hand. "Please, no. Don't say anything more. And don't come close. I can scarcely think for all you've already told me."

The cup rattled in its saucer, and she set it aside.

"I can't breathe in here," she said.

"I'll open a window."

"No, it's not that." She stood and turned toward the door. "It's just . . . I need to think. I never imagined anything like this."

"It's been a long day, and I've laid a great deal on you."

"It's been a long two months. I can't believe that's all you've been here, but it is."

Without turning back to him, she went out,

paused as she looked at the bedroom that was serving as a nursery, then hurried down the stairs. Stone followed. Lauren and Garrett met them in the downstairs hallway.

"Isn't she the most beautiful creature you've ever seen?" Lauren asked. She spoke lightly, but the assessing look in her eyes said she was anything but casual.

"She is," Annie said. "She's precious."

"You know," Lauren said, "it was when I saw my brother holding her that I finally began to understand him." She looked at Stone. "He's got a lot of softness beneath that hard exterior of his. When I was growing up, he was always trying to boss me around. I thought he was pure meanness, but I was very young."

"He was right to do it," Garrett put in. "I'd want someone like him looking over my own daughter."

"I don't know that I'd go quite that far," Lauren said with a laugh. "But I do know that if he doesn't work out any other arrangement"—Stone cringed at her words—"I'll do my best to help him raise her, and I'll probably do it the way he tried to raise me. I don't know if you've noticed, Annie, but my brother and I have made our peace."

Stone felt that he should be putting in a word somewhere, but he couldn't find a good place. He needed to toss Annie over his shoulder, the way he had out on the road, and carry her off where he could finish telling her what he wanted to say. He hadn't been able to do it earlier, though the words had come to his lips a thousand times. First, he had to know how she felt about his child.

Annie looked back up the stairs to where Stone had come to a halt.

"I guess it's my turn to say we have to talk," she said.

"I'm willing."

Before he could say more, the front door burst open and Tanner hurried inside.

"All of you bundle up and get to the ranch as fast as you can. Doc's there, along with the lawyer. He says Pa won't last through the night."

Chapter Twenty-three

By early dawn they were all gathered around Tom's bed, Doc Price and the lawyer Bill Hanes, Chase and Faith, Tanner and Callie, Lauren and Garrett, and Clare, of course. She was pacing at the back of the room as if some demon were driving her. She even whispered to herself and wrung her hands at her waist. Stone had never seen her in such a state.

Out in the hall Tiny watched, a silent sentinel. No such sentinel was needed. If the McBrides had an enemy, it was an enemy within. Outside the house the foreman Jeb Riggs and the ranch hands had gathered. As he'd passed them, Stone had seen Clare's lackey Manuelo standing away from the others, as always taking in everything without being a part.

In Tom's room Stone stood close to Annie, near the foot of the bed. She hadn't wanted to be there. She wasn't family. But he had insisted. And Lauren had practically dragged her in.

Most of them had been there since midnight. Tom had spent the hours drawing ragged breaths, stirring restlessly on occasion, then lying still. Now he was lying quietly beneath the covers, still breathing, but just barely. Doc Pierce looked around the room and slowly shook his head.

Tom raised a hand as if he were reaching out for someone. Stone hurried to his bedside and took the hand. His father parted his lips, as if he would speak.

"You don't have to say anything," Stone said. "We're all here. Just as you wanted."

"Need to talk." The words came out rushed and low, an edge of desperation in them.

Hanes spoke up. "Don't exert yourself, Tom. I can tell them what they need to know."

Tom shook his head impatiently. "Need to talk." This time his voice was stronger, as if he were rallying, as if an inner force were giving him strength. Clare stopped her pacing and stared out the window into the gray light of early day.

"Tiny . . ." he began, then broke off.

"Let me tell this part," Hanes said. "You've got enough to say." And then to the others,

"Tom's worried Tiny won't be taken care of. I've told him someone will take him in."

"Of course," Lauren said, and several others nodded in agreement.

"They go a long way back," the lawyer added, looking through the open doorway to where the cook was standing. "Tom came across him on a ride back from one of the early trail drives. It must have been shortly after the war. There was a son with him, a sickly child. Tom never found out what happened to the mother, nor how Tiny lost his voice. He helped him out. Years later, when Clare was hiring and firing cooks, the job came open. Tiny showed up. I figured she gave him the job because he couldn't talk back, like some of the others she'd picked."

"And the boy?" Callie asked.

"He'd already died. Didn't reach his tenth birthday. I don't know how Tom communicates with the man—can't get more than a shake of the head myself—but they get along."

"Tanner uses sign language," Callie said, taking her husband's hand.

"So that's why Tiny is always so protective of Papa," Lauren said.

"That's right," Hanes said.

"We'll take care of him," Garrett said.

"More than one of us," Faith put in.

Stone looked toward Clare, to see if she had

anything to say. But she was standing rigid as a post and still staring outside.

Tom stirred, and Stone forgot about his father's wife. "I don't hear any of you arguing," he said. "Could be you're finally getting along?"

"It's more than just could be," Stone said. "I'd say we're working through some difficulties."

"You've got more than you think," his father managed. "I've done some bad things in my life. Didn't give any of you what a father should." He drew a few shallow breaths before going on. "I'm not asking for forgiveness. But a man gets ready to meet his Maker, he thinks of things. Mistakes, mostly. I didn't make one getting you all back here."

He fell silent. It had been a long speech. His hand grew lax in Stone's. Stone rested it on the bed and backed away while Doc Pierce bent over his patient.

He straightened and again shook his head.

"Papa," Lauren said, "don't talk any more."

"I'm not done."

"All of you know how Tom is," Hanes said. "He's got something he wants to tell you. You might as well listen. He's not leaving 'til he gets it said."

Tom tried to lift his head. "Prop me up," he said.

Doc Pierce gave signs of protest, then did as

he was told, putting an extra pillow behind Tom's head.

The dying man looked around the room, his pale eyes taking on a hint of the blue that had once enlivened them, before illness sapped him of color.

"You came back for the ranch. Admit it."

"Some of us more than others," Stone said. He felt Annie draw close, and he rested his arm around her shoulders.

"You came back for nothing, damned if you didn't." A weary smile passed quickly across Tom's lips. "Shouldn't be saying damned. Not now."

No one spoke. No one moved. Except for Clare. Whirling, she hurried to his bedside, her lips pulled back in an angry snarl.

"What are you talking about, you old fool? The ranch is out there. Unless"—she smiled triumphantly as she looked around the room—"you mean it's not there for them. You changed your will, didn't you, and left everything to me."

"I'd be leaving you nothing but debts." He looked at Stone. "You figured there was trouble, didn't you?"

Stone nodded. "I had my suspicions."

"Tell 'em, Bill," Tom said.

The lawyer looked from McBride to McBride. "He's not lying to you. That snowstorm a few years back just about broke him. He borrowed more than he could pay back. Lots of ranchers around here did and had to sell out. A Fort Worth bank holds the mortgage on the place. It's my sad job to tell you they'll be calling it in any day."

Stone glanced at his brothers. Tanner shrugged, and Chase shook his head. Stone almost laughed at himself, thinking about all he and his brothers had gone through over the past week, all the arguments he and Tanner had endured, all the denials from Chase about caring for the place.

So why had Tom called them home? To get the last laugh? No. That was too simple an answer. His father was a more complex man. If Stone hadn't known it before, he knew it now.

A look of contentment settled on Tom's face. His gaze turned slowed to Annie. "You told 'em for me, little lady. Family is what matters. Hope they were listening. The only legacy they're getting from me is each other. It'll have to be enough."

With that, he fell silent, but his words hung in the air. After a moment, a tremendous sigh shuddered through him. He lay still. Doc Pierce checked his pulse, then looked up at Stone.

"He's gone."

Lauren turned her tear-streaked face into her husband's chest. Callie took Tanner's hand, and Faith leaned close to Chase.

Stone turned to look at Annie, but before he could speak, Clare let out a bloodcurdling shriek.

"I curse the day Thomas McBride was ever born." Her eyes burned with hatred as she stared at Stone and then at Tanner. "He destroyed my mother. He ruined my life." Her voice turned wheedling. "I loved you." She tore at her dress, all semblance of reason gone. "I would have given you everything. But you were too stupid to know it. May you burn in hell."

She pushed her way out of the bedroom, and they heard her stumbling down the stairs.

"Go get her," Callie said to Tanner. "There's no telling what she will do."

But Stone was already on the way. The three brothers got to the front of the house in time to see Manuelo help her onto the seat of the Circle M's wagon, then crack a whip over the horse's rump. The wagon shot across the frozen ground, then began to slip crazily as it rumbled down the road that led to town. Manuelo seemed scarcely in control.

"The arroyo," Stone said.

Jeb and Zeke were already bringing saddled horses out of the barn. The brothers mounted, riding side by side in pursuit of the fleeing pair. The cold snapped at them. Over the pounding of horses' hooves, they could hear Clare's mindless cry.

But they were too late to catch them. They watched in horror as the wagon neared the sharp precipice, skittered from side to side, then tilted to the left and dropped over the edge out of sight. Once again Stone heard the nightmare sounds that had haunted his waking moments for five long years—the creaking wagon, the terrified neighing of the horse, the crash of wood against the rock wall of the arroyo. Last came the silence, the terrible silence that was louder than a scream.

He was off his horse in an instant, scrambling down the wall, his boots catching against the protruding rocks, his hands grasping at roots and brush to break the speed of his descent. When he came to the upended wagon, its wheels spinning in the gray air, Tanner and Chase were close behind.

To the side, they could see Manuelo lying in a heap, small moans issuing from him. Miraculously, the horse was struggling to free itself from the traces. Tanner went to help. When the animal was loose, the three men lifted one side of the wagon. Clare lay motionless beneath. Stone knelt to feel for a pulse. Her head was twisted at an impossible angle and her eyes stared up at him, blank and sightless. No need to check further. Her neck was broken. Like her husband, she was dead.

Chapter Twenty-four

Later, when the bodies of the two McBrides were laid out in separate rooms, when Manuelo's injuries had been seen to by Doc Pierce and determined serious but not fatal, the family gathered in the parlor. No one spoke much, each of them seeming too stunned to do much talking.

The doctor came down the stairs. "Sheriff, you might want to question him. He's been doing some talking. I think you ought to hear what he has to say."

Chase went upstairs. Stone and Tanner followed. Manuelo was lying quietly in the bed that had belonged to his dead mistress. Bandages were wrapped around his head, and one arm rested atop the covers in a sling. His dark eyes shifted to the men, then down to the injured arm.

"Doc says you've got something to tell me," Chase said.

"She is dead," Manuelo said flatly. He spoke in a heavy accent, but the words came out clear enough. "There is no reason not to talk."

"She. You mean Mrs. McBride."

"She hated being a McBride. No one knew her real name."

"Clare Brown, wasn't it?" Tanner asked.

"You were all fools. Raines was the name. She called herself Brown so that you would not know."

"So that's why she spoke of her mother," Stone said. He told the others about long ago finding a letter from a Mary Raines, one of Tom's women friends. Apparently, she had been abandoned by him and was begging him to return.

"He did not," Manuelo said. "Already she had a husband, a cruel man who tossed his wife and child into the street."

"Clare being the child," Stone said.

"They had been good to me. I followed."

The brothers listened in silence while Manuelo spun out his sad tale of a broken woman and her young daughter, of hard times, of other men, of the mother's death when her daughter was fifteen.

"Señorita Clare was *hermosa* . . . beautiful. The men came."

"Including Tom," Stone said.

"No, señor. She went to him. She made him love her. She could do such things."

"But she didn't love him," Tanner said.

"She wished to destroy him." Manuelo looked at each man in turn. "She wished to destroy you all. She kept the rooms, the flowers, the same, to remind all the McBrides of the woman they had lost. Then you were gone and she had almost won. Until Señor Tomás brought you home."

Stone did not have to hear more. He could imagine Clare's fury. He had seen evidence of it, especially in the lies she'd told Annie about him. Her hatred had poisoned the room in which her husband was about to die.

"You hit Annie, didn't you?" he asked.

"I was commanded to learn what I could about you and the woman. The señorita returned too soon."

The door opened and Doc entered. "He told you about Emily yet?" He was looking at Chase. "About how she died?"

"The wagon," Tanner said.

Manuelo nodded. "She knew about your mother's journeys into town. Señor Tomás kept Clare not far from here. He was with her the night before the last one."

"What did Tom do?" Tanner asked. "Complain about me not fixing the wheel?"

Manuelo nodded. "He was using my Clarita, as he had her mother. But he kept her hidden. He would not divorce his wife. Clare did what she had to do. She turned to me."

"You undid Tanner's repairs," Stone said.

Again Manuelo nodded. "I was to examine the wagon and do what was necessary."

Chase leaned close to the bed. The man's voice was getting weak. "Say it. Say what you did."

"I made certain the wheel would break. The next morning, I hid in the bushes beside the road." His eyes lit with a sudden fire as he looked at Stone. "You did not see me. I let the snake slither from its bag. All went as I knew it would. The horse bolted. And Señorita Raines became Señora McBride."

A silence fell across the room as the depth of Clare's evil and hatred filled the air. Her hatred and her lackey's blind devotion. They were still palpable things, even after her death.

"Have you heard enough?" Doc Pierce asked.

Chase nodded. The men turned to leave. But Manuelo was not done.

"I killed her." He stared into empty space. "She had lost. She would not wish to live. It was not an accident that the wagon fell, no more this time than before. But one thing I did wrong. I should also have died."

He closed his eyes, and Stone knew that he was done talking. Leaving the doctor to his patient, he left the room, his brothers behind him, and went down to report what they had learned to the family that Clare Raines McBride had tried so hard to destroy.

Annie was standing by the corral, watching a pair of horses frisk about in the cold, when she heard approaching footsteps. Pulling her cloak close around her, she turned as Stone came to a halt at her side.

"You disappeared," he said.

"It was a time for family. You had much to discuss. Much to think about."

He nodded, then hooked one boot on the bottom rail of the fence, rested his forearms on the top, and stared at the horses. The wind caught his hair. The fading bruise was still visible. The lower part of his face was covered in bristles. His eyes were sunken from lack of sleep. He had never looked so good.

She had never loved him so much.

"You heard about what Manuelo said?" he asked, and she nodded.

"Hanes told us Tom had begun suspecting her a couple of years ago, but he couldn't prove anything. It seems he decided before I did that

Tanner was innocent. He also told Tiny. Tanner said that shortly after he got here, Tiny indicated something to him like *it begins*. Tanner didn't understand it at first. Now he knows it was Clare's downfall that was beginning. Tom set it up by calling us back."

"Why didn't he just throw her out?"

"He didn't know the truth for sure. Besides, he had a weakness for her. I guess some might call it love. I'd call it an obsession. The strange thing is, he knew she felt the same way about my little brother. When Tanner finally got back, Tom did what he could to keep them apart. He wanted her to think he was jealous. But he was doing what he could to protect his son."

"Tom loved him more than he loved his wife."

Stone shrugged. "I wouldn't go that far."

"He did," Annie said more firmly. "He loved all of you. Didn't you hear him? Family is what matters. It was almost the final thing he said."

"Yeah. It was just like Pa to confuse me right at the last."

Annie grinned. "You called him Pa. Not Tom. Pa, the way you used to."

"Somehow it seems right." He looked at Annie. "You pick up on things, don't you?"

"Sometimes. Not always."

Something new settled on him, something warmer than the flatness with which he had been discussing Tom. It was in his eyes. It was in the way he held his mouth.

"Do you know what I'm going to say next?" he asked.

Her heart stopped and she shook her head.

"I love you," he said. "I couldn't tell you sooner because of Emily. I needed to show you to her first. And her to you."

She held on to the rail, but her gaze was locked with his.

"I'm not much of a prize," he added.

She almost laughed. He was all she wanted in the world, everything she would ever need, but the words caught in her throat.

"The ranch is mortgaged, I've got a little girl who's pretty much got me wrapped around those tiny fingers of hers, I'm quick to judge without listening to all the facts, I tend to want my own way. You care to add to the list of flaws?"

"You're stubborn."

"That, too."

"And private. How long have you felt this way about me?"

"Since the moment I saw you in your father's store."

"Don't be silly. That was over ten years ago. I'm serious."

"So am I. Part of my stubbornness is not admitting to feelings. This time, while I was thinking things through in my mind, I just about lost the most important thing of all. I mean you, Annabelle Chapin. I went crazy when I found you had sold out and gone. I'm hoping you'll be the crazy one now. I'm hoping you'll consider being another McBride. I can't offer you a roof over your head, not for long, but I'm offering you me."

She took a deep, steadying breath, but it didn't begin to do its job. "Don't you want to know how I feel about you?"

"You love me."

"You're sure of yourself."

"I'm sure about you. What we've been doing the past few weeks, it wouldn't have happened if you didn't think I was the greatest man who ever rode into Sidewinder."

Her heart began to sing. "What do you think of my judgment?"

"Not much. Like I said, I'm not much of a prize."

"I love your little girl."

"Now, that I can believe." A glint came into his eyes. "Anybody else?"

"I love the greatest man who ever rode into Sidewinder. You, Stone McBride. I love you."

She couldn't stand it any longer. She threw herself into his arms. He kissed her. Not just once but again and again, so many times she lost count. When they were done with kissing, or at least had decided to postpone it for a while, they began to talk about a life together, of how they made one another complete, about caring for little Emily. And then they were talking about caring for one another, and they even disagreed about which one loved the other the most.

With the morning sun rising over the distant hills, spreading warmth across the earth, they commenced kissing again.

After Tom was laid to rest beside his first wife and Clare was buried in the cemetery outside Sidewinder; after the will was read, with no surprises coming out; after Stone and little Emily moved into the Circle M ranch house, with the approval of the other owners, Stone and Annie were wed in the parlor. The traveling preacher from the boardinghouse conducted the proceedings. Josefina served as matron of honor and Tanner as best man. The guests from town included the doctor and lawyer, Chase's deputy, and the widow Simpkins, who said as usual that she would be moving on one of these days.

Annie's brother Sam and his wife and son came all the way from New Mexico for the ceremony. They wouldn't be lingering long, though Annie told them it was a far distance to travel for only a few days. But Sam insisted that after the wedding, they would be staying at the boardinghouse, then leave on the next stage west.

"I got to get back to the store," he said. As she looked at him, all suited up, his fair hair combed into place, she could scarcely remember the harum-scarum youth he had once been. Love and family and, yes, responsibility could certainly settle down a man.

After toasts had been made to the happy couple and the wedding feast consumed, Stone and Annie feigned reluctance in bidding everyone good-bye. Feigned to everyone but little Emily. Lauren was taking her back to the San Reanido for a few days, though Annie doubted that, eager though she and Stone were to be alone, they would be able to stay away from her so long.

When they were upstairs in the room they had chosen as theirs, at least for a while—the one Stone had used when he was growing up—she played tentatively with the buttons of her white gown.

"Promise me one thing," Stone said.

"I already promised to love, honor, and obey. You want more?" She was teasing, and he knew it.

"Never wear black again."

She looked toward the wardrobe, where her beautiful new dresses were hanging. They had been trousseau gifts from her sisters-in-law. They came in every color but black.

Last, she looked at the white lace nightgown waiting on the bed.

"I promise."

"Don't stare at that nightgown too long. I doubt if you'll get it on."

Annie blushed. "You're shameless."

"Sweetheart, I'm full of shame. I'll spend the rest of my life making up for leaving you the way I did. But I'm not in the least ashamed about what I am going to do to you now."

"You're very sure of yourself."

"With you, yes. Finally."

He made short work of the buttons and of the rest of the undressing, taking care of them both. When he was done, she pushed him back on the bed.

"You might ask yourself, dearest one, exactly what I plan to do to you."

She threw herself on top of him. The bed creaked and sagged ominously. But it held. During much of the night they put it to several severe tests. It passed every one.

Sometime during the lovemaking and the laughing and the sweet whispering, she got her husband to admit he would never be a loner again.

Epilogue

The day before the wedding uniting Annie and Stone, Manuelo had been moved to a small room behind the kitchen, in preparation for his recovery and removal to the Sidewinder jail.

He never got out of bed.

"He wasted away," Doc Pierce explained to the family. "After Clare was gone, he just didn't see any reason for going on. I've seen it happen that way, when a man loses everything he values. A woman can do it, too."

Instead of jail, he was put into a grave next to the mistress he had adored.

Two weeks after the wedding, the McBride brothers rode into Fort Worth and presented a strong case to the Fort Worth bank for giving them an extension on the loan. The bank would be more assured of regaining its money if they were given time to bring the Circle M back from the edge of bankruptcy. Stone did most of the talking, but it didn't hurt that Chase was standing nearby, the picture of rectitude with his sheriff's badge shining brightly on his shirt.

Tanner threw in an argument or two, and at last the banker came around.

Garrett Lassiter had offered to pay off the debt, but the brothers had declined, thanking him for his generosity but declaring this was something they needed to do for themselves. And together. That was the most important part.

Much as she wanted to give them extra help, Lauren had agreed with her brothers' decision.

Two years to the day after the new bank agreement was struck, the entire clan gathered at the McBride ranch house to burn the paid-off mortgage. Annie made accommodations in one of the rooms for the new generation of McBrides—the son Daniel she had borne Stone six months before and, only a month younger, Matthew Tanner McBride, named for Callie's late brother. The smallest, and only female, was Eugenia Lassiter, Lauren and Garrett's daughter, at three months the only redhead in the group.

Heavy with her first child, Faith was close to adding to the brood.

Down by the corral, with Luke and Jeb Riggs watching over her, four-year-old Emily romped. Occasionally Stone stuck his head out the front door to make sure she was all right.

In the parlor, wine was passed and the glasses lifted.

"To the family," Stone said. "The McBrides and the Lassiters. We couldn't have done what we did without everyone pitching in."

"And to Tom," Annie said. When no one responded right away, she added, "Without him, we wouldn't all be here. There wouldn't even be a Circle M, not the way it is now."

Stone looked at her and then around the room. "Anyone have any objection to that?"

Chase, the bastard son, the one kept on the outside by his father though he had given him his name, was the first to respond.

"To Tom," he said, giving an extra lift to his glass.

The others responded in kind.

"To Tom," Stone said, chiming in last. "He wanted us here as a family once again. I thought I never would say anything like this, but I'm glad he got what he was after."

That got a few wry smiles, especially the one he and Tanner shared.

As they drank and began to talk amongst each other, Stone studied his growing family. As alike as they were, they each had separate dreams. Tanner was planning to take his share of the ranch's income and buy land adjoining the Circle M. There he would build a new ranch house for his wife and child.

In the meantime, he had repaired and added on to the line cabin where he and Callie and their son lived.

While Chase was spending more time riding the range with his brothers, he swore he was contented being a lawman, the only thing he had always wanted to be.

As for Lauren, her focus was on her husband and baby. But it didn't keep her from riding over and giving advice about the horse stock she envisioned for the ranch. Garrett was the expert there, and she was learning more and more every day about breeding stallions and broodmares.

Last, Stone looked at his beautiful wife. She was dressed in yellow today, a shade that matched her hair. After Daniel's birth, her figure had grown fuller, a fact she regularly pointed out to her husband, especially when they were in bed.

In the first months after their marriage, she had been reluctant to change anything at the ranch house. But everyone, Lauren most especially, had insisted she make the house her home. Gradually the new coverings for the furniture, the new draperies, the new rugs had been brought in and put in place.

But there was one momento of the first Emily McBride that would always hold pride of place: the flower vase that was meant to hold bluebonnets in the spring. Outside, the late February air was cool with a hint of that upcoming season. Before too many more weeks, the wildflowers would begin to dot the hillsides, then cover them in carpets of color—the bluebonnets, the red paintbrushes, the yellow-and-white buttercups with their tinges of pink.

Soon the vase would be as full as Stone's heart.

"It's time," Tanner said, drawing him from his reverie.

The family gathered in a semicircle in front of the fireplace. After some argument over who would do the honors, Lauren took the mortgage papers, held them in her hand for a moment, and with a dramatic gesture tossed them into the flames.

At the same moment, a cry came from upstairs. Every woman looked away from the ceremonial blaze to see Tiny standing on the top step and gesturing for help. As a group, Annie, Lauren, and Callie abandoned the men.

Faith followed, saying to her husband, "I need to learn all I can. Before long, that cry will be coming from our child."

Left alone, the men poured another round of drinks.

"To our wives," Stone said and was met with nods.

Tanner was the first to set his glass aside. "I ought to go see if everything's all right."

"Me, too," said Garrett.

They led the procession up the stairs.

At that moment, Emily bounded into the parlor, closely followed by Luke.

"Where's Mama?" she asked.

Stone scooped her into his arms. "We'll go find her." He extended his hand to Luke, and the boy, ten years old now and trying to look like a man, took it. "Come on up. We've moved the party upstairs."

The nursery was crowded, but the women made room for the men.

Annie gave up Daniel to Stone in exchange for their daughter Emily. The four of them stood apart from the others, as much as they could manage, not to separate themselves so much as to get a better view of everyone.

It was a scene of contentment until Daniel decided he wanted to get down to practice his newfound skill of crawling.

"Daddy," Emily said in her most officious voice, "Da-Da"—the name she had given her brother—"wants to play."

"And you think I should let him?" Stone asked.

"Yes. But Tiny and me'll watch him. You and Mama can go night-night."

Annie's cheeks turned red. "I don't know where she gets such things."

"Me either," Stone said, enjoying his wife's embarrassment. "Imagine going to bed in the middle of the day."

"She's like her father," Lauren said. "She likes to order everyone around."

Stone tried to look offended.

"Don't bother to deny it, big brother," Tanner said, then to Annie, "Did I ever tell you about the time . . ."

He launched into one of his stories about the past. Surrounded by a loving family, Annie listened and smiled.

EVELYN ROGERS

He rides out of the Yorkshire mist, a dark figure on a dark horse. Is he a living man or a nightmare vision, conjured up by her fearful imagination and her uncertain future?Voices swirl in her head:

> They say he's more than human.
> A man's life is in danger when he's around . . .
> And a woman's virtue.

Repelled yet fascinated, Lucinda finds herself swept into a whirlwind courtship. Yet even as his lips set fire to her heart, she cannot forget his words of warning on the night they met:

> Tread softly. Heed little that you see and hear.
> Then leave.
> For God's sake, leave.

Whether he is the lover of her dreams or the embodiment of all she fears, she senses he will always be her . . . devil in the dark.

___52407-4 $5.99 US/$6.99 CAN

Dorchester Publishing Co., Inc.
P.O. Box 6640
Wayne, PA 19087-8640

Please add $2.50 for shipping and handling for the first book and $.75 for each book thereafter. NY, NYC, and PA residents, please add appropriate sales tax. No cash, stamps, or C.O.D.s. All orders shipped within 6 weeks via postal service book rate.
Canadian orders require $2.50 extra postage and must be paid in U.S. dollars through a U.S. banking facility.

Name____
Address____
City_______________________State________Zip____________
I have enclosed $__________ in payment for the checked book(s).
Payment must accompany all orders. ☐ Please send a free catalog.
CHECK OUT OUR WEBSITE! www.dorchesterpub.com

EVELYN ROGERS

I haven't always wanted to be a writer, but I've always been a reader. Mother must have put books in my crib; I can't remember a time when the printed page didn't captivate me. Right out of college I was a reporter for a crusading West Texas newspaper, a trial by fire if there ever was one, and I soon switched to the noble profession of teaching.

In the early '80s, with children grown and husband devoted to his work, I decided to try the creative process. Right away I was hooked. It took a couple of years for my prose to find a publishing home. Five years later I quit my day job (middle school librarian) and here I am still hooked by the whole idea of creating a story for others to read.

Readers can write me at the following address:

8039 Callaghan Road, Suite 102
San Antonio, TX 78230
URL: http://www.romcom.com/rogers/

Secret Fires

In the midst of the vast, windswept Texas plains stood a ranch wrested from the wilderness with blood, sweat and tears. It was the shining legacy of Thomas McBride to his five living heirs. But along with the fertile acres and herds of cattle, each would inherit a history of scandal, lies and hidden lust that threatened to burn out of control.

The Loner

As first born, Stone had always tried to do the right thing, but that hadn't stopped his brother and sister from turning on him. And it hadn't kept the woman he loved from turning him down. In the years since, Stone had learned to go it alone; a gambler was better off that way. He'd returned to the Circle M for the money promised in his father's will, not for the family he'd once fought to protect, and certainly not for the vulnerable beauty his heart could never forget.

www.dorchesterpub.com

$5.99 US
$6.99 CAN
£5.99 UK
$12.95 AUS